# *CHASING*
# *PAINTED*
# *HORSES*

# CHASING PAINTED HORSES

A Novel by DREW HAYDEN TAYLOR

Cormorant Books

 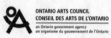

The publisher gratefully acknowledges the support of the Canada Council for the
Arts and the Ontario Arts Council for its publishing program. We acknowledge
the financial support of the Government of Canada through the Canada Book
Fund (CBF) for our publishing activities, and the Government of Ontario
through Ontario Creates, an agency of the Ontario Ministry of Culture, and the
Ontario Book Publishing Tax Credit Program.

LIBRARY AND ARCHIVES CANADA CATALOGUING IN PUBLICATION

Title: Chasing painted horses / a novel by Drew Hayden Taylor.
Names: Taylor, Drew Hayden, 1962– author.
Description: Originally published: Toronto, ON: Cormorant Books, 2019.
Identifiers: Canadiana 20200235400 | ISBN 9781770866089 (softcover)
Classification: LCC PS8589.A885 C49 2020 | DDC C813/.54—dc23

Cover design: Angel Guerra, Archetype
Interior text design: tannicegdesigns.ca
Printer: Friesens

Printed and bound in Canada.

CORMORANT BOOKS INC.
260 SPADINA AVENUE, SUITE 502, TORONTO, ON M5T 2E4
www.cormorantbooks.com

*To Ms. Kappele.*
*Amazing what a couple glasses of wine*
*at a dinner party can produce.*

# CHASING
# PAINTED
# HORSES

## CHAPTER ONE

HOWEVER IMPOLITELY, "IT'S COLDER THAN A CHRISTIAN'S heart" is how Ralph Thomas's childhood friend William would have described this morning's weather. Ignoring the theological and politically incorrect implications, William would have been essentially correct. And though Ralph was several hundred kilometres and two decades away from where and when his friend had said that, it was indeed a very cold morning, religious affiliations notwithstanding.

The temperature at present was hovering somewhere around a brisk minus ten or so on the Celsius scale, creating an urban landscape of huddled masses struggling to stay warm in the bright sunlight. Across the city, its denizens walked the streets bundled up in scarves, coats, heavy sweaters, and all sorts of unflattering woollen and fake fur hats, trying in vain to ward off the climate. Evidently, being Canadian had its downside.

Somewhere in that Canadian city known as Toronto, not that far from where Ralph Thomas was planning to start his working day as protector of the public, sat a man.

Social workers, politicians, statisticians, and people with spare change would call him a typical — whatever that may mean — homeless man. A panhandler. A street person. A representative of those who have slipped through the safety nets in a supposedly sympathetic society. Though covered in layers of mismatched, dirty clothing, this man smiled out at the world as he sat on his kingdom, commonly known as a sidewalk grate, a cloud of steam making him appear oddly unfocused and mysteriously hazy to the occasional passerby. He was known to the world — the world that cared, mind you — simply as Harry, due to his bushy beard, eyebrows, and unkempt hair that peeked out from underneath a worn cap saluting a local hockey team that did not deserve such saluting, which obviously did little to protect his ears from the climate. But no matter. He was a survivor. What's a pair of cold ears to a man who every day walked the tightrope of life? As an Aboriginal man, he was a contradiction in stereotypes — on one hand, he met the cliché of being down-and-out and looking for other people to supplement his condition. On the other hand, the rumour that Native people did not have body or facial hair did not apply to him.

A long time ago, when Harry could remember and was remembered, he'd come from a Cree reserve far out in the direction where the sun set every evening. He'd wandered in the direction of the rising sun to seek his fortune and had landed here on the shores of an inland sea, his fortune unfound. His financial empire now consisted mostly of donated spare change, a hodgepodge of mismatched, discarded attire that he had come across in past years, and disjointed memories. It has been said by a man far smarter than Harry that some are born to greatness, others achieve it, and there are those who have it thrust upon them. The same could be said for destitution. Harry had his thrust upon him with violent determination, courtesy of a negligent and schizophrenic society confused in its understanding of the relationship between Aboriginal peoples and everybody else. But no matter. He was where he was, and, all things considered, he was happy. Cold, but happy. The vast majority of the world's population could say they were cold, but only a few could say they were legitimately happy. Harry smiled.

Like most people, the forgotten man had talents. Some were recognizable: coming from an oral culture and having spent years with multitudes of multicultural down-and-outers who had been pushed aside by what prided itself as a just society, a cultural mosaic, he could imitate any number of accents. It often helped in panhandling. Amused patrons were more generous when he spoke with a Jamaican patois or an impressive Scottish burr. Other talents in his possession were not so obvious. He could see people. Not dead people, or aliens, or demons, or anything Hollywood, or what a psychiatrist or social worker would find worthy of their billable hours. Instead, Harry saw people as they really were — what emanated from their souls, not what they appeared to be to everyone else.

Once he'd been about to receive a few quarters from this lovely woman in a checkered sweater, until a man he'd assumed to be her husband angrily pulled her away, irritably mumbling something about "not encouraging those types." What the woman in the checkered top didn't seem to see was something that was only too evident to Harry. The man had no eyes, just dark apertures out of which dripped ominous obsidian drops of pure malice. It was like his spirit was slowly escaping from his body and leaking out through the two orifices where most people's eyes usually were. Harry had watched the couple disappear into the crowd of spring shoppers, leaving a trail on the pavement of the smouldering blackness still slowly oozing from the front of the man's head. Harry was blissfully unaware that sometime later the man had killed the woman in a rage, afterwards setting fire to a cottage they shared in Muskoka.

But such sight wasn't all bad. Another time he'd spotted a little white girl, no more than nine years old, just across the street, petting a smallish dog tied to a tree. The poor creature was panting and very uncomfortable in the August heat, so the little girl gave the dog her vanilla ice cream cone. Dietary concerns aside, the dog gratefully accepted the cold, somewhat moist offering, quickly devouring it, tail wagging constantly. The girl looked across the street at Harry and smiled. Harry smiled back. To his eyes, she was glowing, her tiny body surrounded by a multi-hued aura of some sort. Somewhere in that little girl, surprisingly close to the surface, sat the spirit of someone who would do good works in her future, changing people (and, it seemed, dogs), places, and times for the better. It was the rare kind of spirit Buddhists would venerate. If there were a bell curve of good and bad, this little creature would somehow transcend it.

Harry didn't know if his unique talent was a product of his Aboriginal heritage, several decades of altering the chemical balance of his brain, or merely being the ultimate observer of society due to his privileges as a bystander. It merely existed, and existed in him. There was little he could do about it, so he did his best to live with it. Besides, he had other problems to deal with.

Winter days like this made being a Canadian homeless person exceedingly difficult. The vent that he called home was a double-edged sword. It provided a certain amount of warmth, but the steam made him and his clothing damp. Dampness and cold weather do not go together. He had many friends who had lost fingers and limbs to such a combination once the bitter winter night fell. Sometimes they'd lost more. And worst of all, people of society often had their heads down and were in such a hurry that they seldom saw him, both as an actual physical presence and as a person of need. Still, like everything else in his life, there was little he could do about it; he merely accepted it. Privately, he loathed the season. Though his people had been born to the frozen wastelands of the Prairies, Harry had enough white blood flowing through his veins to make this time of year difficult. Luckily, not everyone shared his sentiments. At the other end of the spectrum, there were some who found the yearly tilt of the planet away from the sun a rather enjoyable experience.

Such a person was the aforementioned Ralph Thomas, currently navigating piles of dusky-coloured snow alongside the kilometres of urban sidewalks. The man liked really cold days, particularly the way they made his senses more aware and awake, the way they made his skin tingle and his nose hairs stick together after a deep breath. It was a feeling of life or survival, not like those stupefying, humid days of summer that zapped his strength, draining his will to do anything. He knew most people usually cursed cold Canadian winter days, but not Ralph. Ralph Thomas had grown up on a small, isolated reserve several hours north of Toronto, a place called Otter Lake. So on some genetic, cultural, and personal level, he knew he could take the worst this city and the tilted nature of the planet could throw at him. His people had faced, fought, and triumphed over the Canadian winter since their fabled beginning known as Time Immemorial.

Taking a deep breath, he uttered to no one in particular, "Oh, that feels good." This was Ralph's element, his environment. Ever since he was a child, winter had been his favourite season. Half jokingly, he'd asked his father, when he was still alive, if there wasn't some Inuit blood floating through their family.

As proof of his resilience, Ralph's jacket wasn't zipped up, and all that separated his legs and torso from the frigid air was a thin layer of wool combined with polyester, the blend of his Toronto Police Service-issued uniform. And a bulletproof vest. To Ralph, long johns were for long treks in the woods or hours on a snowmobile, not for short jaunts from a house to a mall, a bus, a Tim Hortons, or his division. Long johns in the city were for wimps, he often joked and really believed. Today was no different. Enjoying the briskness of the morning, Ralph noticed passerby after passerby, heads down low, elbows close to their bodies, ignoring the world around them as their feet made short, hesitant steps on the snow-caked sidewalks, hoping not to slide embarrassingly into a salt and pepper snowdrift. As usual, he seemed to be the only one enjoying the morning.

And why not? All things considered, life was going pretty well for the Aboriginal man. Yes, he was of average build and a bit lean for his own personal tastes, but he knew that at the age of thirty-one the whole future lay ahead of him, for the most part. In two years, it would be his tenth anniversary as a member of that thin blue line that kept the forces of chaos and anarchy at bay. Eight years earlier he had started his career, after several years of education, as a constable policing the windswept streets of Dead Rat River First Nation. But after three years, the novelty had worn off. Too many people calling him an "apple," too many domestic disputes, and, living in the actual community he policed, there was no real way of developing any serious Ralph time or space, let alone friends or girlfriends. So, after some paperwork and retraining, Ralph found himself walking the streets of Canada's biggest city, packing heat, authority, and a certain amount of attitude. He was a First Nations man authorized to toss white people in jail. Yes, indeed, it was good to be alive.

During his younger years, after high school, Ralph had surfed the world he existed in by mostly doing contract work here and there, frequently employed in odd jobs that tested his sense of monotony more than his intelligence. When asked, he considered his multitudes of mini-careers … "seasoning." But even at that young age, it was becoming apparent to Ralph that he was dangerously close to simply going through life, not actually living it. Additionally, his sister, Shelley, had told him repeatedly that it is possible to become over-seasoned, which frequently can make things inedible. She would know. She was a pretty good cook.

So, after much thought, the young man had decided to make something of himself and find an actual destination in life, rather than just journeying through it. So here he was, living in Toronto, a cop. Ralph Thomas. Officer Thomas. Police Constable Thomas. A protector of the innocent and punisher of the evil. And let's not forget stalwart guardian of construction sites.

"It's better to be a cop than to need one" was the saying one of his instructors had frequently, laughingly drilled into students. Everyone seemed to agree. At this point, so did Ralph.

Up ahead, he saw the Queen streetcar clang past the corner where he would frequently grab a coffee. As resilient to the cold as the man was, one does not spit into the face of the Canadian winter without proper armour. Armour bearing the insignia of the great ice warrior Tim Horton. Since it wasn't that cold a day, regardless of what everybody else seemed to think, Ralph decided to walk to the subway sans coffee. His shift maintaining the safety of a seventeen-storey condo under construction was over, and there was no point in challenging the caffeine gods to a test of wills. Many of his coworkers preferred to drive home, or Uber it, especially when in uniform. And, on occasion, so did Ralph. But today was too good a day to waste sitting inside something. He'd put in a couple of kilometres on his Fitbit, helping to keep the belly demons at bay, before jumping on the subway. His family had a tendency, after the age of thirty, to put on roughly a pound with each passing year. In that tradition, Shelley was definitely an overachiever, as was her husband, William. But unlike many fellow cops, Ralph could still bend down to tie his shoes without everything going hazy.

With that in mind, he started following Niagara Street to Richmond and headed east. Ralph had been making some extra cash, as many of his brethren in blue frequently did, as a concrete and steel nursemaid. Four hours of standing street-side of a huge pit lined with girders, watching early-morning traffic and people pouring past. His real shift as a police officer began in four hours. Time enough for a nap, shower, food, and maybe some Netflix. Again, life was good. This wasn't the life he had expected when he'd joined the force, but then again, reality tends to be a harsh teacher.

Ralph's eyes scanned the houses and buildings with interest, because this part of the city was new to him. Geographically he knew perfectly well where he was, but he'd never actually walked these side streets before. The cop in him took in the world around him and stored it. He never knew when he might find himself here without the opportunity for such a leisurely assessment of his surroundings.

Following Richmond Street, he began zigzagging through the smaller streets, intending to make as direct a line to the subway as he could walking on north-south and east-west streets. The snow made its distinctive crunching beneath his shoes, letting him know the immediate temperature of the city. No doubt back home it was a good five or six degrees colder, and maybe you could hear the trees crack in the cold. The way sound travelled over a snow-covered forest was like nothing else. He missed that. Here in the city, often the sounds he heard only reminded him of the alien world he lived in.

Often Ralph was of two minds about living in the city known as Toronto. There weren't a lot of Korean or Vietnamese restaurants back home in Otter Lake. Jokingly, he would say there was more sweetgrass than lemongrass. Not even what could be called a real Chinese restaurant: the nearest, in nearby Baymeadow, was one of those ubiquitous Chinese-Canadian restaurants that dot the expanse of Canada. He chose not to eat in those establishments. His relatively few years in Toronto had taught him what real Chinese food was, and he had little tolerance for soggy stir-fried broccoli or sweet-and-sour chicken balls with their radioactive red sauce. When he had first arrived in the city, he'd been shocked to discover that the Chinese from China had never heard of sweet-and-sour chicken balls or chop suey. As with many urban Aboriginals, Ralph Thomas had, over time, become a food snob.

In addition, here amidst the concrete mountains there were movies he could see at noon, all kinds of stores to shop in, and a lot more women he was not related to than there were back home. When it came to encouraging Native students to attend the finer institutions of higher education, Ralph was always surprised that universities and colleges never showcased these elements when canvassing for Indigenous students. He was sure that, with proper publicity, enrolment would shoot up and dropout rates would plummet.

Still, Otter Lake had its incentives. For all his whining about the quality of ethnic food back home, it was almost impossible to find good Native Canadian cuisine in Toronto. Retail deer or moose meat was practically non-existent, unless you had a source, a connection. Trying to locate and purchase wild meat in Toronto felt to Ralph like looking for opiates, and he needed a pusher of non-prescription meats. His sister, Shelley, could make a shepherd's pie like nobody else. Her meatloaf wasn't just a mainstay of settler middle-class life, in Otter Lake it was a work of art. When people came over for dinner, they often requested it.

For sure, what Shelley could do for everyday cooking could bring any chef to tears, Ralph believed. All three of her kids were well on their way to plumpness. In fact, thinking about her cooking was making him hungry. He increased his pace to the subway.

Back home, there was quietness. The stillness of the country. There was fresh air, the lake itself, and lots and lots of family. It was a long trip home, but he hadn't been home in months, not since the summer. Ralph had sworn he wouldn't become one of those types who only came home to the reserve once, maybe twice a year, gradually drifting further and further away from the people they had grown up with. Weddings and funerals frequently acted as a lighthouse, showing people the way home. Members of his family had long ago given up remembering the names of people they or their parents had grown up with; they now complained about what the government was doing to First Nations people in other parts of the country. But right now, Ralph wanted to get to his home here in the city. He was hungry, and, in his hunger, he was positive he had some of Shelley's chili in the back of the fridge, cautiously stored since last summer for just such emergencies. The battle against crime required a lot of calories. That's why Batman, Superman, and all the other superheroes were always so skinny.

Hands deep in the pockets of his regulation jacket, Ralph made his way up a back alley. It was still early, and the city was just beginning to wake up on this lazy Saturday morning. Running alongside him, on the walls and garage doors that lined this back street, he noticed the graffiti. Lots of it. It seemed there weren't two square feet of empty brick or aluminum siding left unadorned, representing the innate need for humanity to continuously illustrate and comment on life. He had read somewhere there had been graffiti in ancient Egypt and Rome.

Intrigued, Ralph slowed down, taking in the complex symbols spread along the walls. The bright and dazzling images that surrounded him were startling, even breathtaking. A dozen or more different artists had created entire universes. Red and blue seemed to be the dominant colours, but there were others. Lots of others. Rainbows of shades and multitudes of images, one after another. Directly in front of him was a painting of the CN Tower as a rocket blasting off into outer space. Beside that was what appeared to be a family of three, all with the bodies of dogs. Behind him, concrete trees. Ahead, two people kissing, their heads morphing into a loving heart.

Ralph had seen graffiti before, even in Otter Lake, and in one of his justice classes he'd learned it was a misdemeanour. But here, all around him in this space, it wasn't a public disgrace; at least, it didn't seem to be. Yes, there was quantity, but, more importantly, there was also a stunning array of quality. The hearts and the minds of an entire subclass of Torontonians had come to this spot to express themselves. And Ralph had to admit, as gaudy and haphazard as it might appear, there was something awesome about each of the images staring back at him. Beautiful, even.

One by one, he took in the startling representations. Somebody with exaggerated facial features waving to him from a convertible car. The guy driving looked kind of goofy. Unlike the picture of what appeared to be a witch-like character, yelling down at four shrinking children — Ralph assumed they were children — cowering below her. Scattered amidst the more obvious and easily recognizable reproductions, he saw others that were more abstract. Paint on the wall that evoked a feeling rather than recognition. Swirls and random letters within letters. Maybe, he pondered, a more street-smart form of a Rorschach test. And what was even more interesting to the police officer was the notable sense of respect that each artist expressed for the others. No image dared to encroach on the paint of its neighbour. There was no overlap, and occasionally one vision would complement the one beside it.

Pictographs, Ralph thought. Or petroglyphs. He smiled at the realization. It was true: the more things changed, the more they stayed the same. What his ancestors had done so long ago on rock walls, this generation of this society was struggling to do on brick. To make their mark on this world, show their point of view. Only these declarations would be lucky to last the winter.

One after the other, the policeman explored all of them with his eyes. They were amazing. Ralph was puzzled that he'd never heard of this alleyway. He could feel the joy and the agony coming off those few millimetres of paint layers that adorned the walls. Directly in front of him, he was looking at an image of a Christ-like figure with arms outspread to the heavens. Except Jesus seemed to be black and in a wheelchair. And the angels were Asian. And his disciples were ... Native, possibly. And heaven looked like the skyline of Vancouver that he'd once seen — skyscrapers and mountains vying enviously as they reached for the sky. Ralph was positive there was an interesting story behind this one. A multitude of people using their artistic visions to comment on what their actual eyes saw. For a moment, he felt a twinge ... a small quiver in the back of his mind, as if looking out on a large pond and seeing the ripples on the surface made by something he hadn't seen but knew was there.

Almost immediately, his attention was once again captured by a dozen different forms of calligraphy that peppered both walls. What wasn't covered in pictures was coated with letters both recognizable and unknown. Some illegible. The varying scripts took different styles, shapes, and characters, depending on which samples he was looking at. Some resembled Cyrillic, others Sanskrit, and the rest reminded him of an alien language he'd seen ages ago on an episode of *Star Trek*. What any of these "words" actually said was a mystery to the man, thus rendering the original purpose of written language moot, it seemed.

As he moved further down the alley towards the street, the frequency and the freshness of the graffiti began to peter out. Posters and flyers began to litter the walls, hiding more and more of the older artistic impressions; as he neared Bathurst, the walls were almost completely covered with advertising for some band Ralph had never heard of that had played at a Toronto club called Grossman's two months ago.

Feeling little tendrils of cold working their way into his muscles, Ralph decided it was time to speed up his sidewalk sojourn and find the subway that would take him to his apartment. Though not technically chilled, Ralph knew the simple act of shivering (which in itself to him was a sign of defeat) was perhaps only minutes way. This had been an odd but interesting detour, and, for some reason he couldn't quite fathom just yet, a little unsettling too. It was almost like reading the diary of someone he didn't know and not having a full grasp of what was being written, other than it was personal in a public way and needed to be said.

The corner of Queen and Bathurst lay ahead of him; a few blocks further down was the subway. It would be nice to take off his police belt, weighted down with heavy police paraphernalia. Add to that his hefty Kevlar vest and jacket. Metaphorically, he and other cops frequently felt they were carrying the weight of society on their shoulders ... or their waists, maybe. Looking to his right, he saw and then felt in the pavement beneath him a streetcar roaring down the street, eager to take people home for the cost of a token. And that's when a flash of colour from the wall reached out, tearing the former Otter Lake resident from this world, forcing him into a long-forgotten place.

At first, out of the corner of his eye, Ralph noticed something peeking out at him from beneath the torn and weary posters. About five feet up and six feet from the building's corner, peering at him from around tape, was what appeared to Ralph to be a large, wild eye. An eye painted of dark blue and purple with a little white. About five inches across. Staring at him. Glaring. The eye looked out of place. But there it was, a dozen or so feet away.

Once again, something in the back of Ralph's mind quivered uncomfortably. He had no idea why an errant eye from a wall of brick hidden behind old posters would do that to him, but there was definitely something in that simple, if disturbing, image that caused a shiver of memory. But, like the eye, maybe it was just a hint of what was hidden. The memory reluctant to come, almost like it was afraid to. Either way, that did not bode well.

*And the eye, was it hiding?* That was a bizarre thought to have, Ralph suddenly realized. Had somebody tried to conceal it?

Moving a few feet closer, Ralph peered deep into the eye. It was layered with circular swirls of blue and purple, softening where they overlapped and became a shade of grey or white, like a photo of a hurricane. It had the eerie effect of watching him, standing there in the urban winter morning, staring back.

*This is silly*, Ralph thought. But he knew the eye, somehow; or, more accurately, he knew he should know the eye, or what it represented. The knowledge was swirling in places his mind stored things that might cause discomfort, trying to get free. This was more than a few layers of paint. He approached the wall like a police officer and, hesitating for two seconds, grabbed two handfuls of weathered paper, tearing them violently off their anchors. They came away from the brick quite easily, the adhesive long ago having lost its effectiveness. Handful after handful of frail paper drifted to the ground, collecting at his feet. Officer Thomas was sure a case for littering could have been made against him, but he didn't care. The more he tore away from the wall, the more he revealed the owner of the eye.

In less than a minute, the wall was bare and the cold northern wind channelling down that alleyway was blowing the shredded paper all across the street and onto the streetcar tracks. Not from the wind, Ralph shivered. He spoke his second set of words of the morning, very quietly and soberly and not nearly with the same enthusiasm as his first.

"Christ, it's you."

The strange memory in the back of Ralph Thomas's brain was no longer twitching to be noticed. It was out. It was at the front of his mind, screaming. Now he was no longer a member of the Toronto Police Service; he was very much the boy who had grown up in Otter Lake. He gazed at an old but never forgotten friend ... though what he was looking at didn't look particularly friendly. Not at all. It had grown in both size and attitude since he'd last seen it so long ago, and though the paint was chipped and peeling in places and poster paste had left scars all over its body, it was still a very powerful image. Winter had nothing to do with the coldness he felt.

Near where the heart would be on such an animal, he spotted something that confirmed his suspicions. A painted image of a hand, a small, delicate hand, complete with faint fingerprints and a slightly crooked little finger, a finger that had been broken once or twice a long time ago. He knew that hand, and this Horse. His childhood, like the wind blowing down the alleyway, came rushing to him.

Once more, his voice was lost in the cold winter wind. "Danielle. What happened to you?" Though he had asked this question out loud, Ralph wasn't sure he wanted to know the answer.

DOWN THE STREET, Harry was counting his change. Saturday mornings weren't usually that profitable. Cold and irritable people, unlucky enough to work on weekends, who staggered down the street still half asleep, weren't usually in generous moods. He usually had to wait until the shopping and brunch crowd started emerging from their comfortable environments. Still, he had enough for some coffee and donuts. The hot brew and carbohydrates would help keep him warm for the rest of the morning. Sometimes that's all a person needed in life. Hobbling painfully to his feet, he noticed a flow of paper shreds blowing past him along the street. Then he observed Ralph across and down the street a few dozen metres, staring at the wall. Not moving.

"Oh, oh. That police guy found the Horse," Harry muttered to himself. Still carrying the tattered remnants of a

Catholic upbringing, he crossed himself. In a brief second, the old man saw what could only be the glow of self-confidence inside the man replaced by something akin to regret, flavoured with guilt, peppered with a growing sense of fear. A veritable potpourri of dark emotions. He'd seen it all happen before. A lot of people who looked at that Horse knew badness was somehow attached to it. Yeah, it was made of a few layers of spray paint, but that didn't mean anything. It's never what it is that's dangerous, it's where it came from and what it means that can be the problem. Viruses can't be seen. They're smaller than those few layers of spray paint but can cause a lot of damage.

That was understandable. Harry remembered the night he'd come upon the girl — she was a woman, but in so many ways she appeared to be just a young girl, barely taller than his waist — painting the Horse, a number of spray paint cans at her feet. Instinctively he didn't like the Horse, and the Horse didn't like him. And it had taken him a moment to realize that in actuality, there was no woman-girl standing there, glaring at him from in front of the wall, there was only the Horse, disguised as a little girl. And something about that wasn't right to Harry. Giving the girl and the Horse a wide birth, Harry had turned and left, very anxious to relocate to a safe distance. There were other grates in this city with less provocative neighbours. Toronto was a city of grates. Eventually, though, the grate he still operated from was like his own patch of home. No other hole in the sidewalk felt right, and slowly he gravitated back to his corner. An unspoken detente had developed between him and the creature on the wall, so he resumed occupying his small patch of home, continuing to sit here, observing but never crossing the street. This was the agreement.

He wondered only briefly if he should warn the man, because it seemed to Harry the man was taking far too much interest in the Horse, more than a casual glance or appreciation might warrant. Harry feared for the police-man because of the Horse. Yes, Harry could see the man had a gun, a bulletproof vest, a baton, all the usual accoutre-ments for aggression and self-defence. But what could they do against the Horse?

Crossing himself once more for reasons he could barely remember, he declined to warn the man, as that would require him to venture near the Horse, which was against the agreement. *We all choose our own paths*, Harry thought. *We can't choose them for other people.* Instead, Harry shuffled off to the nearest Tim Hortons, where life and problems were much simpler. He planned to take two crullers and call it a morning.

The less Horse in his life, the better, he thought. A double-double in addition to the crullers, on a cold day like today, would solve most of his problems for the moment.

As he walked to the Tim Hortons, the always-smiling Harry realized that he wasn't smiling anymore.

## CHAPTER TWO

RALPH THOMAS WAS ABOUT TO TURN ELEVEN IN A MONTH and was fairly typical, as far as any ten-year-and-eleven-month-old kid on the Otter Lake reserve. He ran. He played. He watched television. He longed to be older. And he fought with his sister. As indicated, a fairly normal existence familiar to most kids, despite their culture.

His sister, Shelley, was seven months into her thirteenth year. And, as is frequently the case between siblings in different grades, the two didn't spend a lot of time together at the reserve school. In fact, she barely acknowledged her younger brother's existence. The priorities of teenage girls frequently conflict with those of younger brothers.

Luckily, this did not trouble the smaller boy, for he had his best friend, William James Williams. William was a bit bigger and rougher than Ralph, and he came from a much larger family. Somewhere in the middle, William was one of the eight kids of Justine and Floyd Williams. More importantly, you never called him Willie, or Billy, or any variation on the name. He would answer only to William.

The two boys had little in common, but, being ten, that didn't matter much. Friends during the summer, winter, and all seasons in between, they did everything together. William practically lived over at the Thomas house and took great delight in being an honorary member of their family. All except for Shelley. It would be polite to say they did not like each other. While it could be said brother and sister tolerated each other, that could not be said about the arrangement between Shelley and William. "Grubby little kiss-up" was Shelley's opinion of her brother's best friend. And "know-it-all bookworm" expressed William's attitude towards his friend's sister quite succinctly. *Hate* is too strong a word to use for such young minds, but it wouldn't be an exaggeration to say that if one never saw the other ever again, few tears would be shed. Alien abductions were frequently hoped for by both parties.

It was a Tuesday in the dark days of late January. Snow had come early and hard two months before, and the land was blanketed by millions of snowflakes. As a result, the roads were liberally sprinkled with salt and sand. Near the school, a snowplough had generously pushed all the snow from the parking lot up into one gigantic hill, perfect for the ancient and honoured contest known to children around the world as "King of the Mountain," proving once again that Darwinism was still practised and embraced on this little patch of the Canadian Shield. The snow mountain in question must have been a good three or four metres high, perfect for battles of altitude and advantage. On the other side of the school was a shallow hill where students, though it was forbidden, occasionally took sliding trips down to the bottom. Somehow, flat pieces of cardboard would find their way to the top of the hill for use as impromptu toboggans. With this being an Anishnaabe school, all the students were well aware the word *toboggan* was actually an Anishnaabe word, so they took to the task of hurling themselves down that little hill like fish to water, teachers be damned (though they would never ever say that to their faces), telling themselves they were celebrating their linguistic and cultural heritage.

Both Ralph and William loved tobogganing, but not today. Today's recess was definitely a King of the Mountain day, and, as usual, William was winning. Since he was always willing to push a little harder and shove further, few liked to play with him at that particular game. Except for Ralph. Trusting his friend would never really hurt him, and believing that all things are possible, Ralph took a running start up the side of the snow mountain. He reached the top for less than two seconds before William sent him tumbling down to the bottom. Years of experience and a do-or-die attitude in life had made William a martial artist of piled snow.

"Anybody else wanna take a shot?" William shouted victoriously. As usual, nobody else did.

Ralph rolled over onto his hands and knees slowly, a little bruised here and there, covered in snow but still determined one of these days to survey the world from the top of that frozen mountain. Someday, somehow, William would be defeated. If there was one thing his brief academic study of history had taught Ralph, it was that eventually, all rulers, tyrants, despots, and kings — snow mountain or otherwise — were defeated. Sometimes it just took a little longer. And maybe a better set of boots.

It was while in that position that he noticed a pair of boots standing next to his head, about a foot or so from his shoulder. He knew those boots well. Light brown and white, rubber soles but kind of a fake suede top. "Hey, Shelley, whatcha doin' over here? Wanna play?" Looking up, the prone boy saw a disapproving look on his disapproving sister.

"Yeah. Like I would. Look at It up there. What a jerk."

"Is that why you're over here? To tell me he's a jerk?"

"I think you know that already. Everybody does except … It." Shelley always referred to William as "It", if an It can be a person. And there was always a little dramatic pause before uttering the word, like it was an unpleasant effort to even mention his existence. "Listen, I don't want to be here any longer than I have to … do you need help getting up or something?"

Ralph managed to get to his feet. The last thing he needed was other kids seeing his sister help him stand up after his best friend threw him down a snow mountain. Upright and facing his sister, he asked her, "What?"

She was looking at the pile of snow. "What a stupid game. So boyish. Anyway, I went home for lunch, and Mom … well, she has this idea."

Ralph rolled his eyes. "A 'Mom' idea?"

Shelley grimly nodded. "Yeah, a 'Mom' idea."

Liz Thomas, to put it politely, was a bit more free-spirited than most Otter Lake residents. If she were white and living in the 1960s, *hippie-ish* might be the best adjective.

She was the first to introduce tofu to the reserve, with limited success. Most community members believed Indian tacos were not created with tofu in mind. In her philosophy, the world was an open book, and she wanted to read every page, as well as making her children and husband do so. Tye Thomas had long ago accepted his wife's unique interests. When things got bad, there was usually a hockey game to lose himself in. Actually, sometimes there didn't seem to be enough hockey games.

Some theorize that's why he took up golf.

"What now?" said Ralph.

"She's painted the bottom half of the wall next to the refrigerator black."

"She did? Black? Why did she do that?" Damn it. Ralph could feel snow deep in his boot. It was melting.

"It seems we now have our own kind of chalkboard." Shelley waited for her brother to react.

"Oh." He paused for a moment, contemplating what his sister had just said.

"Why do we have our own kind of chalkboard?"

"Because she wants us to draw pictures." This succeeded in getting a furrowed brow from Ralph, the snow water in his boot now forgotten.

"Pictures? Of what?"

Looking over her shoulder to make sure Vanessa was still talking to Julia and hadn't wandered away, Shelley was already bored with talking to her brother. It seemed she always had to explain stuff to him. "Of whatever. I don't know. Our mother, for whatever reason, wants us and some other kids to draw pictures to let out our inner artist.

She now calls it the Everything Wall."

There was a moment of silence as Ralph processed this information. "The Everything Wall. What the heck is that? I don't think I've got an inner artist. Or an outer one. Oh, god. Shelley, do something!"

"Can't. Already tried. It's done. You know Mom. So you and I have been told to invite people over after school to draw pictures."

"Pictures? That's embarrassing."

"Yes. I am aware of that, but there's more. I think she knew we'd feel this way, so as some kind of lure, there will be a weekly prize for the best picture."

"Prize? What kind of prize?"

"Again, I don't know. Ask her." Shelley could tell William was watching them, but glancing up at him high atop the snow might indicate she was aware of his existence in this universe. "I'm going now."

She turned to leave. Ralph followed her for two steps. "Shelley."

"Nothing I can do, Ralph. But just do me a favour." She stopped, taking a deep breath. "For God's sake, don't invite … It." She visibly shuddered. "I see enough of … It as it is." With that, Shelley walked away in the direction of her own friends, most of whom would not be seen dead standing atop a pile of dirty snow.

Ralph stood a moment, pondering the repercussions of Shelley's message. Drawing? Chalkboards? Prizes? Obviously he loved their mother, but he frequently wondered if all parents worked at embarrassing their children. Some, like William's, had raging fights in public.

The one they'd had in church had become a local legend, repeated frequently by adults over cans of beer. But most parents, he thought, had a much lower embarrassment rating than his and Shelley's.

He remembered the time his mother had gone out and bought a cow, hoping to have their own milk and, who knows, down the road maybe make some cheese and butter. There were two additional acres of land behind their house, and it had seemed like a good idea at the time. Liz had been in a holistic, organic state of mind. It all made perfect sense to her. Again, at the time. Unfortunately, she bought the wrong kind of cow. The bovine wholesaler had misunderstood her missives about providing for her family and had delivered a cow fattened for slaughtering, not milking. Though the whole family ate and adored beef, the idea of taking the life of Angus, both the cow's name and breed, seemed tantamount to harvesting a pet for appetizers. After much embarrassment, it was decided the cow would go to a nearby petting zoo; thus ended a very expensive experiment, but the legend continued for months and years after.

"Hey, whatcha thinking about?" With nobody to challenge him, William had come down the mountain in search of something interesting.

Ralph sighed. "My mom again."

"I like your mom." William shoved his hands deep into his jacket. Being the middle child — actually the fifth in a line of eight — he lived in a house of perpetual hand-me-downs. And somehow, gloves never made it past the third or fourth brother.

"You like anybody who will feed you. You're like a stray dog."

"Woof!" William smiled at his own joke.

The snow deep in his right boot had officially melted completely. Ralph would spend the rest of the day with a wet sock as well as having to look forward to whatever his mother had concocted when he got home. Supposedly there was a test or something next period in geography, about places he quite probably would never have the chance to visit in person. "William, you can draw, right?"

He nodded eagerly. "Yeah, I can draw. Everybody can draw. Just some people like me do it better. Why?"

"Well ..." And Ralph told his friend about his mother's latest escapade, despite his sister's adamant request.

Unlike Ralph and Shelley, William's reaction was considerably more positive. "Cool. I like prizes. I'll be over right after school."

Suddenly the school bell rang, indicating the end of recess, and all fun stopped within a twenty-metre radius of the building. Abruptly, Ralph felt William, his very competitive friend, slap his shoulder while running past him, almost knocking him over. "Race you to the school doors!" And then he was gone, sprinting across the parking lot. Years of being William's friend had taught Ralph many things, including never to let a challenge go unchallenged. One of the things William admired about his buddy, though the bro code of that age would never allow him to admit it, was Ralph's determination to somehow beat him at almost anything, or at the very least to try to keep up. It would never happen, of course, but he had to give Ralph an unvoiced, "I respect you for your attempts, and by all means, do keep trying."

Almost immediately, Ralph bolted after his friend, hot on his heels. William tried to dislodge and lose him as he slalomed between the teachers' cars, but Ralph was determined, practically fixated on the back of William's head. Staying directly on his friend's tail, centimetre by centimetre he almost caught up to him near the last line of the teachers' cars, but William quickly ducked behind a large van and suddenly doubled back.

Ralph, instead, ran full blast around the van and directly into a little girl. An irresistible boy met an immovable girl, and both went down in a flurry of arms, legs, and toques, one young body bouncing off a Chrysler LeBaron. Ralph was first to get up, convinced he had caught ever-elusive William, and turned, ready to pounce. Instead, Danielle Gaadaw lay sprawled at his feet. Best described as small, thin, waifish, practically elf-like, Danielle was easy to miss in any crowd. But here, alone, her back against the LeBaron tire, surrounded by a now-ripped bag of potato chips spread liberally out on the ground in a semi-circle, she was quite obvious. Danielle blinked a few times, not quite sure what had happened.

"Oh, geez, sorry ... uh ... Danielle. I didn't mean to knock you down. I was running and ..." Ralph ineffectively tried to pick up her soiled chips into something salvageable. Danielle was almost a year younger than him and almost four inches smaller. He knew her slightly from school. "Are you okay?" She nodded, managing a small smile, and slowly managed to crawl to her feet. Most of the clothes she was wearing seemed baggy and worn, except for her snow jacket, which was too small. They all looked like they were meant for anybody but her. Ralph could see she was shivering.

That realization quickly evaporated as the final buzzer rang, giving the tardy kids a thirty-second warning. Off in the distance, he could see William standing by the door, looking around for him, grinning victoriously. "We'd better get inside. You'd better hurry up. Sorry again." Quickly he thrust the mess of potato chips he'd collected at her and ran for the door. Most of the crushed potato chips dribbled through her fingers and down the front of her coat onto the damp, snowy ground. By the time Ralph got to the school door, Danielle had been forgotten.

Back in the parking lot, the little girl stood quietly, so quietly that not even the snowflakes falling gently around her took notice. "That's okay," she said to the empty parking lot as more potato chip crumbs fell off her to the ground, along with the snowflakes. Then, putting one foot in front of the other, she made her way across the deserted playground, almost disappearing behind a variety of snowmen and forts. Casually brushing the bits and pieces of her meagre lunch off her faded dirty white jacket, she politely deposited the now useless chip bag into a big garbage bin. The young girl wasn't worried about missing the bell. Danielle seldom got in trouble, because the teachers either felt sorry for her or didn't think it was worth their time and effort. Sometimes being anonymous has its advantages. But not often.

"SO, DID YOU invite some of your friends?" asked Liz Thomas, mother of Ralph and Shelley. She was cutting back and forth across the kitchen, like a yacht tacking to find the right wind. Stocky, but still possessing the energy that could fuel a thousand bingo games, Liz put away the groceries she had bought that day.

Shelley, drinking a cup of tea her mother had just poured for her, nodded. Her face was deep inside a magazine, reading about places and people far away from her mother and the black stretch of wall next to the refrigerator.

"And?" Liz had played this game with her daughter countless times. The world was more interesting than Shelley was willing to believe, and part of a mother's responsibility was to show that to her children, no matter the cost to elementary school prestige. In later years, she was sure they would thank her. But for now, like going to the dentist, it meant some drilling.

Sighing, Shelley looked up from the table. "Louise and MaryAnn might come over later. Sheila definitely was not interested." Under her breath, she added, "Very embarrassing."

"What about your brother? Did he invite his friends?"

Now, attention back deep in the magazine, Shelley took a moment to respond. "I don't know. You'll have to ask him."

"Didn't he say once that William was a good artist?" Liz asked, washing her hands in the sink.

"Once again, you'll have to ask him. But I did tell him."

Now drying her hands, Liz looked at her daughter. Though there was definitely an atmosphere of disinterest and perhaps a little scorn at her idea, she was pretty sure her daughter would quickly gain interest in the project. After all, what kid didn't enjoy drawing? Liz certainly had. Back in her day, she could name all the Native artists that were changing the face of Canadian art. Somewhere in the attic were her assignments on Roy Thomas, Benjamin Chee Chee, Daphne Odjig, and a dozen others who deserved to be honoured and venerated. It was only her early marriage, pregnancy, and crushing lack of talent that had prevented the woman from exploring a career in art. It simply did not occur to Liz that possibly twelve-turning-thirteen-year-old girls might not share her enthusiasm.

Pausing for a second, with a box of macaroni in one hand and something green and leafy called kale in the other, she looked at her daughter. She was well aware of her daughter's antagonism towards the Williams boy, and, admittedly, it amused her. "Shelley, why don't you like William? He's your brother's best friend. He's energetic, funny, and a good influence on Ralph." She opened the fridge and put the kale and macaroni in it. "But then again, all little girls hate little boys, I suppose. I remember this one boy, George, my goodness, I haven't seen him in years. Anyway, I absolutely —" She opened the fridge door and removed the macaroni.

Standing up from the table, Shelley gave her mother a proper, bordering-on-teen, stern look. "I am not a little girl. I am almost thirteen. And I don't like … It because It is mean, rough, and just a nasty little boy. He's a bully. What other reasons are there? You're just too blind to see it. Trust me, you just don't know the real William."

"Well, at least you said his real name. That's a beginning."

If it were possible, Shelley would have given her mother an even sterner look.

"Look, *kwesans*, why don't you give the Everything Wall a try? Just draw something. Anything. For me? I'll love you even more if you do! You'll be my favourite today. Promise." Liz opened a cupboard door and placed the box of macaroni on the shelf.

The stern look gave way to a quick rolling of the eyes. *Kwesans* meant "little girl" in Anishnaabe, and for both Liz and Shelley, it was the equivalent of bringing out the big guns. Shelley now had no option.

"Fine," came her exasperated response. Reeking of reluctance, the young girl dropped the magazine on the table and grabbed a piece of yellow chalk. Shelley knelt down to where the black wall began. Rolling the chalk between her fingers, she studied the Wall, looking for inspiration. It eluded her for a minute or so, then she began with a few hesitant lines, bright yellow streaks against the dark background. Inspired, Shelley reached over to the box of chalk and grabbed two more pieces, red and blue. And then a fourth, green.

Smiling, Liz watched her daughter's hands fly up and across the Everything Wall, a layer of fine dust gently falling to the floor. Within another three minutes, Shelley was putting the finishing touches on a rather unflattering image of what had to be William. Practically grinning with mischief, Shelley stepped back beside her mother, and together they surveyed her efforts.

"Well, what do you think?"

"I think the horns are a little too much, don't you?"

"I am trying to catch the inner William. Almost an improvement, I'd say."

Silently, Liz raised an eyebrow. "I saw somebody use this term on television once. I think it's from a book, but I thinks it pretty much sums up your creation."

"Yeah, what's that?"

"Methinks thou dost protest too much."

Shelley was silent for a moment, rolling the sentence around in her mind. "What the heck does that mean?"

"Look it up. And thanks. The Everything Wall has officially been christened. Today, you are officially my favourite, my daughter." Technically, being Liz's favourite had little cachet, as the privilege changed back and forth between Ralph and Shelley on a daily, sometimes hourly, basis. Grabbing her own tea, Liz left the kitchen after giving Shelley a quick kiss on the top of her head. Shelley returned to her work and added another touch here and there until satisfied. Finally, the only other thing she could do was to utter the word, "Perfect."

About an hour or so later, Ralph and William came in the door, or, more accurately, exploded through the door, soaking wet from various messy adventures in the snow. Ralph even had snow in his hair. "No fair. You hit me from behind."

"All ninjas do. It's part of the job description. A back of the head hit is completely allowed. You should have ducked."

Taking off his boots, Ralph shook the snow from his head. "Who ever heard of an Ojibwa ninja before? And how can you duck when the snowball is coming at you from behind? Geez."

"Not my problem." William's jacket and boots went flying into the corner. "Hey, what's that?" He was referring to Shelley's creation on the Everything Wall.

Now Ralph saw it. Both peered at it closely.

"I don't know. It's pretty good."

Shelley suddenly appeared, coming from the living room. The television could be heard in the background. "If you must know, it's a monster. A horrible, evil monster."

"A wendigo?!" said William. "My grandfather used to tell me about those all the time."

Shelley shook her head. "Worse than a wendigo."

"I like the horns."

"Hey, William. It kind of looks like you." Ralph was staring at it closely.

"Does not." He looked closer. "Does it?"

Laughing, Shelley went back to her television show in the living room. William studied the chalk image. "Nah, I look a lot better than that. Way better. But wow, she's a worse artist than we thought. My turn!" Showing an eagerness born of someone desperate to be acknowledged, William grabbed a handful of chalk from the counter and, down on one knee, attacked the Wall like a beaver does a birch.

"What are you drawing?" inquired Ralph.

"I'm not drawing. I'm creating. Big difference. All artists know that. But you'll have to wait and see." The tip of his tongue protruded from the left side of his mouth as William chose his colours carefully. The boy only needed four — white, red, dark blue, and grey. Now fully squatting in front of the Wall, William started on the outside of whatever he was drawing then drew closer to the centre. Intrigued by his friend's unusual concentration, Ralph watched William, intrigued by how his somewhat brutish and physically aggressive friend was now channelling his energy elsewhere. Into something that didn't require Ralph or anyone else losing a battle of some kind.

As best Ralph could tell, William's creation was a lot more detailed than what Shelley had drawn. Ralph sat on the floor beside his friend and watched William contribute to the Everything Wall, the only sound in the kitchen the ticking of a clock and the scratching of chalk on painted wood. There was a focus on the young man's face Ralph had never seen before. Somewhere overhead he could hear his mother putting clothes away from the morning laundry. In the other room, he could hear one of Shelley's silly afternoon programs. A few more minutes passed before Ralph realized he was thirsty. Inside the refrigerator he found a can of pop, a local low-cost cola. Mom rarely went for the big-name brands.

"I'll take one too," said William, still intent on visualizing his creation but not passing up the chance for a free pop.

A few minutes dragged into five, then ten, and finally fifteen before William emerged from the creative blanket that had surrounded him with a look of superior achievement. "There. It's done." That's when he realized he was alone in the kitchen. "Ralph! Ralph! I'm done. Come take a look."

It took a second or two before Ralph made his way into the kitchen. "It's about time." He looked at William's creation. "What is that? A boat?" Indeed it did look like a boat, but an odd one, with the bow looking unusually long and stocky but powerful, not dissimilar to William himself.

"Good eye, Ralph. They're called Cigarette boats. They're used all the time down in Florida. Remember that old show *Miami Vice*? They go real fast. Drug smugglers and racers use them all the time. They're so cool. I'm gonna get one someday. Can you picture me racing down Otter Lake in one of those?"

Though Ralph was unfamiliar with the type of boat William was describing, the chalk image looked remarkably detailed for a ten-year-old. He had to hand it to his buddy, the boy could draw. Sitting behind the boat's hood were two small, almost indistinguishable characters.

"You gonna draw anything or just give up now?" With his boyish grin working at 120 watts, William knew whatever prize was being offered for best drawing was his. Nobody in the house or maybe even the village could lay a hand on him or anything he could create. His school notebooks were famous for the intricate KISS and AC/DC depictions on the covers. He'd even had a few requests from friends to illustrate their notebook covers, and he would, obviously enjoying the attention. But even William would draw the line at anything girly. No unicorns, unless they were battling to the death. No kittens, unless they were in a dog's mouth. And especially no Britney Spears or anything remotely like her. He, like all artists, had standards.

"Well?" he asked again.

"I'm thinking," answered Ralph.

"Think all you want, but it ain't gonna help."

Suddenly Shelley appeared in the doorway from the living room. "It drew a boat. A weird-looking boat ...."

"No. Not just a boat. A Cigarette boat. Fastest boat around. Kinda cool, huh?"

Shrugging, Shelley got a pop from the fridge and returned to the living room, not giving William the bonus of a verbal response.

"I don't think she likes me. Her loss."

"What is it with you two, anyway? She's my sister. I have a reason not to get along with her. But you two ... I don't get it."

"Ask her. I'm just here for the pop and the chalk. When do I get my prize?!"

Ralph was clearly frustrated. Sometimes Shelley was right; William could be so annoying. "I don't know. You'll have to ask my mother. Want me to call her?"

William sat down at the kitchen table. "That's okay. I can wait." Once again, he smiled expectantly. "When's your father coming home?"

"In a few days. Says he'll be home for two weeks this time." Tye Thomas was a long-distance trucker and spent extended periods of time travelling the highways of the country, transporting milk, paper towels, diapers, batteries, and, once, an entire trailer full of Bryan Adams CDs. All the essentials for a comfortable Canadian existence. A few centuries earlier, Tye's ancestors had done a similar thing with voyageurs and fur traders, but in today's society, the truckers' union made his work a little less labour-intensive. Still, it meant long periods of time away from his family. What he couldn't give in quantity, he strove to deliver in quality.

"You must miss him."

Ralph gave his friend his best shrug. "I guess." There was a pause. "Don't you have someplace to go? Like a home of your own, maybe?"

William was silent for a moment before responding.

"Sometimes, when my father's away … I kind of like it. Don't get me wrong. I mean, he's my father. But the place is a lot quieter. Not as much — I don't know — fuss, I guess."

Tye Thomas had once described William's family as being like a mountain range, with huge peaks of emotion, frequently followed by deep valleys of moodiness. The family lived in a cycle of domestic activity that many thought existed only on television. That's why William's almost constant presence annoyed only Shelley. This week, it seemed, the Williams family was only smouldering.

Ralph looked at the clock on the wall. "Isn't it about dinnertime at your place?" William's family usually ate early so almost everybody could get out of the house for a few more hours. Even Justine Williams, William's mother, took a remedial Anishnaabemowin class, not out of a love for her ancestors' method of communication but to remind herself there were other people in the universe.

"They won't miss me. They know I'm here. I'm always here. What's for dinner?" William drained the last of his pop then crushed the can.

OUTSIDE THE THOMAS house it was snowing gently, almost picturesquely. The sun was just setting, and the shadows were getting longer and more abstract in appearance. Additionally, the temperature was getting colder, as was wont to happen when darkness gripped the land. An occasional car drove down the odd road here and there, but most Otter Lake residents were safely ensconced in their homes, enjoying the warmth and dinner.

Danielle's right foot was cold, very cold. There was a hole somewhere in her boot, and even though she'd tried many times to find it and somehow plug it, the hole always seemed to defeat her and reappear. Bigger every time, she was convinced. And even though the ambient temperature was well below the melting point of snow, somehow her foot always managed to get wet. She had only three pairs of socks in the world; one was already wet from her walk to school this morning, and this one was wet from recess and the walk home. She still had one more set waiting at home. Thank God for small mercies, a distantly remembered grandmother had once told her.

As she ambled by the house where that boy she'd talked with at recess lived, she hoped there'd be something to eat when she got home. That was always a question. A crapshoot, as an also barely remembered grandfather had once said, though Danielle had never been able to quite decipher the meaning of that term. Even though Ralph's house was bundled up with storm windows and closed doors, she could still smell something coming from the house that had to be dinner. Whatever it was, it had onions in it. Danielle liked cooked onions.

The shadows across Otter Lake were growing long, far too long for elementary students to be making their way home after school, but this was Danielle's normal practice. She'd stay at school as long as she could, reading, playing by herself, drawing, whatever she could, until the janitor would gently tell her it was time to lock the doors and close the school for the night. Then the young girl would put on her boots, one usually soaking wet from an earlier recess excursion, and make the long walk back home, shivering all the way, frequently stretching a twenty-minute walk into a good forty-five minutes.

Sometimes, if it rained pretty hard, she'd hide under the awning at the band office until the weather cleared; if she was really lucky, she might find a stray dog or cat to play with.

Walking into her house, at the far southern end of Otter Lake, was another matter. The only good thing waiting for her in there was a dry pair of socks.

# CHAPTER THREE

HARRY WALKED OUT OF THE TIM HORTONS, HIS BLOOD fortified with substantial amounts of caffeine as well as dangerous amounts of sugar and starches. Over the years he had developed a good relationship with the rotating staff of the franchise. They tolerated him, frequently letting him hide in a back booth during the particularly cold periods of the season, during Toronto's infamous Extreme Cold Weather Alerts. Due to his unique talent, he could tell which staff were more tolerant of his existence and which had souls that were less developed. Sandi, the assistant manager, was such a good person, occasionally slipping him something day-old on days when the public were less inclined to redistribute some of their wealth. Poor Sandi was prone to deep periods of depression, he could tell, frequently relying on prescribed pharmaceuticals to keep her making lattes and smiling. Her aura kept changing colours. It wasn't fixed. Everybody should have a fixed aura.

It was later, almost lunchtime, when he emerged, as this

was an excellent time to exercise his profession. Taking up position beside his grate, Harry got out his sign — ALMS FOR THE POOR/LOONIES FOR THE SOCIALLY DISINCLINED. He actually didn't know what the sign meant, but a buddy he had met a long time ago in a shelter had made it for him. It seemed to make people laugh — and that was good in his vocation. Such amusement frequently equalled the juice from a bean grown an ocean away. Modern commerce commonly confused Harry.

Across the road, he saw the police officer, still standing there. That was why he'd gone into the donut place. This man, looking at the Horse, had made Harry uncomfortable. The man hadn't left. He was now taking a picture of the painting. Conflicted, Harry leaned back against a brick wall. Everything in his sixty-four years of existence — if that was indeed how old he was; he just remembered from long ago a song about being sixty-four — had taught him to stay away from the Horse. Most silly people thought it was just a picture on a deserted building. Not everybody was as smart as Harry, but this guy .... There was something different. It wasn't just idle curiosity. Even from across the busy street, Harry thought he could see a look of recognition. From both the man and the Horse.

Constable Ralph Thomas took two more pictures. This was weird. It couldn't be the Horse, but there was no doubt, it was indeed the Horse, right down to the handprint. Both Shelley and William weren't answering their phones. For personal and professional reasons, Ralph would frequently use the camera app on his phone just for such emergencies. He would email these to the couple when he got the chance. Maybe they would have a reasonable explanation for what he was looking at.

"Hey, you! Police boy! I need to talk to you."

Surprised, Ralph turned around. Across the road he saw a short man, bushy and faded. The sitting man was gesturing at him, urging him to cross to his side of the street. More oddly, the person, obviously street familiar, kept looking over Ralph's shoulder at the Horse, somewhat fearfully.

"What?" Ralph yelled back.

Yelling, but whispering at the same time, Harry put his hands around his mouth. "No, over here. I can't go over there. Come here!" Once again, he gestured for Ralph to cross the street. "It's about your friend." Harry pointed at the Horse. For a second, the constable wasn't sure if the old man was referring to the Horse or possibly to the person who had drawn it. Logic told him there was only one way to find out.

Crossing the street, Constable Thomas was well aware that he was jaywalking. The irony was not lost on him. Situations like this required unorthodox responses. Four lanes and a few seconds later, Ralph stood over the sitting man.

"You're awfully pushy for someone looking for loose change."

Harry almost laughed. "I don't want your money, but I thought I should warn you. You should be careful over there. The Horse ... he likes you. He doesn't like a lot of people, but still, he's got a temper. Best to stay away."

The world stopped spinning. Ralph turned his full attention to the worn but oddly happy old man. Harry shifted the cardboard mat beneath him in order to let more heat rise from the vents below the grate. Ralph paused, barely able to get the words out.

"You know the Horse? You've met her? I mean the person who drew … that?"

"Him, you mean. I know he looks like a her, but the Horse is a him. A dark him. You should count yourself lucky."

Kneeling down, Ralph locked eyes with the unusual fellow. "Do you know something about that Horse? Do you know who painted it?" Ralph asked, in full cop mode. His words sounded inadequate to his own ears, his voice weak. He didn't sound like he was in control of the situation.

Harry could see the policeman better. He was just a boy. Indian … he could tell the boy was Indian, both by sight and glow. He knew that term was out of time, but that was what he had grown up hearing and that was what was burned into his memory. Political correctness was low on the priority list for those living on the streets. This boy standing in front of him was an Indian cop. Harry didn't see a lot of this type patrolling the streets. The times were changing. Moving beyond that, everything Harry could see at the police boy's centre told him this man was good. A bit lazy. Once had focus but now was more or less treading conviction water. Had family he cared about. But now was worried about something. It took a second, but Harry quickly deduced the situation. "You weren't expecting to see the Horse. That's why you're looking so shaken, huh? He reached out and grabbed you. Scary, huh?"

Ralph stepped back, startled. He was taller than the old man sitting in front of him, a good thirty pounds heavier, some thirty-five years younger, and substantially better trained and armed, if it came to that. Still, it was prudent to be wary of those possessing the kind of knowledge they, under normal circumstances, should not possess. Crawling to his knees and then standing on his feet, groaning noticeably, Harry stood eye-to-chin with Ralph. "I can't go over there. He won't let me. But I can tell, he knows you. He'll allow it."

Unable to control his actions, Ralph once more looked over at the Horse on the wall. It had not changed. It was still there, unmoved, but managing to stare at the two of them. The old man talked like the image was alive. And had a gender. Ralph felt a chill unrelated to the climate. Was he, Constable Ralph Thomas of the Otter Lake First Nation and long-ago viewer of the Horse, afraid of it? No, that was ridiculous. It was, after all, a spray-painted image. Even so, whatever it represented — then and now — was no threat to him. How could it be? He was simply shocked by seeing it again, after all these decades. That's what scared him. As for this transient in front of him ...

"Sir, who are you?"

"I'm Harry."

"Harry what?"

Once more, Harry smiled. "Out here, you only need one name."

"Why won't the Horse let you cross the street?"

"I think the more interesting question is, how does he know you?" For a few seconds, Ralph wondered how to answer a question like that. But luckily, Harry asked a question easier to answer.

"Do you like chili?"

Much like his earlier comment about the Horse, Harry's question took the constable by surprise. "Uh, yeah."

Harry grabbed the police boy's arm, gently leading him down the block, back to the Tim Hortons. "Good. On cold days like today, donuts just aren't enough. A day like today calls for something more substantial. Like chili. Any man with matching socks can obviously afford to treat me."

*This guy smiles a lot*, thought Ralph, disappearing through the doors with his new buddy. The good thing was, Ralph really did like chili. The bad news was just not at this very moment.

A short time later, Harry and Ralph were sitting by a window. Harry was turning out to be an expensive date. The world was walking by, but Ralph only had eyes and ears for the odd man devouring his second bowl of chili, as well as the bread and coffee he'd ordered with it. Meanwhile, Ralph was patiently waiting, warming his hands on a large black coffee, dark roasted. He had patiently waited for the strange street dweller to quell his appetite, but now he wanted a return on the investment of his time.

"So, tell me about the Horse."

"He likes you, you know. I can tell. He doesn't like a lot of people. That's why I think he knows you. You know him from a before time, don't you?" Harry's spoon made scraping noises on the cardboard container, getting the last of the kidney beans into his grateful stomach. Ralph would have been surprised to know Harry hadn't drunk in years. Over the years of self-abuse, the man had reached a point where the alcohol opened more portals in his mind than it had once closed, or was supposed to. Most people drank to forget. Unfortunately for Harry, his drinking proved to reveal too much of the world to him.

"You sound like it's alive or something." Ralph tried to figure out this bottomless pit sitting across from him. In many ways, Harry fit the profile of a homeless man, but in other ways, he differed. Substantially.

Once more, Harry smiled at Ralph's comment. "No. That would be crazy. Alive, no. There's no blood or pulse there. But that doesn't mean he can't be watching us. Existing. That's different. You don't have to be alive to be dangerous. Don't they teach you guys anything?"

"And how is that ... Horse ... dangerous?"

Harry put his empty container down and burped. "You know."

Ralph tried another tack. "I don't. The artist who drew that picture. Did you see her?"

The smile slowly evaporated. "Her? How do you know it's a her?"

"Are you saying it isn't? That a girl ... a woman didn't draw that Horse?" Ralph leaned forward, anxiously awaiting an answer.

"Once maybe. Maybe once." Harry looked out the window, across the street to where he could see just the head of the animal looking around the corner of a roti shop. No normal woman, or man for that matter, could have drawn an image like that. This police boy should know that. It was time to have a talk about the facts of life with this young man.

"Police boy," Harry said, turning his attention to the man nursing his coffee like an amateur. "Why did you become a cop?"

*CHAPTER FOUR*

IN THE SCHOOL PLAYGROUND, RALPH AND WILLIAM WERE loitering, bored with themselves. The game of King of the Hill had been officially banned by the Powers That Be who ran the school. Always a rebel of sorts, William was willing to poke the beast of school authority for the thrill of pushing classmates down a dirty pile of snow, but Ralph was not. Poking any type of beast was not one of his favourite activities. So instead, they leaned against the swings where the younger kids would occasionally play, looking out at the playground.

Without adrenaline to get his heart pumping and muscles moving, it turned out William was not a very articulate conversationalist. There they stood, the both of them, watching the elementary school world go by. "Hey, did you hear? There's talk of the school getting the internet!"

William seemed unimpressed. "Nope, what's that?"

"Some sort of computer network thing. You can learn and find all kinds of things. Mrs. Kendrick described it like having an entire library in your typewriter. And ... and ...

you can send messages and all sorts of cool things out to people."

William thought for a moment. "Kinda like Spock's library computer on *Star Trek*?"

Now Ralph thought for a moment. "Yeah, kinda. Supposedly it's been popping up all over the world. All you need is a phone line. It's in Baymeadow already."

"Big deal. Nobody will care."

"How come?"

"Nobody will want to do all that typing. All that information, sounds too much like being in school all the time."

Recess wasn't for standing around. It was for running around. Doing things. And what was wrong with King of the Hill, anyway? Nobody ever got hurt ... well, not badly, anyway. "So do you know what the prize is gonna be?! The one I'm gonna win?!" William smiled eagerly.

"You are so sure it's gonna be you."

"Yep. Gotta admit, that Everything Wall was a good idea. I like your mother sometimes. Geez, seems practically everybody's drawn some sort of picture there. None of them very good, of course." Absentmindedly, William grabbed a handful of snow and began making a snowball.

"Yeah, my mother says it's where imagination comes alive." Intentionally, Ralph exaggerated his mother's mannerisms, getting a laugh from William.

"Yeah, that sounds like your mother." Liz Thomas, in one of her annual home beautification attempts, had planted all sorts of new and interesting flowers around her house, determined to make her and her children's home visually arresting. Unfortunately, one of the flowers she'd chosen to line the front of her deck was a particularly lovely strain of poppy. And it wasn't long before somebody made the connection between poppies and heroin. Almost immediately, rumours began to fly about what Liz was really doing with those flowers, completely disregarding the fact that there are dozens of varieties of the poppy plant, of which only one carries the addictive alkaloids that, properly processed, lead to opium, morphine, and heroin. A visit from the local cops failed to put that gossip to rest, and within a week of their blossoming, the poppies were relocated to the compost heap.

William yawned. "And you still haven't drawn anything. What are you waiting for?" William suddenly flung the snowball at a tree, hitting it dead on, showering its roots with bits of lumpy snow.

"I tried three times, but nothing came out. I don't know ..." Unfortunately, Ralph was beginning to feel a little inadequate about his dormant sense of talent and non-existent contribution to the Everything Wall.

"Don't sweat it. Some people know how to draw. Others don't. And I'm happy with that."

Suddenly the bell rang and recess was over. "Is it my imagination or is recess getting shorter and shorter?" said William.

Both boys began walking towards the front doors of the school. Sitting on the steps of the slide, nearby but hidden from where the two boys had been standing, was Danielle. Standing up, she finished off her delayed breakfast, another bag of chips — this time a little more exotic brand of salt and vinegar — and watched the boys travel further away. She watched them leave with a certain longing. It had been a long time since she had walked anywhere with anybody.

"The Everything Wall …," she said. For a brief moment, she seemed happy. Then the second bell rang, and she began walking towards the school. "Imagination comes alive …," Danielle repeated, deep in thought, almost forgetting the wet, squishing sound her right boot made.

FIVE DAYS HAD passed since the creation of the Everything Wall, and the Thomases' wall was alive with life and imagination. Easily two dozen different images of varying styles and talents had been squeezed onto the surface of the black wall. There was still one day left until the winner would be chosen. A motley selection of drawings crowded the kitchen, but it was obvious the boat William had drawn was by far the best. Two of Shelley's closest friends, Vanessa and Julia, had drawn, or more accurately had attempted to draw, their pets, a cat and a dog. Other various friends and family had populated it with animals and objects. Most had laughed at the idea, claiming they were "too old for this kind of thing," but pretty soon, with a little prompting — and occasionally without prompting — somebody would eventually kneel at the Wall, chalk in hand, opening the doors of imagination and letting through what may.

Liz Thomas was pleased. Her little gift to youthful artistic expression was proving surprisingly successful. Part of her was glad William's boat was so good. It was rather obvious he was better at drawing. This way, by picking him, she wouldn't be hurting any of the other youngsters' feelings.

Still, William couldn't continue to win the prize every week, she thought. She'd have to make some rule about that later. More importantly for the moment, her husband was due home that night. It had been three weeks since he'd last slammed the Thomas door behind him, not out of anger but because it had been a windy day and the elements had wanted him to leave with a more emphatic send-off.

This afternoon, she began her usual ritual. Pork chops. Scalloped potatoes. Peas. And, of course, pie. Maybe apple. Possibly a strawberry rhubarb mixture. Liz would make most of the traditional welcome home dinner herself, except for the pie. Her dexterity in the kitchen for some reason did not extend to the baking arts. Experience had taught her her limitations. Those pies came from a small shop in Baymeadow. Once she had made the mistake of bringing home something called a Key Lime pie. Due to its unique appearance, all in the family had refused to call it a pie. And who ate green pies? So that non-pie quickly fell by the wayside.

Tye Thomas's life was one of simplicity. Drive trucks. Come home. Eat the same food he'd been eating for the past four decades. Get to know his kids again. And wife. Catch up on local gossip. Watch some hockey. Laundry. Golf when the season and the weather allowed. And then head out again to parts of the continent where it was his responsibility to prevent product shortages. The eighteen-wheeler he drove was the twentieth-century cargo ship travelling across the land instead of the sea. The Thomas house, located on the Otter Lake reserve, was his home port. And if the projection in his phone call was correct, Tye Thomas should be pulling his own personal cargo ship — a Ram 1500 — into port in the next few hours.

Liz's life was just as simple. The only difference? She wished it wasn't. There was a wayfaring spirit hidden somewhere deep under her polyester blend Baymeadow sweatshirt, struggling to break free. Rather than a cargo ship, she wanted a catamaran, a schooner, a real sailing ship to explore the world, see new things, and have adventures. There were precious few adventures to be had in Otter Lake. She had to live them through her children; thus, the Everything Wall.

A television show about some far-off land played in the living room, and when she craned her head as she was preparing the scalloped potatoes, she could catch some of the visuals as well as the audio commentary. In her heart she kept a list of places that, should she win the lottery, she planned to take her family. There were several of the usual places one would expect: Greece, Australia, New Zealand, England. Some unexpected countries also appeared on that list: Iceland, Ireland, Easter Island. The show currently captivating her interest talked about some ancient civilization in India, which was now on her unofficial list. The world was so fascinating. She loved Otter Lake, but ...

LATER THAT AFTERNOON, Ralph, William, and Shelley were sitting at the Thomas living room table, playing a game of cards, a unique local game called Anishnaabe Rummy. The rules had developed in the community over a number of years and they involved the ability to swoop in on your neighbour's cards, picking the tastiest one, whenever an ace turned up.

Outside, it was a cold, drizzly day. The very first hint of spring had arrived extremely early with a temperature slightly above freezing. Thus, the rain created a dampness and cold that ate through even the best winter gear. As a result, it was an afternoon meant for indoors and cards.

"You're cheating!" yelled Shelley at William.

"Prove it ... I mean, am not!" he replied to the accusation.

Shelley threw her cards down in frustration and stormed away from the game. "I want to go to Vanessa's. I bet they're having fun over there."

"Go right ahead but take an umbrella or a scuba outfit. It's very wet out there."

Looking out the window, Shelley sighed. "I wish somebody could drive me over."

Ralph shuffled the cards once more. "Then you'll have to wait till Mom or Dad gets home. Want another game?"

Depressed that her life had come down to either forging out through the winter rain, or playing cards with her little brother and It she rested her head against the glass. Apathetically, she answered, "I guess." Even this had to be better than reading the book she'd been given for English class. Shelley never understood how a lot of the books they were given to read in school related to her life in Otter Lake. Yes, the human experience was universal, as her teachers tried to drill into her class; but, seriously, a book about a group of stupid boys stranded on tropical island, getting meaner and meaner. If that was of interest to her, there was William to study. He was his own Lord of the Flies. As for the Shakespeare she'd had to read ... cry havoc and let slip the dogs of boredom.

Shelley sat down at the table for another game of Anishnawbe Rummy, there was a slight noise, possibly from the direction of the front door, possibly not. Almost a scratching sound, like a tree branch rubbing against an outside wall. Or the cat trying to get in — if they'd had a cat. "Did you hear that?" she asked.

"Hear what?" William was busy sorting out the cards before dealing them. Despite his talent with chalk, manual dexterity was not his forte.

"Ralph?"

"No. I didn't hear anything. What did you hear? Maybe it was the furnace." Shelley was about to answer him when the mysterious sound repeated itself, this time slightly louder. "I heard it that time. I think someone's at the door."

"What, a mouse?" snorted William, getting ready to deal. "I think I'm first, right?"

"Dealers are never first," Shelley snapped. Leaving her hated enemy, Shelley went to investigate the mysterious noise. Curious, she opened the door to the front steps. Standing on the stoop was a little girl, looking very soggy and uncomfortable. It took a moment for Shelley to place her. She was from their school, but several grades back. All the kids from the reserve and a few from nearby settlements went to the school, and almost everybody knew everybody in one way or another. But not everybody was as unremarkable as Danielle. Somewhere in her almost thirteen years, Shelley had passed this girl on the street, in the hallway, or at some function, but she couldn't seem to recall the tiny creature's name. But at the moment it was a very wet and cold Danielle that was standing at their door. The two boys could hear her teeth chattering from across the living room. Even though the young girl was looking down, Shelley could tell her wet, stringy hair was plastered across her face. She could also see water running down the unfortunate girl's neck. She was shivering with the cold.

"Hello," said the puzzled Shelley. "Who are you?"

At first Danielle didn't respond, and then when she did, her chattering teeth made her difficult to understand. The two boys put down their cards and listened, curious about who Shelley was talking to.

"Christ, that's what's-her-name. Danielle. Isn't it, Ralph?"

"Yeah. What's she doing here?"

Ralph shrugged as Shelley invited Danielle in out of the rain, though that move did little to stop her shivering. "Danielle, is that your name? Oh, you poor thing. You're soaked through to the bone. Let me get a towel. You stay right here."

Shelley closed the door behind Danielle and left the room. The little girl stood in the living room, a puddle of water growing around her feet. William and Ralph looked at each other, not sure what to say.

Ralph finally worked up the nerve. "Hey, Danielle …"

Nervously, she looked up and managed a small, slight smile before Shelley came back, towel in hand. "Take that coat off. Let's get you dry. What are you doing out on a day like today? It's horrible outside. You shouldn't be out there."

Danielle tried to answer, but quickly found a soft, fluffy towel being rubbed across her face, muting her response.

"Are we playing this game or what?" asked William, with a freshly shuffled deck. Shelley and Ralph ignored him.

"There," said Shelley, taking another look at the now semi-drowned girl. "You look a lot better. Almost human." She smiled at the tiny creature in front of her, but wasn't sure if she got a smile back.

"Thank you," said Danielle, too low to be heard clearly.

"I don't think I've ever seen you here before." Shelley took Danielle's tiny jacket, heavy with rainwater, leaving a trail of water as she walked across the room. "What can we do for you?"

There was no response while Shelley hung the girl's coat on the back of a chair over a hot air vent, hoping it would drip reasonably dry with some prodding from the furnace.

Danielle's attention, however, was elsewhere. She had spotted the Everything Wall once the towel was taken from her face. Clearly visible from the front door, across from where she stood, was a black chalkboard with many dubious expressions of art and what appeared to be a welcoming space for one last attempt. Her eyes, unusually alive, almost eager, scanned the images that populated the surface. Near the bottom right of the Wall, close to the humming refrigerator, there was the only untouched space. The little girl smiled and turned towards Shelley. "The Everything Wall."

Shelley nodded. "Is that why you're here? You want to draw something?"

Danielle smiled even brighter. There was a brief and hesitant nod. "Please."

"The chalk box is on the counter. Right there."

Shelley escorted the little girl across the room. As the Wall grew closer, Danielle's smile grew bigger. The tiny girl quickly grabbed the chalk. Shelley thought she heard her say, "Thank you" again, but was unsure. This little Danielle sure was a soft speaker. The older sister looked over at her younger brother, who seemed as puzzled as she was.

William looked impatient, eager to get back to the game he was winning.

"Come on! Are we playing or what?"

With the chalk in her hand, Danielle knelt down, facing the blank spot. Everything and everybody around her seemed to fade away, for at that moment in her life the universe consisted only of her, the expanse of painted plywood, and the chalk, which was her passport to what could be innumerable worlds of wonder. There, she stayed, kneeling as if praying, looking at the Wall.

Puzzled by the girl's sudden appearance and her reaction to the Wall, Ralph watched her. To the young boy, it almost seemed like she was looking not at the Wall but into the Wall. In her left hand a white stick of chalk was clutched, but it didn't move. Danielle was motionless. As if waiting for something.

"She's weird," whispered William.

Shelley glared at the sitting boy. "Shut up. Geez, you're an idiot. She's not weird. Just quiet. Ralph, who is she?"

She was weird, thought Ralph. Everybody knew that.

But weird isn't always a bad thing. Weird could simply mean different. And different could mean special. And special could mean extraordinary. But a lot of the time, William was right. Weird was weird. "She's in our school. I think she's a grade behind me. She comes from down towards Hockey Heights. Other than that, I don't know much about her."

Shelley asked the age-old question unique to Native communities. "Who's her parents?"

"Oh, man. What's their names? William?"

Unlike a lot of questions posed in school classes, this was one the boy could answer. "Yeah, let's see, her father ... I think his name was Albert. Albert Gaadaw. At least I think it was. My father knew him. He died, I think, about four years ago. Construction accident of some kind. And her mother's name ..."

"Hazel," finished Shelley. Even though she'd been only eight, Shelley remembered the accident and everybody talking about it. Something to do with him being buried in a hole in the ground. Hazel Gaadaw. Practically everybody knew of Hazel Gaadaw. And not in a good way. Albert's death had devastated her and had left its repercussions on the woman and, by association, his daughter. Looking again at Danielle, Shelley's immense sense of compassion for anybody other than William became infinite.

"She's awfully skinny," Shelley mentioned, looking at Danielle.

"Yeah, and you're awfully fat. Come on, are we gonna play this game or what?" William was no longer the focus of the afternoon, and that needed to be addressed.

"All right then, let's play your stupid game. Honestly, Ralph, I have no idea how you put up with It. I don't know how It's family puts up with It either."

"My mother tells me I'm adorable. That's why." Smiling, William disappeared into the living room, followed by his fellow Anishnaabe rummy players.

"And I'm not fat!" came Shelley's voice from the other room.

Alone in the kitchen, Danielle was forgotten, which was fine with her. Her eyes were riveted to the Wall and all its potential. She barely breathed. But there was more than the Everything Wall in her eyes. That was merely the door, hiding so much more. There was something else that hid beneath its surface. Something special waiting to come through. Most people saw what was. It was a precious few who could see what could be or even what should be.

Another second passed, then a few more. All the world was silent except for the hum of a fourteen-year-old refrigerator and the squabbling of kids in another room. Danielle raised her left hand to the Wall and slowly drew a curved white line. A second later, another line followed, then another. Faster and faster came the chalk impressions on the Wall, dust like small snowflakes slowly falling to the ground. Grabbing a handful of other chalk pieces, Danielle smiled as the image began to take shape. She could almost see the Horse.

More importantly, it could almost see her.

AFTER HALF AN hour, Ralph was tired of listening to Shelley and William bicker over the card game. At first it had been amusing how everything about one seemed to irritate the other. But by this point, it had become annoying. Every time all three got together — as Shelley would have absolutely nothing to do with William unless Ralph was directly involved — it was the same sequence of events. Shelley would say A. William would respond with a snarky B, usually resulting in Shelley's annoyed C. William would ignore her and move on with D. As predictable as an election on the reserve. Despite Shelley's insistence that he always be around, it was almost like Ralph didn't exist when Shelley and William were together.

Ralph couldn't understand why they bothered hanging around each other so much if they didn't like each other that much. People didn't make much sense, Ralph had wisely concluded, based on his ten, almost eleven years on the planet. His parents were a similar case. His mother, kind of unconventional in many ways. His father, so conventional in other ways. Yet, sixteen years and two kids later, they still managed to move forward in life together. Ralph wondered if his father would be bringing any presents home with him tonight. Sometimes he did and sometimes he didn't, depending on where the trucking company sent him. Admittedly, not a lot of exciting things to buy kids when in Lethbridge for the night, or Hearst.

To give himself some peace, the younger brother quietly slipped away from the living room coffee table, as Shelley was now deeply involved in yet another spirited discussion over William's occasionally unique interpretation of the rules to Anishnaabe rummy.

"You can't do that!" yelled Shelley.

"Sure I can," responded William. "I saw it in a movie."

"What movie? *How To Play Cards Stupidly*?" And on it went. Shelley had a whole set of other friends she preferred to play anything with, but on such a miserable day, it was best to spend time staying home and dry and warm and being miserable with William and Ralph.

Ralph had a mild thirst that if properly exploited would have an additional beneficial effect. This manoeuvre involved moving away from the anarchy of the living room and obtaining water from the tap in the quietness of the kitchen.

The other two did not notice Ralph leaving the table as William practically shoved a seven of clubs into Shelley's face, intent on proving his point, even if unsuccessfully. Part of Ralph was hoping the rain had stopped; this would permit his sister to go over to Vanessa's, leaving him and William to get into their own brand of interaction. Boy stuff. Less bickering.

Once he crossed through the doorway into the kitchen, he saw Danielle partially hidden by the refrigerator. Still kneeling, chalk in hand and in motion. *Oh yeah*, Ralph thought, having completely forgotten about her, as had the other two. She had been so quiet and discreet in the kitchen, her appearance and eager participation in the Everything Wall had faded from their immediate consciousness. But there she was. Her hand fluttering against the Wall. Adding final touches.

When Ralph cleared the refrigerator, he stopped dead in his tracks. He was transfixed. All thoughts of his sister and William and that glass of water just evaporated. Ralph stood some six feet away from the little girl, staring at the Everything Wall and its new citizen. There are few times in a ten-year-old's existence when time and space bend. When all their imagination has taught them no longer is relevant. A child's imagination is powerful for sure, but on rare occasions, it can be overpowered. Augmented with new parameters. The Everything Wall swallowed up ten-year-old Ralph. He disappeared into it long enough for William and Shelley to wonder what had become of the third member of their awkward triumvirate.

"Hey, you playing this hand or what?!" asked William as he entered the kitchen.

Right behind him came Shelley. "I don't know if I want to play cards anymore. It looks like the rain has stopped. I might want to go over to ..." Shelley noticed Ralph's fixed and unresponsive expression. "Ralph, what's wrong?!"

"You got anything to eat?" said William, dodging around Ralph, aiming directly for the refrigerator. He hoped there might be some chicken left over from last night's dinner with the Thomases. There were always leftovers in the Thomas fridge, unlike in his house. The definition of leftovers in the refrigerator at William's home was condiments.

Then William saw the Everything Wall. "What? Geez!" Not many things took the tough boy's breath away, other than a punch to the breadbasket.

Only Shelley had not yet set eyes on what Danielle had created on the Everything Wall, but it was obvious by the reactions of her two male companions that something very different had been added. Off the top of her head, she could not remember either of them stopping so suddenly dead in their tracks, so frozen. This was very un-Ralph and un-William. Curious, and a little concerned, she looked around her brother to the black wall where she had left the quiet little girl from their school to labour away.

"What are you two up ..."

Now Shelley crossed over the border from the annoying and boring world of playing cards and rainy days into what was waiting for her on the Everything Wall. She, too, was silenced. The only sound in the kitchen was the slight, raspy scraping of chalk on wood. A darker tracing here, a thickening border there, defining an edge more clearly near the eye, adding more colour. Despite the reactions of Ralph, William, and Shelley, the Horse was still a work in progress.

All three stared at the Horse. They stood in their tracks, stock-still, taking in Danielle's creation.

To call the creation a horse would have done it and every horse in Creation a disservice. It was the kind of horse every person on Earth would have wanted to ride, but never could. It looked like it was leaping across the Wall, blazing freedom somehow emanating from it. Out of four shades of chalk, Danielle had managed perfectly to sculpt the image of a magnificent steed, every muscle, every sinew, and every hair. The image was better than a photograph. A photograph rendered reality, and reality was sometimes lacking. Danielle's drawing was much better than any artist they had ever seen or read about could have done. The creature on the Everything Wall seemed alive and conscious, real and powerful.

In the drawing of the animal, Danielle had managed to incorporate other images on the Everything Wall. In some cases, the Horse swallowed them up. The Horse was huge, covering the entire Everything Wall. The other images, drawn by Shelley and William and other friends, barely registered; they appeared between the Horse's legs or beyond its back, as if standing aside, making way. It was unlike anything the three had ever seen or even imagined was possible, let alone on the wall of a house on the Otter Lake reserve. But there was the Horse on the Thomas wall, now staring back at them.

Ralph, the first to see it, had been immediately swallowed up by what Danielle had created; he was completely unaware of the arrival of William and Shelley. The creature appeared so noble, if that was the right word. It looked protective and strong, but also kind and caring. There was also wisdom and love captured in Danielle's drawing on that plywood wall. At first, Ralph wasn't sure how he could have come to that unusual understanding — wisdom and love — then he realized it was the eyes. Somehow everything the Horse was, its very essence, poured out of its eyes.

And Danielle's, too. There was an intensity, shining through brightly, Ralph noted, that was not normally seen in shy barely-ten-year-old girls. For a brief moment, Ralph could see through what some have called the crack between the worlds. Fleetingly, he saw what Danielle saw and what she was endeavouring to re-create on their wall. The Horse was everything the girl wasn't. Everything she needed. Everything every person in that room, and perhaps the world, needed, all wrapped up in a chalk drawing. It was obvious, but not in a conscious manner, that what she was creating was the girl's best friend, protector, father, and, were she older, lover. The Horse filled all the missing parts in her life. As the artist, she would call it forth with such mundane equipment as chalk, plywood, and black paint, and it would come. It was as real to her as anything was to anybody. And by some means, this registered on Ralph and the other two witnesses.

The Horse took Shelley's breath away. She'd ridden a horse precisely once during a weekend stay the year before at summer camp. She'd done this with more fear than excitement. But her experience of the creature on the Wall was nothing like that. The Horse's mane was like fire. The hooves like a ballerina's delicate feet. The chest and shoulders massively strong, strong enough to ride into the night and through to the next morning without breaking its stride. Many have said there has always been a spiritual connection between girls and horses, and this animal was the Mount Everest of what that connection could be. Though it was just chalk, Shelley wanted to reach out and touch it, to make sure it really existed. But her arms couldn't or wouldn't move. She continued to look, her eyes doing what her fingers couldn't.

"Holy ...," she managed to say.

William, the least philosophical and imaginative of the three, was equally bedazzled. This little girl he had barely acknowledged or given any thought to, who had by her arrival thrown a wrench into his afternoon activities, had somehow created something that timid little girls shouldn't be able to create. The style and the way she brought it to life didn't just overshadow what he had contributed to the Everything Wall earlier, it practically destroyed it. It wasn't fair. And yet it almost seemed like the Horse was looking at him, staring him down, mocking his effort. Regardless of who had drawn it, the Horse was definitely cool. Cooler than it should be. William couldn't deny that. Dangerous, too. He should have drawn it. That should be William's Horse. But it wasn't. Danielle had brought it into this kitchen, into this world. It taunted him.

"Shit," he managed to say, his voice quiet, full of wonder and envy. Normally that would have earned him a slap on his ten-year-old shoulder from Shelley, but it was unlikely she even heard it.

The three of them did not notice the gradual slowing of Danielle's hand and the return to normal of Danielle's countenance. With a few final touches added to the Horse's tail and right hoof, she put the chalk down. She was finished. She looked it over one last time, visibly pleased at what she had created. Smiling, she got to her feet, gathered up all the pieces of chalk, and neatly presented them to Shelley with a grateful nod. The older girl put her hand out to accept them, not really conscious of what she was doing.

"Thank you," said the little girl, smiling again. She gathered up her still-damp coat, put it on, and walked across the rooms to her equally damp boots and put them on too. Then she turned and opened the door to the outside, far cheerier than the level of moisture in her clothing warranted.

"Wait ...," whispered Ralph.

Danielle stopped and turned around.

"How ... how did you do that?"

Danielle looked again at the Horse, her interest obviously fading. "I dunno." Then, almost as an afterthought, she nodded towards the image on the Wall. "Ask him," she answered, with complete sincerity. Then, just as suddenly as she had arrived, Danielle Gaadaw was out the door.

William was the first to break the silence that permeated the kitchen after the little girl's departure. "I'm not going to win the prize, am I?"

Both Shelley and Ralph slowly shook their heads in agreement.

ALMOST TWO HOURS later, the trio were still admiring Danielle's contribution to the Everything Wall. Used plates, cups, and empty pop cans littered the floor and table, evidence that a few of their baser instincts had kicked in. All three were still in awe of the Horse.

"It's almost like it's alive," said William.

"Where'd she learn how to do that?" asked Shelley.

"Not from our art teacher," added Ralph.

More silence followed.

"What do you think Mom will say when she sees this?"

Ralph thought for a moment. "She will love it. How could she not? She'll want to frame it."

William leaned forward from his seat on the floor to the right of the chalk drawing and hesitantly reached out, touching the tail of the creature. The action instantly caused cries of concern from the other two. His index finger left a small smear of dark brown chalk leading away from the

Horse. "I'm sorry. I just had to touch it. Make sure ... something."

Instantly, Shelley was trying to repair the smudge. "Make sure what?!"

"Make sure it was real," answered Ralph for William.

"Yeah," the other boy acknowledged.

"Well," said Shelley protectively, "it's real."

Some twenty minutes later, Liz Thomas came home, car laden with groceries. Time, as it usually did, had foiled her original plans. The scalloped potatoes she had made earlier were still in the refrigerator, waiting to be popped in the oven. But coffee with Janine Magneen had eaten up more time than expected, and the restocking of the pantry for her husband's return had consumed what precious few minutes were left. Impatiently, she honked the car horn twice, inviting her children to assist her in transporting the food from her vehicle to the kitchen counter. She knew from long experience that after that, she was on her own in distributing the staples and produce to their proper locations. She honked a third and final time, and Ralph and Shelley, along with William, came out of the house to help her. But something was wrong. Liz could see that. They weren't running down the stairs and to the car with excitement. And Shelley and William weren't fighting. William wasn't wrestling with Ralph. Instead, they seemed quite placid, almost reflective. Instantly, Liz hoped this wasn't a portent of something horrible.

"Okay, what's wrong?"

Shelley answered for them all. "Nothing. Absolutely nothing. Hurry up. You gotta see this!" Each grabbed a bag of groceries and entered the house, quickly but orderly. All three stopped inside the doorway, patiently waiting for Liz to follow. This was unnatural. "You're scaring me," said Liz, locking up the car.

"Hurry," said Ralph.

"Yeah, hurry," added William with an eager nod.

Liz entered her house, puzzled and concerned. Still silent, all three kids put their grocery bags on the table, then stepped back, once again looking at the Wall, hidden from Liz's view by the refrigerator.

Expecting a hole, or maybe a dead squirrel — it had happened before — Liz joined the children and met the Horse. She, too, said nothing as she gazed at what was on her Everything Wall. Immediately struck, bewildered by the image and by the ability and talent of the person who'd drawn it, Liz struggled to process the figure now located on her kitchen wall. She was uncomfortable. Frightened? She realized that the ice cream in one of the bags across the table was melting, but at this point it seemed an unimportant issue.

"Who did this? William?"

For a brief second, William's innate nature almost made him claim ownership, but he knew it was a claim impossible for anybody to believe, including himself. He was already learning that reality frequently has a way of keeping people honest. "No. Not me."

"Shelley? Ralph?"

"No," replied Shelley.

"No," replied Ralph.

"Then who?"

"Danielle Gaadaw." Shelley spoke the name of the little girl she was coming to think of as an artist.

It took a moment for Liz to process her daughter's statement of fact. "Albert and Hazel's daughter? I haven't seen her in ages. She did this?"

Ralph nodded. "I watched her do some of it."

The girl definitely had talent, the mother thought. "What did she say? I mean, did she say anything about it?"

William answered. "No. She doesn't talk a lot."

"Yeah. Just said, 'Thank you,' then she pretty much left." Ralph felt they should have thanked her instead.

"She's really weird," added William.

"This is quite an achievement for sure." Liz walked around the children, looking at the Horse from a different angle. "Do any of you know her much? Do you play with her?"

Shelley shook her head. "She's three grades below me and one below Ralph and William. I don't think I've ever seen her play with anybody."

Liz now knelt down, just a few inches away from the image. "Wow."

Ralph agreed. "Yeah. Wow."

"Do you know her?" asked Shelley.

Liz shook her head. "Not really. I see her walking around the village sometimes and think to myself, what a poor little girl. She always looks so small and cold. Even in summer. I always meant to ask somebody about her, but I always seemed to forget. I knew her father a bit. He dug our septic tank."

"And what about her mother? Hazel, right?"

For the first time since entering, Liz took her eyes off the chalk drawing and looked at her daughter. "That is a sad story. Poor Hazel. She really did love Albert. So sad."

Shelley and Ralph looked at each other, not quite understanding.

Ralph expressed their confusion. "What do you mean?"

With barely a shrug of her shoulders, Liz tried to explain the impact tragedy can have on a person. "When somebody you know and love is suddenly gone, sometimes it can leave a vacuum. And sometimes what rushes in to fill that vacuum is not necessarily a good thing. Hazel looked for comfort in some pretty bad places."

"My father always told me to stay away from their house. Says they're bad people. Crazy, even. A lot of drinking, he says." As always, William was nonchalant in relaying his father's opinions.

"Yeah, William, I heard that too. I'm surprised nobody's looked into their lives by now, I mean about Danielle's welfare."

"It can't be all that bad. Look what she can do."

"Yes, William, I am looking at what she can do. I wonder where" — Liz gestured to the Horse — "where this came from."

It was the dripping of melted ice cream on the floor that managed to drag Shelley back into the world of Thomas kitchen reality. "Mom! The ice cream!" Straightening up with a groan, Liz got a cloth from the sink while Shelley attacked the lost dessert. Ralph and William, barely tearing their attention away from the Everything Wall, put the rest of the groceries away, surprising Liz. This was a monumental day in more ways than one.

Once the disaster was dealt with, Liz looked over her shoulder at the Horse. "Well, gang, I guess we have a winner for this week. It is sure gonna be hard to top that. Does everybody agree? Danielle gets the prize?"

They all nodded, including a rather glum William.

Liz opened the refrigerator a foot before pausing. "It's sure going to be a shame to wash that away. It'll bring me to tears for sure."

Ralph looked at his mother. "There's no reason we have to." They all glanced at him. "I say we leave it up. I got no problem with that. There'll be lots of room left to draw. Shelley, William, Mom? What do you say?"

"That's a nice thought, Ralph, but I'd hate to play favourites with all the kids participating, even you three, by favouring one kid's drawing over another. It wouldn't be right."

In the silence that followed, Liz suddenly thought to herself, *Those scalloped potatoes should have been in the oven twenty minutes ago.* She looked at the drawing one more time. "It definitely is worth saving. You guys sure?"

One by one, they nodded their agreement with varying levels of enthusiasm.

"I wonder what she'll draw next?" pondered Shelley.

"That," admitted Liz, "is a very good question."

THE LIBRARY WAS attached to the school the three kids attended, though it was kept as a separate institution. Usually, it was only open for ninety minutes after the school closed during the week, but it was hosting a meeting today — something to do with government attempts at increasing literacy rates in First Nation communities — so Ralph, Shelley and William raced along the frozen roads as fast as they could, knowing time was growing short. The library would be open but not for long.

"Why are we going there again?" asked William.

"You know why. But in case your sad little brain can't figure it out, Ralph, tell It why."

Once again forced to be the mediator, Ralph took a deep breath, partly because of the cardio experience resulting from the half-kilometre power walk and partly because of familial weariness. Sometimes being the bumper nation between two warring parties can be draining.

"Uh …"

Looking up to the sky in a uniquely teenage combination of frustration and annoyance, Shelley practically growled at the two younger boys. "Oh for — Boys. It's absolutely amazing how you guys make thirty cents on the dollar more than we do." As usual, both boys had no idea what Shelley was talking about. Unlike her, they did not, on occasion, watch the evening news with Tye and Liz.

Struggling to keep up with the girl's longer legs, the stocky William shouted at her, "I don't understand!"

Under normal circumstances, William's statement would have been a prime opportunity for the girl to further eviscerate her brother's best buddy. But even Shelley, despite her contempt for William, felt that under the circumstances it would be too easy. Besides, they were in a hurry.

"I just wanna see if maybe we can find a picture of that Horse somewhere. Maybe in one of those books.

That was so amazing, maybe she copied it from something."

William looked to Ralph, sharing the same unspoken thought. *Actually, that was kind of smart.* But neither dared to speak it aloud.

# CHAPTER FIVE

TYE'S RETURN TO THE BLISS OF HIS DOMESTIC LIFE WAS A little different this time. Usually the kids would welcome him back with hugs and kisses. Presents, if any, would be handed out, and of course there would be a kiss from Liz with hints of more passion to follow. But this time, when Tye drove up the long driveway in his truck, there was a different feel to the house. Physicists say the universe vibrates at a certain recognizable resonance, and so, like all families, did the Thomas family. But for some reason, as the man exited the cab of his pickup, he could sense a different rhythm emanating from his home.

Entering, he smelled the welcoming aroma of the pork chops and scalloped potatoes he treasured, but even those, he would later argue, had a different taste to them that evening.

"*Aaniin*!" he announced, entering the kitchen. Usually the family could see and hear his vehicle pulling into the driveway, followed by the driver's door slamming shut and the screen door opening. Today, however, everybody seemed to be running on a lower setting. There was Liz, manning the kitchen like a pro, smiling at the sight of her husband. Frequently they would take turns with the cooking, but it was their custom for her to go all-out on his return.

"Welcome home, my sweet."

Off came his jacket, and Tye leaned over the counter to give his wife a polite but welcome kiss. Normally she would have come around the counter and given him something more appropriate to his being away for three weeks, but her hands were deep inside oven mitts. The scalloped potatoes required her attention, as they can be a harsh mistress to those who are not familiar with their secrets.

Standing a full six feet, Tye still looked as fit as he had when he'd played hockey a few decades back, despite the hours spent behind the wheel of his eighteen-wheeler. He tried to work out when he could on the road, but the anonymous motels he usually found refuge in seldom offered decent athletic facilities. Still, somewhere in his ancestry there was an individual who was thin despite all the moose and fish he ate, and somehow that gene had ended up in Tye's DNA.

Tye surveyed his domestic kingdom, looking for problems, or some new purchase his wife had made, or clues to some adventure she had embarked on. Returning home was frequently an act of gambling. So far nothing nearly as tragic or dangerous as that Greek guy who spent ten years trying to get home. But frequently, what awaited him on his return was uncomfortably surprising.

"Hey, honey. Is everything all right?" Despite spending

three-quarters of his time on the roads of North America, the man still swam through the ocean of the English language with a fairly strong Otter Lake accent.

"Yes. Why?"

He looked around the kitchen. "I don't know. Something feels off. Usually the potatoes are done. Are you just taking them out? And where are the kids? Are they hiding?"

Opening the oven door, Liz Thomas did her best to briefly explain the current situation. "Well, Tye, it's been an interesting afternoon." She closed the oven door, a steaming tray of potatoes and other carbs held in her oven-mitted hands, and navigated her way around the kitchen island to her husband.

Instantly, Tye narrowed his eyes, suspicion making them squint. "What did you do?"

Smiling, she embraced her husband after putting the tray down. "I did nothing."

"My nothing or your nothing?" Though still guarded, Tye returned her hug, relishing the feel of her warm body in his arms. Though not overtly sexual — that would come later — the warmth of her body, the chemistry of their scents, forgave a lot of misadventures. When Tye held Liz in his arms, spooned with her in bed, and held her hand in the movie theatre even after sixteen years, he could forgive her anything short of a homicidal rampage in the local Tim Hortons.

The hug held comfortably for a time, then, without saying a word, Liz took a step back and turned Tye around to face the Everything Wall. Hidden by the refrigerator, he had missed it when he'd walked in. "What the hell?"

Liz watched her husband's eyes take in the Horse.

"I call it the Everything Wall. I came up with the idea last week. You know how parents are always punishing kids for drawing on walls and things like that. I thought, why do we do that? I mean, kids should have the right to draw where they want, right? So this is where they had to tear out a part of the wall to get at the water pipes last spring when the leak happened. And we had never gotten around to fixing it proper and painting it to match. So I painted it black and told the kids they could go nuts there, you know, hoping to encourage their artistic selves. It was a hard sell. Harder than I expected, 'cause you know kids today. William took to it instantly, but the others had to be coaxed. But, of course, the real amazing thing, that one, the Horse, was done by Danielle Gaadaw. Remember her? Albert and Hazel's daughter. Poor thing. I wasn't here, but she just showed up this afternoon and did that. Have you ever seen anything like it? It just took our breaths away. That's kinda why everything is late. We sort of lost track of time, looking at it, talking about it. Sorry, my sweetie. The kids should be back any moment. Actually, they should have been back about half an hour ago. They went to the school library to find books on horses. Hey, did you hear, the reserve may be getting the internet? Anyway, there's some sort of meeting happening tonight, so it's open. Well, that's sort of been what we've been talking about today. What do you think?"

The entire time Liz was explaining the day, Tye had been looking at the Wall. Shelley's rendition of William, William's boat, three dogs, a dream catcher, what might have been a portrait of Brad Pitt, and a plethora of barely recognizable images. And, of course, the Horse, around which all the others seem to be orbiting. But he said nothing.

"Tye?"

"You know …," he said slowly, "… there's a reason most people don't let kids draw on their kitchen walls."

The smile on Liz's face began to fade. "You don't —"

"I mean really, Liz. You want our kitchen to look like this? Some of the places I drive through, this kind of stuff is sprayed on city walls everywhere. And you want to put it in our kitchen? I don't get it."

"But the Horse?"

"Danielle Gaadaw drew that? Seriously? Did you see her do it?"

This was not going the way Liz had expected. Now she was feeling defensive about something that not that long ago had taken her breath away. "No. I was shopping. Ralph says he saw her do some of it. As she was finishing it."

"I think they're putting you on, Liz." Poor Liz, always gullible, it seemed to Tye.

For Liz, the Wall was an entryway for the imagination, but it helped if you had an imagination. Before his career as a truck driver, Tye's understanding of geography had consisted primarily of knowing what cities NHL hockey teams and their farm agencies came from. He loved and adored his wife, but men like Tye didn't really care about what could be; he was too busy dealing with what was.

"The kids like it," Liz responded defensively.

At that moment, the door opened and three bundles of Indigenous youth stormed in the room, two directly into

Tye's arms. "Dad!"

When they'd seen their dad's truck, Ralph and Shelley had thrust their books into William's hands and raced in through the door. William felt a little awkward, putting the books on the table as the family reunion took place. Taking his eyes off the Thomas family, he once again looked at the Horse. It looked back at him, almost taunting him, which he found unnerving.

"I was wondering where you guys were! I thought maybe you found another father or something."

Denials filled the kitchen as Tye half wrestled with his kids. William noticed a slight look of sternness on Liz Thomas's face. Life in his difficult house had taught him to read people, and he knew that look. But he seldom saw it within these four walls. "Did you see the Horse? Did you?" asked Ralph.

Their father's mood changed. "Yes, I did. It's very good."

"Good?! It's amazing!"

"Let's talk about it later. I think dinner's going to be a little late. Come on, let's go in the living room and you can fill me in on your week. You, too, William."

Instantly William was in the other room. Liz could hear Ralph excitedly asking his father, "Did you bring us anything fun?"

"From Brandon?!"

Liz remained alone in the kitchen. She had hoped that somewhere in her husband's experiences and soul existed a small part that could relate to the Everything Wall and, just maybe, the Horse. It didn't look like it. Part of her big fear was that maybe, someday, Ralph's interests might begin drifting towards Tye's universe. There was absolutely nothing wrong with the big guy, it was just that his universe extended only so far. There were borders, like that on the reserve. And his universe didn't include flights of fancy.

Almost forlornly, Liz found herself standing in front of the Horse, sharing her ideas.

"I wish he could see you."

LATER, DURING DINNER, as he told an interesting story about almost hitting a moose on the highway, Tye noticed the three kids frequently looking over their shoulders at the Horse, their attention drifting away a few minutes at a time. The head swivelling became annoying in a remarkably short period of time.

"Hey, are we having dinner in our house or some art gallery? Eyes on the table." All three quickly complied. "That Horse will still be there after we eat."

"Dad! You should draw something!"

"Yeah." A momentous occasion, as Shelley seldom agreed with Ralph on anything. Seems the arrival of the Horse held many advantages for the Thomases. Now it was Tye's turn to look over his shoulder at the Wall.

"Kids, I've done karaoke, I've danced at a few weddings, even did one of those eulogies at my father's funeral, but there are several things I cannot and quite probably will not ever do in the artsy world, and one is draw a picture of anything. My talents lie elsewhere. I'd like to see that Rembrandt fellow drive my big rig in reverse, or Da Vinci figure out how to shift my twelve gears." All three kids laughed. Liz dutifully ate her scalloped potatoes, choosing wisely not to comment.

Tye looked at the image again, sizing it up, trying to put a label on it other than a picture drawn by a small, skinny, weird girl who lived over in the non-status part of the community. Horses like that did not come from such beings. Just before dinner, the three youngsters had meticulously gone through the three books they'd brought home from the library, looking for anything that might give them a clue as to who or what the Horse was, or even where in the world it could have come from. There were plenty of equine representations in those books, but nothing that quite matched the majesty of what was drawn on the Everything Wall. What was most amazing to Tye was the fact that, other than the occasional squabble, Shelley and William almost seemed to be getting along. Almost.

And it was the sister who'd suggested that they broaden their investigation. They were looking at pictures of real horses. Maybe they should look at artistic illustrations of horses. Both Ralph and William agreed this was a good idea. Seldom had Tye seen such joint focus in the three kids. On the surface he liked it, but as with all change, it did elicit some concern.

"You saw her draw this?" Tye asked this as he put more salt on his potatoes. His wife never put nearly enough on.

Liz put her fork down. "Tye —"

"Just trying to get a better context of what's going on. That's all. Well, Ralph, did you? Did any of you?"

For a brief second, all three kids looked at each other before Ralph spoke. "Just the finishing touches. It was almost completely done when we came out here."

"Then how do you know it was her?"

Once again, Liz uttered her husband's name. "Tye!"

"Come on, Liz. You can't tell me you're not a little bit curious. Does that look like a ten-year-old could draw it? Well, how can you be positive that" — he pointed to the Wall — "came from her?"

This was a line of questioning that took the three kids by surprise. It had not occurred to them that what they believed might not be. Liz could see her kids wrestling with the dilemma set before them by their father. But before she could intercede, Ralph spoke up after quickly glancing at the Horse. "She was the only one here. In the kitchen. Shelley let her in."

Then his sister took the baton. "I gave her the chalk. And we saw her start. Right at the beginning, but we were playing cards and forgot about her. We didn't hear anybody else come in."

"Besides." Now it was William's turn to speak. "Who else would draw that? Could draw that? Nobody I know. If I drew that, I'd want everybody to know. Mr. Thomas, I didn't see her actually put that Horse up there, but I am pretty sure it was her. Don't know of a lot of crooks running around, breaking into houses to draw horses on the wall. If so, that's kind of sad."

Liz tried to put her last piece of Shake 'n' Bake pork chop in her mouth, but it was rather difficult as her mouth was currently otherwise occupied with a broad and proud smile beaming across the table. The three kids, whose combined ages didn't add up to her husband's, had presented a logical and moderately impassioned argument.

Tye didn't dare look at his wife. His chop tasted too much like crow.

A FEW HOURS later, Tye came out of the bathroom, a dab of toothpaste on his left cheek. Liz was waiting, still carrying traces of that earlier smile. "Well?"

Tye stopped in his tracks, taking his T-shirt off. "I know better than to ask 'Well what?' This is about your Anything Wall, right?"

"*Everything* Wall, you stupid truck driver. You know that very well. I want it to stay, at least for a while. I know kids, especially ours, and they will probably get tired of it in a few weeks, maybe a month or two, but until then —"

"You realize it's just a form of domestic graffiti. Most parents go out of their way to prevent their kids from drawing on walls. Especially at their age."

"I will never say no to my kids."

"Don't they have an art class at school? Let them draw on the walls there."

Silence found its way into the Thomas bedroom. Liz looked out the window, even though it was late and utterly black outside. "Tye. I want to keep the Everything Wall."

Weary after three weeks on the road and four hours dealing with his wife's current obsession, Tye had little energy left. Once again, the door slammed shut on what was logical and made sense, just to make his wife happy.

"Yeah, sure." He sat on the bed.

"The kids love it."

"I got that impression."

"It fosters creativity."

"Yay." The man slid into bed beside his wife and turned out the light on his night table.

"Tye, you really don't think there's something special about that Horse?"

In the darkness, there was a sigh. "Liz, I don't know much about art, horses, or that Gaadaw kid. If you say it's special, I believe you. I met a driver in Vancouver once whose son could play six or seven games of chess all at the same time. Amazing to watch, but after a while it wore off and life continued."

Liz's voice cut through the darkness. "How horrible."

"What? Life continuing?"

A pillow across Tye's face prevented further conversation.

FINDING DANIELLE AT lunch the next day wasn't that difficult. She was eating a bag of chips near the parking lot, alone as usual, basically occupying time and space until there was someplace else to go, something to do. That's where Shelley and Ralph made a quick survey of the playground and located her from across the field. Danielle gave them a shy smile as they came closer, once again hesitant to meet their eyes. She noticed a large paper bag in Shelley's hand.

"Hey, Danielle," said Shelley.

"Hi," added Ralph.

Danielle smiled, and both siblings could see her saying the word "Hi" but so softly neither of them actually heard it. All three felt uncomfortable at the atypical nature of the conversation. Under normal circumstances, none of them would have a reason to participate in a drawn-out conversation, being in different grades and from different parts of the reserve. Contrary to popular belief, Native communities have many of the same social classes as communities off the reserve, especially when it comes to the complex world of school and its various hierarchies. Colonization had its fingers in all the pies on the reserve.

Shelley cleared her throat. "That was just an amazing horse you drew yesterday. Totally amazing. Wasn't it, Ralph?"

He nodded in agreement, looking for something to add. "You should be very proud." Ralph suddenly realized he had just sounded like his mother. He made a mental note not to sound like that again.

Not really knowing Ralph's mother, the young girl didn't notice, only shrugging at the compliment. She ate another chip, finding the ground in front of her seemingly very interesting.

"Mom says you can come over any time you want, if you want. So do we."

"Thank you." This time both heard it, though again it was barely above a whisper.

"Oh, and we have this for you." Shelley held out the paper bag with something moderately heavy in it. She waited for Danielle to take it. Even more nervous, and not used to this much attention, Danielle took the bag hesitantly, its weight taking her by surprise. It was obvious to brother and sister what she wanted to ask but didn't have the self-confidence to utter.

"It's your present, like an award. For winning the Everything Wall contest. It's from our mother." Ralph nodded in agreement with his sister. "She went and got it first thing this morning. There was nobody even close to what you did on the Wall."

"I think William was a little annoyed."

"Yeah, but nobody cares. Take a look, Danielle. It's for you."

Lowering the bag onto the hood of a nearby Honda Prelude, Danielle nervously reached in and pulled out a large, weighty picture book. She smiled as she saw what the subject matter of the book was. "Look, horses. Lots of horse pictures." She immediately started leafing through the glossy pages, her attention focused. "Thank you."

"Do you ever say anything other than 'thank you'?" asked Ralph, half jokingly. Deep into her book, Danielle didn't respond. Instead, she flipped another page, then another, her eyes taking in all the different images of horses. Briefly it reminded the two of the previous evening, watching her cross back and forth into this other world she seemed to prefer. Shelley and Ralph stood there in the parking lot for a moment, watching her, not knowing what else to say. It felt like they had been forgotten.

"Um ... well ..." Shelley looked at Ralph.

"I guess we should be going." Again there was no response from Danielle. It seemed Ralph and Shelley's existence in her world had been replaced by the photographed horses. The little girl had climbed into the book. Danielle sat down on a red railing that bordered the parking area and rested the big book on her lap. She didn't feel the cold wind, her wet boot, or anything else. Danielle touched one of the photos, horses running along a beach, ocean spray angling up in a V shape on either side. To Ralph it seemed she was no doubt imagining wonderful things.

"Bye, Danielle." Ralph waited for a reaction, but there was none. Shelley managed a half-hearted wave, again with no reaction. All they saw was the top of Danielle's head. Slowly, Ralph and his sister turned back to the school and started walking.

"That is one strange puppy," commented Shelley.

"I guess she just likes horses."

Mission accomplished, they both disappeared into the crowded playground, going their separate ways.

Halfway across the playground, near the swings, William watched them give the little girl the prize book. He was not very happy. That book should have been his. This was so unfair, he thought. She was some little freak, both in what she was and what she could do. William didn't like things that were unfair, or freaks for that matter. What had once seemed a fabulous thing, the Everything Wall, now appeared to make William's life less enjoyable.

Their task finished, the temporary merging of grades and classes came to an abrupt end. Shelley returned to where Vanessa and Julia were hanging out. Ralph made his way to William. He had offered to let him join the brother and sister in presenting Danielle with her prize, but for his own reasons, William had been disinclined. But now there was time to do something fun with his friend during what was left of the recess. William waited as Ralph approached.

"Well, was she weird?"

Ralph had to admit she was. "Yeah, a little."

Trying to shake thoughts of the girl and that stupid Horse of hers from his mind, William started to walk towards the school, urging Ralph to follow. "Come on, Gary and Mitchell have built some kind of snow fort. Let's go check it out." And, as had been the case for as long as they could remember, Ralph followed wherever William led.

SHORTLY AFTER, THINGS returned to normal. Another cold snap came, banishing the rain, replacing it with bitingly low temperatures that left a hard crust on top of the fields of snow and, more dangerously, icy roads. Shelley had resumed referring to Ralph's best friend as It, yet continued to play cards with him in these days of inclement weather. The world was indeed a contradictory place, and the Thomas house in Otter Lake was sometimes at its apex.

During his time off the road, his down time, his domestic time, Tye was busy shovelling new snow and fixing the storm windows the season had found wanting. In addition to his household chores, he had a brother and two sisters he had to catch up with. His next foray onto the Canadian highways wasn't for another week and a half, so he planned to get as much done as was humanly possible. This was his usual routine — sitting in the cab of his truck for ten hours a day, followed by ten hours in various hotels and motels for weeks at a time. Repeat as necessary. Then back to the reserve and doing all the things that make a house a home in as short a period of time as possible.

As for Liz, she had her own set of priorities. The purchase of the book of horses had been, she thought, an inspired idea for Danielle Gaadaw. The prize reflected the girl's art and, she hoped, her interests. But it was a new week and, amongst her other chores, the maintenance of the Everything Wall loomed large. It had to be washed and cleaned for the next infusion of imaginary creations that would flood into their house — starting that very day, Tuesday. Liz would wash all the children's work, except for the Horse, as had been agreed, even through William's gritted teeth. The animal would be left proudly occupying its niche in the Thomas kitchen, where it had spent the last two days watching the Thomas family prepare and eat their breakfast and dinner. Frequently there would be some arguing, laughing, and the occasional song would suddenly erupt, filling the room. Generally, it observed existence pass through this example of government housing.

Tye had stopped to admire it once, making a comment about how it seemed like its eyes were watching him. Tye acknowledged that he had no artistic appreciation for anything that ventured beyond his comfort zone, which included the music of a steel guitar and television commercials that made him laugh. Even though he would deny it if asked, he had to acknowledge to himself that there was something about the Horse, something he couldn't quite put his finger on.

On Tuesday night, with the wind howling outside, the denizens of the Everything Wall became extinct, rendered so by an energetic Liz, a rag, and a pail of soapy water, which proved as effectively genocidal as any large comet — with one notable exception.

THE NEW WEEK brought several juvenile etchings, which had

already popped up here and there across the Everything Wall. It was the usual menagerie of expected depictions, none approaching the artistic quality of the Horse and its effect upon its viewers. It was obvious some form of intimidation had made its way into the drawing ability of other young residents of Otter Lake. In this second week, most drawings were small, half-hearted, simplistic, almost as if no one wanted to put the necessary effort into anything that might be compared to the Horse. As the saying goes, it's hard to shine when you're standing next to the sun. Only in its sophomore week, the Everything Wall was becoming anemic.

"Danielle did that?!" was the common refrain from most of Shelley's and Ralph's friends when they saw the drawing that was still on the Everything Wall. "Geez, that's pretty good" was a popular response. "Wish I could do that" was equally frequently heard. Very few echoed William's assessment of "Weird."

Wednesday afternoon quickly became a reality. Temperatures outside were a serious deterrent to most outdoor activities, regardless of how many layers were worn. Life moved indoors. It was in the midst of yet another card game that consisted of seventy-five percent card playing and twenty-five percent arguing that Shelley somehow, above the din of William's alternating protestations of anger and innocence, heard a familiar gentle tapping at the front door.

"Did you hear that?"

"Nope. Hear what? Wait a minute, I think I'm missing a card." William began looking under the table.

Ralph was thinking the same thing as his sister. "Do

you think?"

"I don't know. Last time, we barely heard her when she knocked."

"Big deal," was William's second contribution to the developing conversation. He was doubly irritated. If Danielle was at the door, waiting to be invited in, it meant potentially another amazing animal would prevent him from winning the drawing contest. In fact, so far this week he had not contributed anything to the Everything Wall. He was waiting to see what the weird little girl would do. He would wait until then to see what kind of master stroke he would need to pull out of his hat to combat this unexpected and slight foe. Now she was here to draw again.

*Bring it on*, he thought.

He was about to win this card game — the card he was searching for was not exactly lost, just relocated — and Shelley and Ralph had obviously lost interest in the game. Their focus was on the girl at the door and not the cards in their hands.

Hurrying across the kitchen, Shelley opened the door, revealing on the other side a very chilled Danielle, looking smaller and colder, if possible, than last time. "There you are. I was wondering if you were going to show up again." Shelley could feel the cold coming in through the mud room, refusing to release its tendrils from the little girl's arms. Ralph showed up on Shelley's right, leaving William leaning against the doorway between the living room and the kitchen, trying to act nonchalant. Danielle gave the older girl a small, shy smile.

"Can I ...?" Her voice trailed off. Danielle seemed too

shy to even finish her sentence.

"Yes," said Shelley, standing aside and holding the door for Danielle to walk through. She closed it when Danielle was fully in the house, standing in the warm kitchen. "So, you want a pop or anything? I think we have a Coke somewhere, if It didn't drink it already." She gave William a menacing glare as she opened the refrigerator door, but he didn't see it. Or possibly he didn't care. He was too busy watching Danielle, who gently nodded her head in response to Shelley's offer.

"Can I take your jacket?" asked Ralph, giving her his best welcoming smile. Danielle nodded and started to take off her winter jacket. Taking it, Ralph noticed it was too small and surprisingly thin, with two small rips in the lining. The Thomas clan was by no means wealthy, but Ralph could not imagine his mother letting him or Shelley out in the Otter Lake winter wearing an inadequate coat like the one he was holding in his hands.

The frail young girl they had all met only a handful of times at school, eating potato chips and poorly dressed, seemed excited, almost animated to be in the house with them, a distinct change. As she progressed deeper into the kitchen, the creator of the Horse suddenly stopped moving, her feet fixed. Blinking rapidly, she was staring at her artwork on the Wall, the one she'd created less than a week before.

Ralph noticed her change of expression immediately. "Danielle, what's wrong?"

Shelley, hearing Ralph, suspended her search for a soft drink in the refrigerator door and looked around, curious.

Danielle was standing in the centre of the kitchen, still shivering from her sojourn in the Canadian winter, displaying a peculiar look of puzzlement and a dash of frustration. William leaned further into the kitchen to try to see what was drawing Ralph and Shelley's attention.

"Danielle?" voiced a worried Shelley.

"It's still here," she said.

They all looked at the Horse on the Wall, not comprehending what the problem was. "Oh, yes," said the older girl. "We all loved it so much, it's so beautiful, we didn't want to wash it away. Our mom totally agreed. We left it up so we could look at it some more." She looked nervously at her brother, "We thought you would be ... I don't know ... flattered."

It did not appear that Danielle was flattered. In fact, she was close to tears.

"But ... but you said ... you said you would get rid of it every week, so other kids could make new drawings. It's not supposed to be here. This isn't right."

This caused serious confusion amongst the three. Shelley, always the better communicator, tried to pilot their ship through Danielle's sea of confusion. "I'm sorry, but we thought —"

"It's supposed to be gone," Danielle said a second time. As if desperate, she turned to Ralph. "Isn't it? Why isn't it?"

This was the most all three of them had heard the little girl talk, collectively, in quite probably their entire lives. Even William was struggling to grasp what the girl was telling them. "But that's your Horse. I don't get it. Don't you like it anymore?"

Then, like a bucket of water thrown on to a campfire, Danielle reverted to the fragile thing they remembered from school. She looked down at the ground. "I'm sorry. I'm being rude. It's just …" She swallowed, then grabbed her coat from the confused Ralph. Quickly donning her coat and zipping it up, she announced, barely above a whisper, "I have to go." Not looking at anyone, she scurried to the door, faster than any of them had seen her move, and was out into the cold before any of them could react. One by one, their gazes returned to the Horse on the Wall. Each of them replayed the last five minutes in their minds.

"Man, if I thought she was weird before, I think she's even more weird now, if that's possible," offered William. Then, without another thought, he returned to a far more pressing matter. "Are we gonna finish this card game or what?"

Shelley was about to tell It to shut up, but lost interest as she continued to study the Horse. Just short of thirteen years of age, she knew there was more to this Horse than a thin layer of coloured chalk on a black wall. No one could put that kind of love and devotion — if she were older, perhaps she would have added the word soul — into the drawing she was looking at and then react so severely for some as-yet-unknown reason and not have it mean something above and beyond a mere child's drawing.

Ralph knew, and, though he wouldn't admit it, William also knew there was a special significance to what was on the Wall three feet away. They both felt this somewhere deep inside, but they just didn't want to know. On some level, William was aware that the more he understood this girl and her Horse, the more difficult it would be to be jealous of her.

Ralph turned to his sister. "Now what?"

ON HER WAY home through Otter Lake's snow-covered and chilly streets, Danielle tried with little success not to cry. She wasn't sure why she was crying. In the cold of the winter, the tears that managed to escape stung her cheeks, practically freezing instantly. She shivered in the growing darkness but was completely unaware of it. She thought only of the Horse and the lost opportunity. Danielle knew the Horse wanted to come out so badly, and she wanted to let it out equally badly. There was something about that house, that home, that made Danielle feel she could draw the Horse there over and over. It felt safe, where the Horse could grow and be healthy and free. Those were good things. Not like the place her mother told her was home. She couldn't let the Horse visit or live there. She'd tried several times, but had got into deep trouble for her efforts. The last time really badly. No Horse could come and visit her. It couldn't thrive there. She knew there had to be other places where it could develop and run free. The Thomas house seemed to be just such a place.

Now she worried that she had been quite rude to Shelley and Ralph, that she had been a rude guest in their home. She was sure of it. Her father, when he'd been alive, had tried to teach her about politeness and the dangers of being rude. Upon reflection, she shouldn't have acted the way she had. It was wrong. Danielle was sorry now. She wished she could tell all of them she was sorry. Everybody there had been so nice to her. Her father would not have approved of the way she'd acted or how she'd left her new friends' house. Could she call Shelley and Ralph and William new friends? She'd have to try to be nicer from now on. If there was to be a now on.

It was so seldom she'd think about her father. Occasionally she dreamed of him, but that was becoming less and less frequent. Mom never mentioned him, especially with her new boyfriend. In some ways, it was like the man whose lap she'd found so warm and comforting, making her fall asleep, had never existed. Danielle no longer missed him with the deep, painful aching that she'd had since he'd died four years ago. It was now just a dull ache. She guessed that was good.

Turning left at the stop sign, she stuck her hands as far down into her pockets as they could go, dangerously straining the stitching inside. Momentarily her finger popped out one of the rips Ralph had noticed earlier. Danielle was used to the cold, but today she seemed lacking in her ability to ignore or fight it.

The house where Ralph and Shelley lived seemed a perfect place for her friend to visit, and today had been the day she was going to draw it again and let it run free. But the old Horse was still there. That was last week's Horse. That wasn't right because her Horse changed. It grew, evolved. Just like people. It needed to stretch and become what it wanted to become, not what it was, and that couldn't happen when the old Horse was there. It had to go. Shelley and Ralph were such nice people, they meant well, and Danielle knew she shouldn't have acted so badly, but she was disappointed. Why had they lied to her? She couldn't understand why they'd said they would make room every week for a new Horse and then hadn't done that. It wasn't fair. Nothing much was fair in her life, but for some reason this felt more unfair than anything else.

The tired and worn wooden steps of her trailer creaked beneath her tiny feet as she climbed the stairs to the front door. She and her mother and her mother's boyfriend lived here. Danielle could remember when the trailer had been a much happier place and she would run home excited. Now she looked for excuses to stay away. But today she was out of excuses, and it was getting really cold, making her teeth chatter. Add to that she was hungry, tired, and had no place else to go. She turned the knob and entered as the warped door scraped open.

"There you are. It's about fucking time. Carla phoned and said she saw you wandering the streets. Get in here, you're making us look bad. I suppose you're hungry too. I made some Kraft dinner for lunch. You can have what's left, on the stove."

The door and the world closed behind her. No Horse would want to live here.

# CHAPTER SIX

"I WANTED TO BECOME A COP BECAUSE ...," RALPH STOPPED midsentence. It had been a long time since he'd had to justify or even explain his career choice. "And what does this have to do with that thing over there?" The Tim Hortons was bustling. The lunch rush was just ending, but the cold was forcing the street people and regular customers alike to search for alternative methods of keeping their bodies warm.

Denizens of Canada's largest city passed their table, throwing the occasional puzzled look in their direction. A noticeably down on his luck, aged man sitting across from a youngish police officer, deep in conversation. For some observers, it was just another example of the egalitarian nature of Tim Hortons across the country.

"I asked you this before, and you didn't answer. Do you know the person who drew that Horse? I'd like an answer."

Harry drank his third ... or was it fourth, possibly fifth coffee of the morning, realizing the Western concepts of quantity were seldom relevant on a morning like this, all the time measuring the immediate scalding nature of the cup's contents against the slow burn of the season's cold bit, waiting outside the franchise's doors. To him, they were two sides of the same coin. "You'd like an answer, would you? Everybody wants answers, but very few would think I have them."

"You keep evading the question."

"Maybe you keep asking the wrong question."

Clearly frustrated, Ralph leaned back in his chair and then, just as quickly, leaned forward until he was centimetres away from Harry's face, almost completely across the Formica table. "What question should I be asking, then?"

A few seconds passed as Harry looked deep into his double-double. For a moment, Ralph thought he'd lost the man in whatever world some street people occasionally lived in, but Harry looked to their right, at the table near the bathroom. A woman was sitting with a younger man, probably her son, talking animatedly. Harry watched them for a second, as did Ralph, trying to figure out what was so interesting about the couple that would draw Harry's attention. The constable was about to inquire when Harry broke the silence between them.

"That woman. Had a very bad childhood. There's a war constantly happening inside her between what happened to her and how it sometimes affects her own life as a mother. Always on the edge of letting the dam she built up break and becoming her own mother. I see that all the time in people. Who they were and who they are. Who they're struggling to be. People can be really fucked up."

The woman looked normal and fine to Ralph. "How do you know this? Do you know her?"

Putting on his best *are you kidding* face, Harry laughed. "You silly man. How would I possibly know her?"

"Then how do you know what you just told me?"

Returning to the woman, Harry sipped his coffee. "That man, I think that's her son. That's the connection I get. At times, I see tentacles and tendrils coming out of her, wanting to hurt him, but they never quite reach him. It's like she's shadowboxing with him. Throwing punches that will never hit. Odd way to live, huh? She wants to be a good mother, but something inside doesn't want her to be. It's a constant battle."

"I don't understand."

"Why did you become a cop?"

This man, this Harry whatever-his-last-name-is, was truly a frustrating individual. *It's a game*, thought Ralph. The man was lonely, on the fringes of society, wanting to talk to somebody, maybe even pull a trick or fool a police officer. It made sense. Quite possibly, he knew nothing of the Horse and who had painted it, re-created it, on that brick wall. *What an idiot I am*, concluded Ralph. Well, enough of this. Putting his hands on the table, Ralph got up, more frustrated with himself than with Harry.

"Okay. I've had enough."

"Enough? We haven't even started."

Shaking his head, Ralph turned towards the door. This morning hadn't turned out quite the way he had antici-pated. The Horse was just a coincidence. It had to be.

He'd read in school that Isaac Newton and a second, less famous man had both developed algebra at the same time in different places, and that Darwin wasn't the only person to come up with the theory of evolution. Darwin published his book before Alfred Russell Wallace did, so the former was remembered and the latter forgotten. It followed that if complete strangers in different countries had separately come up with a complicated language like algebra, or something requiring years and years of research, like evolution, how much higher was the probability that two people more than twenty years apart could draw a very similar, though striking, image of a horse. With the same carbon copy image of a girl's hand on the shoulder. The more Ralph thought about it, the sillier he felt. Under his breath, he even chuckled to himself. It was time to go home.

Looking out the window at the distant head of the Horse, Harry crumpled the empty coffee cup in his hand. "It was a woman. A girl. Actually, not a girl. It was the Horse. The Horse drew itself. But I'm pretty sure it was once a girl. It's kind of hard to hide that. But I don't think she exists anymore. And, how about this, she had the same colour as you."

The world in the Tim Hortons stopped for Ralph. Sounds and people disappeared. The words Harry had said raised a lump in Ralph's throat.

"What do you mean she had the same colour as me?"

Closing his eyes, Harry managed to pull the memory of the night the Horse had appeared on the wall and the person he'd seen call it forth. It had been a hot summer night, and Harry was down to a T-shirt and track pants, his usual uniform for a Toronto summer. He had been packing things up, late into the evening. Like many citizens of the streets, Harry didn't really care for shelters. Too many nasty things happened there. He had a nice little nook hidden away in a construction site not far away. He'd been using it for the last couple of weeks, allowing him to stay out longer, long past the usual curfews set by the shelters.

He knew the alleyway that was to become the home of the Horse. Lots of people frequented the walls there, spreading their messages of dreams and creativity across and along its dingy surface. Many strange and unusual persons had frequented those alleys of the imagination, but none like the bringer of the Horse. He himself had wandered that potholed and broken pavement many times before. It used to remind him of the beauty that could exist in the city. But it had been a long time since he'd been between those brick and aluminum walls.

His eyes still closed, Harry answered Ralph's question, his right cheek twitching. "The woman … the girl was Indian. The Horse is Indian. If horses can be Indian. I know some Indians can be jackasses …" Suddenly Harry burst out laughing, startling Ralph.

*If this guy is wasting my time*, thought Ralph, but before he could finish, Harry looked at him, directly in the eye, as lucid and focused as anybody Ralph had ever met in his life.

"Sit down. I'll tell you more. But you have to tell me, why did you become a cop?"

Not knowing what else to do, Ralph once again sat down.

## CHAPTER SEVEN

USUALLY IT WAS THE THREE KIDS WHO WOULD BURST INTO the Thomas house bustling with energy and pleading for something to eat, but this time it was Liz, chasing Tye. "Let me, please! I want to try it."

Tye seemed quite adamant. "I told you. You can't. It's not allowed."

"What do you mean, it's not allowed? It's your truck. You drive it."

Tye put his coat on a peg in the mud room and waited patiently for Liz to take hers off. "Okay, first thing, it's not my truck. It belongs to the company. I am hired by the company to drive it. And secondly, there are all sorts of insurance and company regulations preventing the wife of a tractor-trailer driver from operating it just for the hell of it."

"I think you're afraid I can handle it. Probably better than you do." Liz took her winter boots off.

"Hey, you want to take a few truck-driving classes, go ahead. The company is always looking for a few more women drivers. We have a handful, and it always looks good for publicity reasons." Tye stopped talking and looked around, appearing puzzled.

"What?"

"It's quiet."

Liz looked around too, suddenly aware of the silence. "School's out, right?"

"Yeah, a while ago." Together they walked into the living room, and not for the first time, Tye had the uncomfortable feeling that the Horse's eyes were following him. While he did not share his family's growing obsession with the drawing, there was something captivating about it.

In the living room, the parents came upon an unusual sight. Three children, one on the cusp of teenageness, sitting in an array of armchairs and couches, their faces buried in books. For a brief half a second, Liz debated whether she should poke the bear and possibly disturb the rare calm of the house. "Ah, hello?"

All three looked up at the same moment.

"Hey, Mom. Dad."

"Hi."

"When's dinner?" said William.

Curious, Liz took the book from Shelley, opening it. She showed it to her husband, whose furrowed brow revealed a certain amount of confusion. Tye decided to poke the proverbial bear a little more. "You guys are quiet. I don't trust you. What's up?"

All three shrugged, but Ralph answered. "Just trying to figure things out."

Liz gave Shelley back her book and then glanced at the two boys' books. "More stuff about horses, I see?"

"Painted horses," added William. "We took the other books back to the library and got these out instead."

Tye sighed. "Is it my imagination or have you three become kinda fixated on horses ever since what's-her-name drew that thing on our wall?"

"Her name is Danielle, Dad, and she was here again today."

Liz leaned into the kitchen to look at the sparse Everything Wall. "Really? It looks the same."

"It is. That's the problem, Mom," said Ralph. "She was disappointed."

"More than disappointed. I'd say she was hurt that it was still there," added Shelley. "It made no sense."

"Shelley and Ralph wanted to try and figure this out, so I offered to help." William turned the page of his book and tried as hard as he could to indicate he was deep in thought.

Shelley rolled her eyes. "Some help."

Tye picked up one of the books and casually leafed through it. "Don't you think you guys are taking this interest in her and horses a little too far?"

Liz kissed Shelley on the head. "I think it's admirable. It shows inquisitive minds. Let us know if we can help." Liz entered the kitchen, still speaking. "I'm gonna start supper. And Tye, your boots are still on. You're leaving a mess through my freshly cleaned house." It was true. Tye's snow boots were still on his feet, and there was indeed a trail of half-melted snow leading into the living room.

"Oops." Tye managed a decent *mea culpa* face that brought a smile to the faces of his children and their friend.

Tiptoeing back into the kitchen in an overly exaggerated manner, he grabbed a mop stored next to the boots for just such an emergency. Off came his boots and down went the mop. In a low voice, but loud enough for the kids to hear, Liz admonished her partner. "And what is wrong with you? Those kids are reading books on art and animals, actual non-fiction books with facts and information."

"I'm just saying ..."

"Well, don't."

All three kids exchanged slightly amused glances. Between mop sweeps, they heard Tye sighing.

Louder this time, their mother addressed them from the other room. "So, any idea why that poor little girl just left like that?"

Tossing her book on the coffee table, Shelley got up, stretching her legs. "Nah, I think maybe we got the wrong books. These just show us pictures. I mean paintings and drawings of horses. Nothing really about why people draw them."

From the far end of the couch, William's voice shouted out. "I found some really cool ones that cave people drew. They're amazing. Who knew? Cavemen! They look more real than a lot of paintings I've seen on walls. I might start drawing like that."

"Makes sense. You are a caveman. No, Mom, we've been trying to figure it out since it happened. She looked so ... I don't know ... wounded ... like we'd done something to her on purpose."

Still leafing through a book, Ralph shook his head. "No, not wounded. Like you said earlier. Disappointed. Yeah, like she was sad to see it still here. She wasn't expecting it to be still on the Wall. In fact, she didn't want it to be here at all."

"Honey, you missed a spot."

The kids heard the mop stop its swishing sound. "Was the floor always this dirty?"

"Just since you got home. So, have you three geniuses come up with any idea of what and why?"

"She's crazy. That's why."

For that comment, Liz stuck her head back into the living room, aimed directly at the only non-blood member of her family. "Now, William, that's no way to talk about a frightened little girl."

"Sorry." Chastened, he ducked down behind his book.

Back in the kitchen, Liz started slicing up some lettuce. Salad was on the menu for dinner. William would not be happy.

"And you're sure nobody said anything that upset her. Nothing?"

Shelley shook her head. "Nothing. Honest, Mom. As soon as she saw it, she started getting upset. Really, I tried to —"

Out of nowhere, Ralph remembered the intense look on Danielle's face as she'd finished up the details of the Horse. He started leafing back through the pages of his book, trying to find a reference he had skimmed over. It was a comment at the bottom of an ancient carving that had caught his interest. After a few seconds he found it. The caption made perfect sense to him. Perhaps the reason for the young girl's actions. He interrupted his sister as the ideas took form. It was so obvious but, at the same time, so bizarre. "I think I might know."

His sister, his friend, and his mother peered at him. Even his father, mop still in hand, glanced around the door frame at his son. They all waited expectantly.

"Yeah? We're listening," said Tye, now curious.

Realizing he might have spoken too quickly, having only developed a half-conceived idea, he was nonetheless committed. Getting up from his big comfy chair, he went to the dining room table, which was actually in the living room, and opened up his book. There, on the page, was the image of a deer carved into an antler bone. All crowded around it.

"She was trying to draw a moose and it came out as a horse?" William's contribution to the discussion was not addressed.

"It's not the picture of the Horse itself that's important to her. Not the Horse that's up there now." They all looked at him, confused. "You see, it's the *drawing* of the Horse that's important to her."

For the second time, confusion danced upon the faces inhabiting the Thomas house. "Ralph, honey, I don't understand. And I don't think Shelley or William do either."

Tye spoke. "Well, if we're taking attendance, let's make it unanimous."

Ralph turned the page to show another large, impractical piece of primitive artwork. This time a whale. "It's drawing the Horse that she likes, not the actual finished Horse. When she's creating it, chalk in her hand, putting it on the Wall, I guess she's imagining it to life, that's what she wants. Do you see what I mean? That" — Ralph indicated the Horse — "means nothing to her now. She wants to draw a new one, create a new Horse, and couldn't because this one, the one she drew last time, was still here. Danielle needs it to be gone so she can draw it again." They all turned to look at the Horse. And it looked back.

"That is so warped."

"You should know." Shelley tried to wrap her brain around what her brother had said. "Imagining it to life." She liked how that sounded, and it made her think of something. "You know, this year in school we learned that some cultures do things like that. They carve or make things that have no logical purpose in their lives, they do it just to set free something inside. Like why a lot of what anthropologists call 'primitive people' carved so much when they were nomadic people and carrying around a whole bunch of carved soapstone or bones or things like that wouldn't be so smart. In fact, it would weigh them down. Literally."

"Yeah, yeah. And model airplanes," said William.

"What?"

Intrigued by what was being said, William spoke up, grasping the idea in his own unique way. "Model airplanes or boats. Kind of the same principle. It would be a lot easier to buy a finished plane or boat, but some people really prefer putting the things together. There's no point in getting one if it's already finished. Know what I'm saying?"

"Crossword puzzles. Jigsaw puzzles. Nobody wants a finished one." Now Liz was seeing the big picture. Even Tye was nodding, once again gazing at the Horse out of the corner of his eye. He, for one, would not be unhappy if it was decided it was time for the Horse to meet its demise via a bucket of soapy water. This was a good step in that direction.

The mystery had been solved, they hoped. For a few seconds, the entire family looked at the Horse. They knew the problem, and they also knew the solution. The Horse they were all fascinated by was yesterday's news. It had to go. It had achieved its purpose, but now it was time for the Horse to go to where all chalk horses must eventually go. Artistic oblivion.

Ralph stated the obvious. "I think we have to get rid of it. If we want Danielle to come back."

"But it's so pretty. Washing it away would be such a shame. A waste." Shelley looked close to tears.

"Shelley, if what Ralph is saying is true, and we wash it away, Danielle will bring it back again. That's what you're saying, right, Ralph?" The ten-year-old boy whose only intellectual claim to fame up until that point had been a strong understanding of how long it would take for a train leaving Winnipeg, travelling at a hundred and forty kilometres an hour, to arrive in Montreal, blinked at his mother's question.

"I think so."

Nodding with the conviction that only the mother of two children can possess, she left the half-chopped lettuce on the counter. "It makes sense to me. Tye?"

"I guess."

"And I think we're all in agreement that we would all want to see that Horse again, in whatever form." Both

Ralph and Shelley nodded, definitely hoping this wasn't the last time they would see the Horse.

Under his breath, William registered his growing disagreement with the popular opinion of the house. "Christ, it's just a stupid horse." Nobody heard him. Liz was busy getting a small bucket from the closet, and Shelley was already running the hot water in the sink.

"Now?! You're gonna do this now?" Once again, Tye, the father, had lost the thread of intention within his family.

"No time like the present. Only take a moment. Shelley, can you get me that sponge?"

Tye, still holding the mop, had to jump aside to make way for Liz and her three-quarters-full bucket heading past him for the Wall.

The daughter did as she was told, she, too, almost sideswiping her father as she rushed past. Ralph, Shelley, and Liz stood in front of the Horse, water slopping over the edge of the bucket and onto the floor. Tye and William stayed back, not really feeling the moment.

"Everybody, say your goodbyes."

Silently, Ralph and Shelley paid their respects to Danielle's soon-to-be-gone creation. Liz said a simple, "Bye, Horse" before condemning it to a soapy death. Anybody not familiar with recent events would have thought the farewell to a chalk image seemed unusually emotional. The first part of the beautiful beast to go was the tail. A wet and soapy sponge of death wiped it out of existence. Then came the rump and hind legs. Slowly, the creature they had all admired was being dissolved into dirty water that ran down the Wall and spread across the kitchen floor.

"So much for me mopping the floor."

"The beauty of the situation is you can always mop it again."

Next, Liz erased the flanks and back, followed by the front legs, the mane, and the neck. All that was left was the head, with those disturbing eyes. Liz found this the hardest part of the Wall to cleanse. But one swipe of the sponge of death and the Horse no longer existed. At least on the Thomas wall.

The Everything Wall was open for business once again.

As he watched the Horse disappear, William shook his head, not understanding the emotionality of things around him.

"Geez, it's not like it's the *Mona Lisa* or anything."

Frustrated, he stormed into the living room. In front of his favourite spot on the couch was one of the horse books. He kicked it away with his foot. The Thomas house wasn't as much fun for William this evening as it had been before.

THE NEXT DAY at school, Ralph kept his eyes open for Danielle, but she didn't make an appearance. Shelley did the same, with the same results. Danielle was a no-show for the whole day. As usual, William didn't really notice or care. It wasn't until the day after that Ralph caught sight of the little girl, walking into the schoolyard. She seemed to be limping, favouring her right foot. A few minutes early for school, he ran up to her, eager to share his news. At first, when she saw him approaching, it looked like she was ready to flee, a look of panic quickly crossing her face, but as Ralph got closer, Danielle seemed to recognize him and was less fidgety. She welcomed him with a slight smile.

"There you are! We've been looking for you!"

Danielle looked surprised. "Me? You were looking for me? I didn't do anything." The look of fear returned to her face, and, upon seeing it, Ralph instinctively tried to calm her.

"No, no. Everything's okay. It's just about the Everything Wall. We've washed it. No more Horse. You can come and draw on it again. If you want."

They stood in the schoolyard, talking, almost like normal kids do, thought Danielle. Other kids from the village passed them by, intent on getting to school on time. A few wondered why Ralph was talking to that strange little Gaadaw girl. They weren't related and had no reason to socialize. And many others still couldn't believe that little girl in the odd-fitting clothes had managed to create the Horse they'd all seen staring back at them from the Thomas kitchen wall. But once out of sight, the thought of Danielle quickly evaporated from their consciousnesses as the reality of school and its normal stresses grew closer.

Danielle struggled to meet Ralph's eyes. "I'm sorry I was so rude. I shouldn't be. You and your family are very nice. It's your Everything Wall. I'm sorry." Danielle looked down at the ground again, still unwilling to meet the boy's eyes, expecting a flood of criticism and anger at her earlier actions. Instead, he laughed. Not at her, but at what she'd said.

"You call that rude?! Wow, I wish everybody was that rude. Forget about it."

Off in the distance, a dog barked. A recent bylaw requiring Otter Lake residents to keep their dogs penned or on a chain had not gone over well with local canine residents.

"So, you gonna come over?"

Behind Ralph, the school bell rang, signalling the start of a new day of education. All around them kids began running, not wanting to be late for another lacklustre day of sitting in a room, listening to their teachers drone on about insignificant facts and formulas.

"Well?" asked Ralph.

At first, Danielle wasn't sure she had heard properly. "You want me to come over?"

Ralph nodded, like it meant nothing.

"Okay then." She managed another smile, a bigger one this time, one of almost pride and a certain amount of eagerness. "I will! I will!"

"Great. I'll let my sister and mother know. Better hurry. You don't want to be late for class." Delighted, Ralph started trotting towards the school, knowing William was somewhere inside waiting for him.

It had been a long time since Danielle had been invited anywhere, so she was quite excited. The second bell rang, indicating there would be no more bells. Danielle sped up, smiling to herself and feeling oddly pleased. She would get to draw the Horse again, and, almost as amazingly, she might actually have friends. Her left hand was already twitching at the thought of picking up that chalk again. She almost didn't feel hungry now.

The day passed slowly with class periods of geography, history, and science. But finally the end of the day came, and, like water from a ruptured container, all the children of Otter Lake spilled out of the one-storey school *en masse*, making their way home, where family, television, and homework awaited them — not necessarily in that order. This flood of Aboriginal adolescents included William, Ralph, and Shelley, making their way down the frozen streets of the village.

"She's coming over? Today? Did she say today? What time?" Shelley was anxious to see the little girl in action.

"I didn't ask specifically."

"Oh, Ralph. You can be so useless sometimes. I could have gone over to Julia's this afternoon instead of walking home in the cold with you two, but I thought you said Danielle was coming over this afternoon. Brothers!"

"She is! She told me she was."

Trailing about a foot behind, William seemed oddly uninterested in the conversation. "I'm bored."

Used to his friend's occasional moody moments, Ralph tried to engage him in the banter. "How come you're not excited about seeing Danielle draw her Horse?"

"It's just a stupid horse." The memory of what had so dazzled the young boy had evaporated over the last few days. Personally, he hoped he'd never see the Horse again. After all, it wasn't that amazing. Boats could go a lot faster than horses and were far more amazing. "I don't know why you want to see it now. You didn't last time."

"Last time we didn't know. What's wrong with you, anyway?"

William shrugged. Idly, he picked up an icy chunk of snow and threw it at the stop sign, missing. Picking up another one, he noticed Shelley was smiling. "What?" This time he flung it harder, and it hit the sign with a palpable bang, exploding in a shower of snow and ice.

"It's because she's better than It. I bet that's why It's acting all funny like this. It's jealous of the way Danielle can draw and all the attention we're paying to her."

"Stop calling me It!" William lashed out, pushing Shelley's shoulder, knocking her into Ralph, who grabbed her instinctively. At the same time, both siblings let out a "Hey!" He had pushed Shelley. All their squabbling over the years, all the fights, all the disagreements had never resulted in any form of physical interaction. This was new, and they all recognized that it was something different. Shelley and Ralph stared at their so-called friend, still processing the push. Realizing he had crossed a line, William tried to explain his actions.

"I'm not jealous of that little weirdo. So she can draw a stupid horse. Big deal. There's more to life than drawing a horse."

Shelley faced the boy, equally angry. "Then let's see you draw one like hers," she said, still smiling, but this time a little more coldly. Shelley's attitude and physical stance seemed to dare him.

"Shut up!" William was fairly sure he wasn't jealous. That was for kids. But he wasn't sure how he felt or why he had pushed his best friend's sister. This was all new territory for him.

For practically everybody.

Once again the mediator, Ralph was relieved to see that just a dozen feet or so ahead was their house. Refuge from the present group friction might not be total, but at least it would be warm, with refreshments.

"Stop it, both of you. Geez, sometimes I don't get you two. Everything I know about brothers and sisters says me and Shelley should argue and fight the way you two do. I don't get it."

Once more William shrugged. "Whatever." He let himself inside the Thomas house first.

"And he calls Danielle weird. I don't know why he's your friend, Ralph." Shelley disappeared into the house, following William.

Ralph, alone on the steps, mumbled to himself, "Sometimes I don't know either," before entering and closing the door behind him.

With their boots and coats removed, William and Ralph lost themselves in some reruns on the television in the living room. Disagreements such as the one that had occurred on the way home from school were frequently forgotten in the search for distractions. Still keeping her distance from William, Shelley caught up on her homework at the kitchen table.

Almost an hour passed before Liz Thomas came home.

"Your father won't be home till later tonight. He's going to some junior hockey thing in Baymeadow. So it's just us." Her news elicited a round of grunts. "I see the village school system is doing an excellent job teaching you the fine art of communication." Once more a series of grunts acknowledged her observations.

"William, are you staying for dinner?"

Shelley mumbled to herself, well aware all could hear her. "Well, duh!"

"Yes, ma'am!" William's train of logical thought followed with an immediate, "What are we having?"

"Well, let's see ... somehow I knew you might be staying, so I got us some —" Liz was interrupted by a soft knocking at the door. She paused for an instant, not sure if she had indeed heard what she'd heard. "Did somebody just knock?! I'm not sure ..." Instantly, Shelley and Ralph's heads turned towards each other, then to the door on the other side of the Everything Wall.

On the far side of that same door stood an excited Danielle, fidgeting in her boots. She was here at her *friends'* house! It was so odd to think that. She had *friends*. And on top of that, she was here to draw her precious Horse. She knew her mother wouldn't miss her if she came home late. She seldom did. And this place was always so warm and smelled so nice. Danielle definitely liked coming here. The only problem was that eventually she had to leave.

The door opened in front of her, and there on the other side, smiling, was somebody new, not Shelley, not Ralph, not even that mean-looking kid. But a woman who, for some reason, seemed delighted to see her.

"You must be Danielle. I have been so looking forward to meeting you. Oh, sweetheart, we loved your Horse."

One by one, Shelley and Ralph came up behind the woman. "I'm Liz, the mother of those two, and welcome." Liz opened the door wider and ushered in the little girl, who was clearly unprepared for such a welcome.

"Th ... th ... thank you."

"Hey, Danielle," said Ralph and Shelley in unison.

Danielle nodded as her jacket was suddenly and forcibly removed from her back by an enthusiastic Liz, almost lifting the tiny girl off her feet. Noticing the worn quality of the young girl's coat, Liz made a mental note to see if she still had any of Shelley's outgrown coats in the basement. Looking around, Danielle noticed William a distance away, leaning against the archway separating the kitchen from the living room. He had a nasty look to him, like he smelled something bad. Quickly, she decided not to look at him anymore. That was probably the best thing to do. If she pretended he wasn't there, he might go away. The opposite of the way she called her Horse. She pretended it was there and it came.

To her right, she noticed the Everything Wall, clean and pristine except for small, unimpressive drawings scattered around its edges. The centre, a good three-quarters of the Wall, was empty. That was where the Horse would be. That's where it had been before and where she would call it forward again. Danielle could almost feel it right now, nudging her to begin.

"Would you like something to drink first or do you want to draw?! I think we have some ginger ale?!" Shelley pulled out a can from the fridge. "It's diet?! Want that?!"

Not really knowing the difference in ginger ales but nodding appreciatively, Danielle took the can. Liz couldn't help thinking that perhaps she should buy some fully sugared drinks specifically for Danielle. If there was ever anybody who needed the extra calories, it had to be the tiny waif who stood in front of her. Her fingers looked as skinny as the pieces of chalk. But for now, her daughter was acting as an excellent host, and the mother decided to let the rest of the afternoon play out by itself.

Opening the can of ginger ale, Danielle noticed everybody was looking at her. This made her uncomfortable. She froze, unable to drink. There was a little tremble to her frame, but not so little that Liz didn't notice it.

"All right, everyone, let's let the girl alone. I'm sure she doesn't want us all looking at her, do you, hon? When you are ready, the chalk is there in the box on the shelf."

They all went back to what they'd been doing. Supposedly. Liz disappeared upstairs while the two boys went back to the television. Shelley sat herself back at the table and turned her attention to the math book lying open before her. Algebra — the math from hell. If A equals algebra, and B equals Shelley, then C must equal all the lost hours in her life that she'll never get back. Why would somebody invent this and teach it to Native kids? Shelley found herself mumbling her father's favourite phrase as she sat there, waist-deep in algebraic formulas: "White people sure are strange." But between logarithms and equations, the corner of her eye still wandered over to where Danielle stood in front of the Everything Wall.

Soon only the muffled sound of the television in the other room could be heard, along with the occasional turning of a page and the *glug-glug* of pop being drunk. Though Danielle couldn't see her, Shelley was smiling. *Good,* she thought, *and I'll have to make sure she eats something before she leaves*. She was so thin! Too thin. Shelley Thomas had a remarkably developed mother instinct even then, barely a year after puberty.

Sipping her pop and now relatively alone, Danielle turned her attention to the Wall before her. Scouting the borders of available space, the girl gingerly picked up the container full of chalk, a multitude of different colours with which to explore the universe. Today, she felt the Horse wanted more blue. She never knew what the colours meant in the creation of the Horse, but the Horse knew and that was good enough for her.

Putting the box on the floor near the Wall, she picked up a white chalk stick first, then looked at the flat surface in front of her. She didn't move for five seconds, a look of deep concentration taking shape on her face as her imagination spread across the black paint. Her focus was so deep she didn't hear the small sound of a twelve-year-old girl turning slightly in her chair to look over her shoulder. Or a slightly younger boy getting up off the couch in the other room to hover just outside the entrance to the kitchen, or the huskier boy who followed him. They were all silent, waiting, wanting to see the creation of the Horse and learn how such artistic magic was accomplished.

Danielle wrapped the fingers of her left hand around the chalk. Putting the pop on the floor to her right, she gripped the chalk between her thumb and index finger. Clenching her right hand and resting it against the Wall, she used it to balance herself as she crouched into position. Her hand opened and, for a second, expanded against the wall itself, as if to feel it.

Then she began. Deep in her mind, she called. Almost immediately, she knew the Horse was waiting. Coming.

One individual's creation is often hard for others to witness and appreciate, let alone understand. Michelangelo was supposedly once asked how he could carve such beautiful sculptures, to which he replied that he simply imagined what he wanted to create deep inside a block of marble and then removed everything that didn't resemble what he had envisioned. Coming from such an artist, the process sounded surprisingly easy.

What Danielle saw on that Wall, or perhaps even behind it, none of the other kids could fathom. They could only watch, gathering a hint of what she was doing. She sketched the outline of the creature, moving sometimes swiftly, other times so delicately and precisely that the observers were left aching for more active and broad creation. After the red came more white, then the blue, and finally the brown. She used yellow to highlight certain areas of the Horse's body. She used her hand to blend the colours together by smudging them in just the right way. Somehow this added shadow and depth, texture and grain. Minute by minute, the Horse took shape on the Thomases' wall in Otter Lake. It was like a portal that magnificent creatures would pass through, granting those precious few a brief audience.

How a ten-year-old girl could know the detailed musculature and anatomy of a horse in such detail was surely a mystery. Even if asked, it was doubtful Danielle would give a sufficient answer. She just did what was necessary. The hooves were delicate, as were the ears and the nostrils, flared, expelling air. She spent ten minutes on the mane alone, making it seem like the Horse was running in full gallop, perhaps down a beach somewhere with an ocean gale chasing it, as in those photographs in the book they had seen the other day. Danielle saved the eyes for last, which many philosophers believed were the windows to the soul. Tongues and ears might lie, but never the eyes. And like the version that had been created last week, they were fierce and protective, almost as if they were warning people away from both him and Danielle.

All three children watched the creation from start to finish, never uttering a word. At one point, her neck hurting, Shelley turned completely around on her chair, but Danielle didn't hear her or the creaking furniture; she was too busy communicating with the being on the Wall. Her body was here, but everything that made Danielle *Danielle* was somewhere on the other side of that black plywood. Shelley's breathing gradually became shallower, almost as if she was afraid her very breath would disrupt the little girl's act of creation. The only time she'd ever felt remotely like this had been a year ago at the arena in town, where her parents had taken her to see some figure skating. Seeing a beautiful young girl, dressed so pretty, dancing on the ice as if gravity and friction were figments of the imagination had made her briefly imagine a world where she could be that graceful and talented. Here, now, in front of her, was something completely different yet so similar. Danielle's hand, gliding across the plywood wall, creating things that ninety-nine percent of the population could never imagine, never mind create.

Shelley felt honoured to be able to watch.

The two boys, with differing opinions on the girl, shared a mutual amazement at what they were witnessing. William watched Danielle's hands like a hawk, hoping against reality that he might be able to, in the way young children (and a few adults) believe is possible, re-create or imitate what the little girl was doing. He had hands. He had imagination. He had chalk and a flat surface to draw on. But that was where the similarity ended. His sense of astonishment was slowly turning into something darker: envy.

Ralph, on the other hand, could almost see where Danielle's hand was going to flow. It was like he could see what part of the Horse she was going to draw next. The Horse was taking shape, and he could almost see it three-dimensionally. Even though he didn't know how, Ralph understood that Danielle felt the Horse was real. And, for that short period of time, the young boy didn't think he could argue against the young girl's belief. Each chalk mark was a caress, each straight line was a map Ralph followed to aid him in understanding what was happening on his kitchen wall.

Now familiar with her medium, Danielle incorporated more of the environment in her conception. There was a mild warping in the wood that Danielle used to her advantage by placing where the head joined the neck of the Horse over the dent. The result was that the head seemed to follow Ralph when he moved. Had somebody taught her that, or was that something instinctive? Or maybe it was in reality part of the Horse, not the Wall.

It may seem exaggerated to describe the sense of captivation the diminutive girl had on the other three children in the room. After all, in the larger context of the world, this was just a small girl drawing on a wall with chalk. For hundreds, maybe thousands of years, children had got in trouble for simple variations of this very same act. But all three were somehow aware that Danielle was taking them someplace, using some power that very few had access to. And they knew they were privileged to be along for the ride.

It was Ralph who, once again, had been fully enveloped by Danielle and her chalk Horse. In ways he was not able to describe, he thought he could see the little girl riding atop that Horse, somewhere in a land far away — the creature carrying her, she holding on tight and caressing its powerful neck. He saw them, horse and girl, together, interacting as more than a drawing and its drawer should. Perhaps there was indeed a crack between the worlds, and somehow he was peering between the two, looking at what Danielle was seeing. Had Ralph Thomas been able to express himself at that moment, he would have said, "It was truly weird." But in a positive sense.

Danielle began to slow down. She was adding finishing touches, details in the tail and around the shoulder to indicate motion. More to the nostrils to make them seem like they were actually quivering in exertion as it ran faster than could be imagined.

Twenty-seven minutes passed in the universe known as the Thomas family kitchen, and then there it was once again, as amazing as last time. Maybe more. The Horse on the Everything Wall looked remarkably similar to what they had seen only a few days ago, except it wasn't a carbon copy. There were subtle differences that marked it as changed. None of the three who'd been watching Danielle surreptitiously could say what exactly the differences were, but they all were certain that the Horse was different, somehow changed; had it grown or metamorphosed in some manner? Were its ears keen to hear an imagined sound? Were its eyes communicating something the previous drawing hadn't been aware of? Had Danielle imbued it with a consciousness that wasn't present before? Had Danielle's talent evolved? Had the Horse?

Danielle made one last adjustment to the tail, roughing in some yellow with two fingers, making it appear to be moving along the wall towards the doorway. Satisfied, she stood up, let out a deep breath, backed away from the wall, looked at her work, and was finished. The Horse was there, and her job was done. Danielle leaned back, assessing what she had created. All was good. He was here. Concluding that she had done everything she had come to do, she replaced the chalk pieces neatly back in the plastic container and put it on the shelf.

Nobody in the kitchen moved as she did this. As she put on her jacket, she said a pleasant yet perfunctory thank-you that concluded the tiny girl's third visit to the Thomas house. "And I liked the book very much. Very pretty." Then Danielle walked through the kitchen to the door, an actual skip in her step, stopping briefly to slip her boots on.

All was silent as the two doors closed behind her. The three usually rowdy and rambunctious children were not so rowdy and rambunctious. In fact, only the hum of the refrigerator and distant growl of the furnace below them could be heard. A few seconds later, Liz entered the room, the only sound and movement.

"Did I hear the door close? Why is everybody so quiet? Something wrong?" Turning around, she saw that the Horse had returned to the Everything Wall. Then it was Liz Thomas's turn to be quiet. Only for a moment. "Wow," was all she could utter.

"Yeah," added William. Shelley and Ralph didn't speak.

ON HER WAY home, Danielle hummed to herself, not feeling the cold winter wind. This had been a good day for her. A very good day. Though she was tired — she hadn't slept well because her mother and her mother's boyfriend had been fighting all night — the only word to describe how she felt was "positive." Very positive. That was a phrase one of her teachers frequently used, telling students that they should always try to make each and every day positive in some manner. For the first time in a long while, Danielle felt she had managed to do just that. She had friends now, not just the Horse. Going home didn't seem to matter so much today. Having someplace to look forward to was better than having nothing to look forward to.

She could see her house down at the end of the street. Her mood darkened as she approached the rundown mobile home that seemed it had only ever been at the end of this lane. There had been far worse days, her ten-year-old mind reasoned, so she struggled to keep the smile on her face. For the rest of that day and night, until she left for school in the morning, she would think of her Horse.

The Horse was a lot more than many kids had, she told herself.

WHEN TYE GOT home from the game that night, the house was as dark and silent as the woods around it. It had been a fun night. His team, peopled with half a dozen cousins, had won. A good time had been had by all. Though far past his prime as an athlete, he still frequently got requests to join this and other teams. He was in good enough shape, and most of the other players were of the same age and definitely of a heavier calibre. But his erratic schedule on the road made commitments like that difficult. As a result, he would go out and support the team when he could, always making his apologies when he couldn't put on the necessary skates and gear.

Someday, when his trucking days were over, he'd have to figure out how to slip back into being a permanent resident of Otter Lake, provided his body would allow him to. But for now he was going for quality, not quantity of representation. Tye had told his wife he would be home a good hour earlier, but the international laws of male companionship dictated two more beers and other stories that absolutely needed to be told that night, or they would not be responsible for what happened to the world. Tye returned to his dark home feeling a little guilty at having robbed his family of an hour of quality time, but he would make it up to them — the battle cry of all late-arriving or absent parents.

Turning the lights and the engine off, Tye coasted into

the driveway. No need to wake any of his family. If he was lucky, and that Williams kid hadn't eaten up all the dinner, there might be something in the fridge for him to gobble on, courtesy of his loving wife. Sometime down the road, he was going to have to do something about William. Not that there was anything wrong with the boy, but he spent so much damn time at their house. Tye knew the Williams house was a loud, raucous place, and his son's best friend was just one log in a boom of other Williamses, but he was at the Thomases' house so much that one of the guys at the game had asked if Tye was going to build on an extra bedroom for the boy.

Entering his home was like being enveloped by a warm and comforting blanket. The night and the pickup's temperamental heater had been cold, so for a few brief seconds Tye stood just inside the doorway, enjoying the warmth of his home, in several different meanings of the word. It was a good home, and he and Liz had worked hard to provide for everybody. He knew the time he spent away was difficult, but work that paid really well was rare on the reserve, and he was glad to have something like this to provide for everybody.

Bonus! There, covered in plastic wrap, was a sizable plate of spaghetti. A traveller of the world, or at least Canada, Tye knew spaghetti seldom tasted better than at midnight in an empty kitchen. Everybody knew that. Seasoning it with salt — Liz was awfully stingy with the salt — and pepper and some extra parmesan cheese, Tye sat down front and centre at the kitchen able to enjoy his wife's culinary creation. Tomorrow would be his turn in the kitchen, and he had to think of something chicken-related to make. Maybe in the slow cooker.

The first forkful of pasta, however, never quite made it to his mouth. Still sitting in the dark for the most part, the kitchen lit primarily by a street lamp some twenty metres away, Tye saw the Horse. It was back where it had been only a few days before. It was staring at him. The creation on the Wall unnerved the man. There was no reason it should. Tye was a seasoned horror movie fan. He had seen all the Alfred Hitchcock classics and he'd read all of Stephen King. He had survived the horrific experience of being with his wife during the birth of their two kids, though his eyes had been closed most of the time. There was nothing left to scare him. But this image was doing a good approximation of causing him to experience a queasy kind of fear.

It looked at him.

The Horse, as everybody called it, had been drawn by a ten-year-old girl who weighed barely more than his boots. It was made of chalk. There was absolutely no reason why that creation should give Tye the willies. Refusing to back down in front of something only a few grains of chalk in depth, Tye put his plate down and leaned forward in his chair to examine it. The way the light from the streetlamp cascaded through the window and onto the Everything Wall gave the Horse a unique glow.

The girl had talent for sure. There was no denying that. Tye tried to remember the last time he'd seen little Danielle. Must have been sometime just before her father had died.

Or maybe at the funeral. Stupid tragedy ... but then, most tragedies are. Tye had been on the road as usual but had heard about it from his cousin who worked with Albert at the construction site. A water filtration system was being installed. Albert, with two other men, had been pouring cement into what would be the foundation. The ground on which Albert stood suddenly gave way. Danielle's father was instantly covered by both earth and cement. His coworkers were there in an instant, digging at the wet cement and dirt, calling his name. But the man had hit his head in the fall. The dual weight of soil and cement suffocated him before he could be pulled from the hole.

As Tye remembered, Danielle had to be looked after by a distant cousin because Hazel was too grief-stricken to be of any use to her daughter. Many would argue little had changed in that department. Hazel still grieved, albeit in a harsher fashion.

It was the eyes, Tye thought. That's what it was. He'd seen eyes like this on a documentary he'd come across in some forgotten hotel room in a forgotten truck stop, about that painting, the *Mona Lisa*. Supposedly, that Italian artist had done such a good job painting that woman's portrait that if you walked across the room, her eyes would follow you. Just like in some photographs.

Whatever the answer was, Tye didn't care. His appetite lost, he haphazardly tossed the plastic wrap over the spaghetti and placed it into the fridge. *William can eat it tomorrow*, he thought. He left the kitchen, relieved at leaving the room now dominated by the Horse and its eyes, eager to find solace anywhere else in his home. Horses hadn't much interested Tye in the past, and what curiosity he might have had in them was rapidly evaporating in his house's current environment.

The man shuddered at the thought of that thing becoming a permanent resident of his home. It wasn't that he didn't like the Horse; it was just that it unnerved him. Little girls shouldn't be able to draw things like that. And the things that little girls drew shouldn't unsettle him, which of course, because it did, unsettled him more. It was a vicious circle.

The other thing that was so puzzling was the blind sense of amazement the rest of the family and, he might as well admit, a good measure of Otter Lake's junior population held for the thing. A handful of adults had been through the house in the past week, and they had had much the same reaction. It wasn't just the children. Tye was very aware that when it came to things like art and non-sports pastimes, he walked a different path than his wife.

William was right. Simply put, it was weird. Everybody seemed to see the beauty, the majesty, but for Tye, something more was struggling to come out of the Wall through the Horse. He didn't know what, but it was there. And possibly, if logic followed a predictable path, it would seem it was somewhere in Danielle. But this was all silly. He was imagining things. That little girl ... it was just a drawing. That's all it was. Tye climbed the stairs to bed.

IN THE KITCHEN, all was quiet. Twenty-one minutes later, Ralph entered. He had heard his father climb the stairs and, after a brief visit to the bathroom, crawl into bed. Though there was a good second level of a house between him and the Horse, he could feel it through the floor panels. Creeping as delicately as the forty-year-old house would let him, Ralph had no idea why he was returning to the kitchen. He wasn't hungry. With the heat turned down for the night, his feet were rapidly becoming cold on the unheated floor. Not wanting to wake anybody, Ralph resisted the impulse to turn the overhead lights on. Instead, he flicked on the light above the kitchen stove, hoping that would provide enough illumination for him to see the Horse.

Sitting on a kitchen chair, his feet tucked up underneath him, Ralph stared at the Horse. And it stared back. Upstairs, the remaining members of the Thomas family tossed and turned while Ralph remained silent and still. As did the Horse. The boy didn't understand why he was here. Both Shelley and William were amazed by the Horse, as was he, but that's where it stopped for them. For Ralph, the relationship continued. It was something deeper. Instinctively, he knew Danielle saw things he couldn't, that it was more than a series of chalk lines on a kitchen wall. It was alive for her. It was alive for Ralph, too, though not as strongly as for Danielle. He, in some way, knew there was more to this than what everybody else saw. And he wanted more.

Was it possible to draw something into existence? Sure, he'd learned in school that big-time designers and architects drew pictures of cars and planes and buildings that eventually came into creation. Was that the same? Ralph didn't think so. He wasn't sure what he was thinking.

Ralph sat alone in the family kitchen for another twenty-two minutes, wondering if he could somehow see what exactly it was Danielle saw. Every once in a while, for a second, he thought he saw something fleeting in the Horse, but just as quickly it flickered and was no longer there, leaving him unsure if the flash he was sure he'd perceived had just been his imagination. But wasn't that what all this was about — imagination?

The more Ralph thought about it, the more confusing it got. Eventually, he returned to bed, leaving the Horse and all its secrets still, biding its time on the kitchen wall.

ACROSS THE VILLAGE, William lay asleep in a fetal position on his bed. On the other side of the room, his brother Jimmy slept, still in his track pants, mouth wide open, appearing to be in the middle of a silent scream. Underneath William's bed, buried deep in a notebook beneath a week's worth of dirty laundry, were sheets of paper testifying to a dozen different attempts at drawing a horse. All were half finished, most with an angry line or two through them.

## CHAPTER EIGHT

IT HAD BEEN A LONG TIME SINCE HARRY HAD HAD SUCH a long, detailed conversation with anybody. Normally he could get by in the day using just four, maybe five pistons in the aged engine that was his mind. Today he had had to use seven, with the possibility of eight creeping up on him. This would have required the grease-soaked dust of several years to be cleaned off as he ushered the long-unused pistons into unexpected use. No amount of sugar or caffeine could sustain such effort for long. The first signs of a headache were beginning to knock on the old man's forehead. For the moment, he chose to ignore them.

To Harry, Ralph's discomfort with this simple question manifested itself visually with little explosions from the pustules protruding out of his skin. That was one thing Harry had noticed about people: when he asked them direct questions about themselves or their motivations, they tended to get very uncomfortable. Exploding pustules were not a good thing. Even if very small and even if on a man such as the one sitting across the table from him.

Harry knew they weren't really there — at least, that's what other people seemed to believe. Who was he to contradict them? Those manifestations of spirit were indeed there, and it wasn't his fault if other people who had bank cards and subway passes couldn't see them.

"Well?"

Ralph was beginning to feel hot. The Tim Hortons seemed stifling. In his time with Harry he had neglected to take off his coat, thinking theirs would be a short conversation. As a result, there was sweat in all the usual places on his body, and he felt clammy and damp inside his clothes, an unusual sensation for this time of year. The cause wasn't only his standard-issue police jacket; some was from the overheated interior of the franchise, as its furnace fought to find a balance with the creeping coldness that snuck its way through the constantly moving doors and the large plate glass windows. The heating system was overcompensating to keep the winter at bay. Admittedly, a good portion of the sweat was the result of the grilling this weird old man was giving him. Why had he become a cop? It had been a long time since he'd been asked such an obvious question.

"Why does anybody become a cop?"

Harry shook his head, particles of donut falling from his beard. "Not an answer."

"Why is this so important to you?"

"Again, not an answer." Harry blinked his eyes repeatedly. The pain in his head was growing worse. He needed to stop thinking soon. If he were to look in a mirror right now, he was sure he'd see holes peeking through the very essence of who he was. That happened a lot when he overtaxed his mind. There was only so much of him to share on any given day, and he was rapidly tapping himself out. "You want to know about the Horse and the person who drew it? It's just not that simple. The Horse is complicated. It's not just a Horse. You may be you, and I may be me, but that Horse is not just a horse. Understand?"

Ralph did not. This guy was making things far more complicated than they needed to be. He still had not heard from Shelley or William, and his time before work was running out. He needed this discussion to progress at a more efficient pace, and he needed to get some real answers. He'd been trained for situations like this. "I became a cop because my father had been a cop, and my grandfather ..."

"You're lying." Harry saw the police boy's pustules start to pulsate. Usually a good indicator of lying. Why was this guy lying to him? Most people lied for three reasons, Harry had learned over the years. One was because they were trying to get something they couldn't get any other way. Two, because they were afraid of something and lying was the best way for them to protect themselves. And third, lying was in their nature. While Harry could read Ralph in his own way, he wasn't psychic, meaning all three of these possibilities remained a factor until one of them was proved.

Ralph was lying. The truth was, he wasn't sure. It had been a spur-of-the-moment decision years ago, and he'd lost the purpose in that time. Less than a decade ago he'd graduated and been posted to the Dead Rat River First Nation in northern Ontario; there, he'd thought he'd bring peace and order to a rather rowdy community, famous for its beaded moccasins and baseball team. His idea of peace and order proved a rather difficult state to achieve. Being single, good-looking, and holder of a regular income, a fair number of local women found him of interest. As a result, a fair number of local men found him problematic. Many difficulties above and beyond his position as a peace officer surfaced as a result of those two strongly held opinions, making his three years in Dead Rat River less than the envious position his fellow graduates believed him to have received.

Knowing the same might happen in any other Indigenous community, Ralph had thought it better to sidestep the noble idea of serving his people specifically and decided to serve them in a larger context. Less Native content and more people of a mixed and varied population. The law, is after all, supposed to be colour-blind. That was how he'd found himself in Toronto, originally with its Aboriginal Peacekeeping Unit; however, finding the unit again too incestuous, Ralph embarked on his career as an ordinary Toronto Police Service officer. In all that time, post–police college, he'd never been asked why he had become a cop.

Harry's eyes were closed again, as if the sunlight beaming in through the windows was hurting them, but Ralph could tell the man was still waiting for his answer.

"Because of Danielle."

Harry smiled. Opening his eyes, he glanced out the window to the Horse. "He'll be glad you remembered her name. That's a good sign."

Ralph's heart was practically in his mouth. "Do you know where I can find her?"

For a moment, a look of puzzlement came over the old man's face. "Now, why would you want that?"

"I knew Danielle, and the Horse, a long time ago, before there was a Horse. I'd like to say hello."

There was no more smile on Harry's face. "The Danielle you knew doesn't exist. One could even ask if she ever did. There's only the Horse."

"What are you talking about?" Ralph was beginning to be frustrated again. He was telling this old man more than he told most people and was getting very little in return. And what the old man was sharing was bizarrely enigmatic and cryptic. Most cops, Ralph included, were not fans of the enigmatic or cryptic. "You keep talking like that thing is alive. It's just a painting, not even that. It's graffiti on a wall. It's Danielle who created it. And why do you keep referring to it in masculine terms?"

Shaking his head, Harry looked defeated. "You don't see anymore, do you?"

"See what?"

"Oh, He's not going to be pleased."

For the third or fourth time that morning, the conversation was going in a completely and annoyingly different direction from the one that Ralph intended. "*He's* not going to be pleased? Who's 'he'? The Horse?"

Harry rubbed his forehead. The headache was now throbbing. "Yes, the Horse. Of course the Horse. Who else are we talking about?"

Before Ralph could answer, Harry with no last name, of the weird disposition and unusual way of expressing himself, fell over, out of the booth and on to the floor. He was unconscious.

Luckily, there was a man sitting across from him who knew something about saving lives. This was the third time Ralph had been in a situation like this. Basic first aid is deep-seated in all officers of the law. The first time he'd battled death so closely had been during his stationing in Dead Rat River. At a wedding dance, an older, substantially overweight man had tried to participate in an ancient form of dance known as the Twist when his heart decided it had other plans. Due to the reserve's location — on land the Canadian Government didn't want back in the 1870s — an ambulance would take a good forty-five minutes to arrive from the nearest non-Indigenous community. So young Officer Ralph, who was working the dance, leapt into action and applied CPR and mouth-to-mouth for the first time in his life. Unfortunately, the man's heart was quite stubborn in its choice of action, and the father of the bride didn't live to see his daughter leave for her honeymoon.

The second time, Ralph was enjoying his first week at his posting in Toronto when his patrol car came upon a man slumped on a set of stairs set along a suburban street. This time Ralph managed to keep the man alive until the paramedics arrived.

Without thinking, Ralph kicked his chair away, kneeling beside Harry. Loosening the man's clothes, trying not to react to the sudden and strong aroma, Ralph tried to find the pulse on his bearded neck. The layer of fat and facial hair made it difficult. Next came the chest compressions followed by what was euphemistically called the Kiss of Life. If asked, it would have been difficult for Harry to remember the last time he'd brushed his teeth or used mouthwash (other than for its alcohol content). So Ralph's artificial ventilation was worthy of a medal of honour in itself.

"Somebody call 911. Tell them what's going on!"

Out of the corner of his eye he saw three or four other patrons look up from their Candy Crush and crullers and quickly switch their cells over to phone mode. The call for help had gone out.

"Come on, Harry. We're not done talking yet."

# CHAPTER NINE

UNLIKE THE WEEK BEFORE, THE WEATHER NOW WAS BITINGLY cold. Winter was making its presence known more forcefully. Windows across the community were covered with frost. Trees creaked when they swayed in the wind. Playing outside was not as much fun as it used to be, except for the diehards. And hot, sticky, mosquito-infested summer months were now being remembered with a fair amount of fondness.

In front of the Thomas house, William and Ralph were in the midst of a snowball fight, with William throwing the bigger and harder snowballs with far more lethal potential. All snowball professionals know it's difficult to force snow into sufficiently lethal projectiles when the temperature dips. The snow has to be packed very hard before it forms a ball, sticking together properly so that it doesn't fly apart when thrown. At one point, Mr. Georges, a science teacher, had tried to explain that adding more pressure raises the melting point of snow. This makes the snow damp and therefore easier to pack together, thus rendering the snowball able to overcome the centrifugal force resulting from being thrown. Somehow it related to the fact that water can be boiled at something like sixty or seventy degrees Celsius on Mount Everest instead of the usual one hundred on the reserve. The point was, Mr. Georges was putting way too much science into something as basic as a good, old-fashioned game of snowball wars.

Ralph did his best to dodge William's projectiles, but was soon overcome with snowy assaults and fell back into the ditch, scrambling and laughing. Not giving any quarter, William advanced, throwing still more snowballs, making them faster and faster, with just two or three strong pats of his hands before throwing them as hard as he could. Ralph kept rolling and twisting as he tried to avoid the rain of frozen water projectiles, but with little luck. For all his faults, William was indeed a fearsome warrior, even capable of throwing left-handed when pressured.

Exiting through the porch door, Shelley saw the juvenile war happening in front of her house and rolled her eyes. Not bothering to acknowledge the two boys and their foolishness, she walked right through the barrage and onto the road, determined to make her way to Julia's house without her brother and It embarrassing her.

Seeing Shelley cross the path of fire, William briefly debated making her a civilian casualty of the war, but the potentially painful repercussions of a carefully thrown snowball in her direction made him change targets. Shelley walked on, and William continued to throw his snowballs at Ralph, who managed to stand up, enabling him to maintain a zigzag pattern as he struggled to evade the frozen mortar shells.

Across the street, behind a reasonably tall snowbank left by a snowplough's recent attempt to clear the street, sat Danielle Gaadaw, watching everything. She smiled as Ralph successfully evaded a snowball and quickly tossed off one of his own, missing William by a mile. She saw Shelley disappear around a corner and wished with all her might that she could run up to her and join the pretty girl wherever she was headed. Instead, she hunched down lower, making sure the two boys couldn't see her, and continued to watch them play. The only sign of her existence was the occasional trail of breath vapour that came out of her mouth, a by-product of such a frigid morning. Luckily, the vapour was the same colour as the snow.

Unaware of the cold and her cramped legs, she watched for a long time, smiling at Ralph and William's antics. Eventually, the boys got tired and hungry; they negotiated a truce, deciding wisely that lunch was much better than war. Inside the house, Liz served them grilled cheese sandwiches. At least that's what Danielle thought they were, seeing only a bit of what was going on through the kitchen window. It had been so long since she'd had a grilled cheese sandwich. Her mouth watered at the thought, even though she could barely remember what they tasted like.

The afternoon passed as most winter afternoons pass. Danielle watched the Thomas house for a while, all the while imagining herself on the other side of the glass in the curtained window. Huddled up into a ball in an unconscious attempt to retain as much body heat as possible, she observed the house. Tye came out, got in the truck, and drove away, returning ten minutes later with a carton of milk. If she tried hard enough, Danielle could almost see her father — what she remembered of the man — in Tye. She was certain they almost had the same walk, though she had to admit to herself it could just be her imagination. But she took comfort from her observation just the same.

A short time later, Danielle spotted Shelley returning home. She looked so confident and not shy. "Not shy" was the only way Danielle could think of to describe her. From the top of her cloudy brown hair to the tip of her freezing toes, the younger girl hero-worshipped the older Shelley.

Pretty soon Shelley had entered her house, where, Danielle was certain, she would be greeted with a freshly made and warm grilled cheese sandwich too. A couple of cars and trucks drove by the hidden girl, kicking up clods of snow in their wake, but Danielle didn't notice them. She was focused on the house and the people in it. Her house had been like that once, she remembered, but not any-more. From her pocket she dug out an almost empty package of Saltines and munched on them as she watched the house and imagined what Shelley and Ralph and William and Liz were saying and doing. She wished very much that she was in that kitchen right then, eating a hot and gooey cheese sandwich, smiling at Ralph's jokes and making girl plans with Shelley. Even William would be tolerated. And a hug from Liz Thomas would be so welcome. These were the thoughts of Danielle Gaadaw as she squatted in the cold snow, across the road from the Thomas house that winter afternoon.

INSIDE THE HOUSE, other thoughts were being expressed. "Think she's any good at drawing anything else? I mean, a horse is easy." William then gave his best "I don't care" shrug.

"So is criticizing. Let's see you draw a horse, then?" dared Shelley, smiling at William's glare. She even reached over, grabbed the box of chalk, and placed it directly in front of him.

The young man backed away, as if the multicoloured sticks might bite him. "I would if I wanted to." William bit into the remaining half of his sandwich. "I just don't want to." He avoided eye contact with Shelley, sitting to his left.

Behind them was the Everything Wall, with the Horse standing proud and very present in the kitchen. As had been the case the day before, few other images dotted its surface. Shelley noticed her mother standing beside the Wall, a half-eaten grilled cheese sandwich in her hand, a concerned expression growing across her features.

"What's up, Mom?"

Liz took a short breath before answering. "Nobody else has really contributed to the Everything Wall. I mean, other than Danielle's Horse and those three drawings by Jennifer, Mark, and Keith, nobody has taken chalk to the Wall this week. Last week the place was hopping. Don't tell me your friends are all bored already. I knew it would happen eventually, but seriously, after week two?"

Ralph shook his head, trying to swallow his mouthful of cheese and bread before answering. "It's not that, Mom.

It's just, what's the point in putting anything up there when the Horse is right there? It's embarrassing. I mean, everybody loves the Horse, but ..."

William finished Ralph's thought "... but what's the point?"

Liz knew that unless the Horse was no more, a thought that saddened her, the Everything Wall was in danger of becoming obsolete. She was conflicted by her choices. On one hand, she had come up with the idea for the Everything Wall to encourage her own children as well as some of the local kids to draw, to participate, to create. She still felt that urge and wanted to see it continue in the next generation. It had been a success the first week. Was the drawing of the Horse so powerful that it kept her own and the neighbourhood children from making drawings of their own?

But to banish the Horse — and by doing that it would mean she was telling Danielle that she could no longer draw her glorious creature — made her very uncomfortable. That solution, if it could be called that, seemed worse. Liz was concerned her words would devastate the young girl, not to mention her own growing interest in an animal that up to now she had barely taken for granted.

Last night, as she'd lain in bed, Liz had gone through a number of options in her mind. Maybe there could be two Everything Walls, one for all the kids and one especially for Danielle Gaadaw. But it was an idea that, when she examined it closely, fell apart. There would still be the problem of intimidation. Nobody wanted to ride their bicycle to a motorcycle rally.

Since the young girl seemed interested in only drawing the creature, maybe Liz could let Danielle draw her Horse and then immediately erase it from the Wall. That was a possibility, but not a very practical one. Liz was afraid to admit it; she didn't know what to do. Her husband had been of little help. Tye had been oddly reticent about discussing the drawing when he came to bed last night. In fact, he'd outright refused to discuss it.

It wasn't just the intimidation factor that worried Liz. She was concerned with the obvious problem that it was quite apparent that once again Danielle was going to win the contest. It didn't help matters that there were so few participants. No one was giving Danielle a run for her money. But it wouldn't have mattered if there'd been two or three times as many drawings this week as the first week. It was doubtful anything could have come close to what she had created the first time around and then improved significantly the second time. Was it possible that she would continue to create something more and more spectacular, week after week? This meant that this week's problem would repeat into the future, more of the same. Liz couldn't keep awarding the prize to Danielle. It wouldn't be fair to the other kids. She had to think of something to do. But for this week ... there was nothing to do but give Danielle the prize.

"Ralph, could you give this to Danielle? It's her present for winning again this week."

"No surprise there," said Shelley. "What is it?"

Liz pulled it out of her large purse and placed it on the table in front of them. It was a modest-sized but inexpensive plaster cast of a tan-coloured horse with a dark brown, irregular spot covering its left shoulder and a neatly combed mane.

"Nice," commented Ralph. "She'll like that."

William did not look overly impressed. "I just wonder if she can draw anything else. That's all I'm saying. Don't you wonder that?" William finished off the last of his sandwich, getting no answer from his two companions. Both brother and sister had wondered that question themselves but would not admit it to William. In the end, it didn't really matter.

"I guess we'll never know," said Ralph, dipping his grilled cheese sandwich in ketchup.

William did not respond.

THAT MONDAY AT school, the morning progressed as mornings usually do in First Nations communities, as well as many other schools across the country.

When recess came, Danielle opted to stay in the classroom while the other kids ran off their pent-up energy outside. Though she could see them through the window to her left, she preferred to lose herself in the book of horses Liz Thomas had given her the previous week. She turned each page carefully after drinking in each picture. An Appaloosa running through the scrub brush of the American southwest. An Arabian posing at the top of a barren cliff. A quarter horse in a corral, appearing to look at the camera intently. A Clydesdale in a pasture, one leg partially raised. They all appealed to Danielle, and although this was the third time she had looked through the book, she wasn't tired of looking at them. She knew the order of the pictures and had memorized everything printed in the book about those horses practically verbatim. The familiarity of reading and rereading those pages was like the feeling she got when she climbed into a warm bed. This was the only book she owned.

On the other side of the window, William was watching her. Around him, the other students were throwing snowballs, trying to surf through the snow, or standing around talking in groups, but he only had eyes for the little girl sitting at the desk near the back of the classroom. He noticed nobody else was in the room. Danielle was alone. The teacher was off doing teacher things.

Danielle turned the next page of her book. There was a picture of a Shetland pony, so cute and tiny. In the background was some kind of festival. Danielle smiled to herself, wishing she could pet it.

"Hey, Danielle."

The voice startled her, causing her to tear a page. Looking up anxiously, she saw it was that big rough boy, the one Ralph and Shelley called William. She didn't say anything. Fumbling with the book, she straightened the tear and then closed it carefully, hoping that somehow the torn page wouldn't be torn when she looked at it the next time. Her fingers were becoming sweaty.

"Looking at your prize, huh?"

Danielle didn't respond, looking down, clutching the book close to her chest. She wanted desperately to leave the room, to be safely away in some other place, but the husky boy stood in the only doorway, watching her. He had a mean smile that she recognized; it was similar to one her mother's boyfriend often showed, especially when he was annoyed or mad.

"Hey, Danielle, I got a question. We were talking about this yesterday. We were wondering ..." He closed the door behind him.

OUTSIDE ON THE playground, Ralph was looking for William. They were in different homerooms, but they usually met up almost immediately after the recess bell went. He quickly surveyed the playground's inhabitants, trying to find his friend's stocky figure among the three hundred kids, but with no luck. This puzzled Ralph. Ralph had a few other friends, but it was usually William who waited for him. William's absence from the playground was strange.

Seeing his sister near the corner of the school building, he ran up to her. "Hey, have you seen William? I can't find him."

Her conversation with Julia and Vanessa interrupted, Shelley looked over her shoulder and gave her brother a glare colder than the snow he stood on.

"No. Go away."

"But —"

"No 'but.' No nothing. Go away! Leave us alone." She turned back to her friends, rolling her eyes. "Brothers!"

Confused but not quite worried, Ralph wandered along the wall of the school, wondering where his friend might be. He had been kind of moody when he'd left their place last night. William hadn't said much, but Ralph knew it had something to do with the Horse, or Danielle, but more probably both. His buddy could sure be grumpy sometimes. But that was the cost of being William's friend.

He passed classroom window after classroom window on his right as he walked along the wall of the school, looking into them and continuing to scan the school population on his left.

On another matter, he wished his sister wasn't so mean. Watching her interact with William sometimes made him happy she disliked his friend more than him, but it still hurt him when his sister was so rude and dismissive. To the best of his knowledge, he'd never done anything to earn such meanness. But something his father had once told him provided him with some solace, though it conjured up more unsolvable questions. "Sometimes sisters are just like that. I know. I had three. Just keep your head down and hope for the best. And if worse comes to worst, you can always outrun them." His father's sister Aunt Rachel had moved away a long time ago, but aunts Carol and Claudia seemed okay to Ralph. They even gave him lots of homemade butter tarts. Now that he thought about it in this context, he had difficulty imagining his sister growing up to be so nice. At least to him.

As he reached the elbow in the school, where the building made a right angle along the street corner and continued down a different road, Ralph stopped walking. There wasn't much time left in recess, and even if he did find William, there wouldn't be much time left to do anything fun. It just wasn't like William to not be around, wanting to do something. Ralph might have had a few other friends, but he was William's only real friend. This absence was very un-William.

It seemed to Ralph that the world had become weird ever since Danielle and her Horse had appeared in their lives. He was sure Shelley felt the same way. And his parents. He could tell by the way his mother didn't seem to know how to act around Danielle. And the way his father had looked at the drawing of the Horse. He knew that Danielle and her creature made them uncomfortable.

Ralph started to pace back towards his sister, still deep in thought. About friends, sisters, strange little girls, chalk horses, and how somehow, some way, they all seemed tied together. Life could be pretty strange sometimes.

Just by chance, or possibly providence, he glanced towards his left and saw his friend on the other side of the glass in the classroom window. William was pushing somebody. That somebody, Ralph realized with a gasp, was Danielle. Ralph stopped in his tracks, surprised to see them together, alone, in Danielle's classroom. He saw William push Danielle again, harshly, towards the front of the room, making her almost fall. For the first time, Ralph could see in William's face an obvious aggressive nature, a willingness to do anything to get his way. This was why some people had called his friend a bully, mean, and other assorted titles. He'd always shrugged it off. William's older brother Robert was a bully. Everybody knew that. He'd been bounced out of at least two high schools. Even William didn't like Robert. But now, on the other side of the window, he could see his buddy being mean and doing mean things to somebody who couldn't and wouldn't fight back.

Instantly, Ralph pounded on the window desperately.

The dull thudding filled the small classroom. William looked up, right into Ralph's face; their eyes locked, just for a moment. Then, looking away and without acknowledging his only real friend, William grabbed a piece of chalk and threw it at Danielle.

Ralph banged hard on the window three more times, his hand hurting with each impact, but William wouldn't look at him or stop menacing the young girl. It was obvious William was upset about something; Ralph had no idea what William meant to do, but instinctively he knew it wasn't something good.

Dodging away from the window, the younger boy raced towards the door of the school. Normally kids, under threat of detention, weren't allowed to enter the school building during recess unless they had permission, but this was not even a consideration for Ralph. He did not have time to get permission to do the very necessary thing he had to do.

As he ran towards the door, Shelley saw him and thought he was approaching her again. She looked annoyed.

"Ralph! I thought I told you —"

Barely pausing, Ralph attempted an explanation. "William's in one of the classrooms. With Danielle. I don't think he's being nice. She's crying ..." Without waiting for a response, he continued past her, aiming directly for the door. He flung open the door and raced down the deserted hall, his sloppy wet boots leaving puddles and the force of his footsteps echoing. Behind him, he heard his sister calling his name. He didn't stop. The room he had seen Danielle and William in was directly ahead and on the left.

Ms. Martel's room.

Ralph stopped just inside the opaque classroom door. Danielle was at the chalkboard, a piece of white chalk in her trembling hand. It was scraping along the black surface. So far, there were only two shaky lines evident. William was watching her intently, standing just a few feet behind the struggling girl. Ralph could feel Shelley's arrival right behind him. She stopped and looked over his shoulder.

Over Danielle's gentle sobs, they heard William's harsh voice, almost laughing. "That's it?! That's the best you can do?!" Danielle had stopped halfway through the third line, unable to continue. The chalk landed on the floor beside her shoe.

Ralph opened his mouth to object. But it was Shelley who spoke first, asking the obvious. "William? What are you doing in here? What are you doing to her?"

William, a triumphant smile on his face, turned to face them.

"Look at that! I told her to draw a dog. Does that look like a dog to you? It sure doesn't to me. So she can draw a decent horse. Big deal. So what? Geez, no wonder she's crying. I'd cry too if I drew a dog like that. I guess she ain't so great after all, huh?" Folding his arms across his chest, he sneered at the pathetic rendering on the chalkboard.

The attempted drawing did look like it had been sketched by the left hand of a right-handed monkey. If it was indeed the beginning of a dog, there was no way of telling.

As if he'd climbed the biggest mountain and beaten the most ferocious monster in the world, William was beaming victoriously. His point, however obtuse, had been proudly made.

Shelley forced her way past Ralph, nudging him roughly into the door frame as she did. She walked directly to Danielle, who was leaning against the far end of the board, her forehead leaning against the wall, her long, wispy hair hiding her face. Her tiny body trembled with what appeared to be silent sobs. The moment Shelley's hand touched her back, she flinched until she realized it was Shelley, who was gently pulling her into her arms. Though there was only a little more than two years' difference between the girls, Danielle seemed to disappear into the older girl's coat.

"You stupid ..." Try as she might, Shelley could not utter any profanity, especially while comforting the little girl. "I could just kick you. What were you thinking?!" Shelley glared at William, furious and intense.

Ralph was scared by his sister's words and her tone of voice, and Shelley's was not a look that made William entirely comfortable.

"What?" He sounded genuinely puzzled.

"Look what you did to her!" Shelley was angry.

"What?! I didn't do anything. I barely touched her."

The smile of success gone from his face, William was experiencing some difficulty understanding why Shelley was so mad at him. He was used to her angry dismissals of him, but this outburst seemed different. More focused and strong. Even Ralph was looking at him weirdly. It was like they didn't understand the laws of the schoolyard. Danielle was just a peculiar little girl, that's all. So what was the problem?

Suddenly, William felt Ralph's hands on his arm, pushing him away from the girls at the chalkboard.

"So uncool, William. So uncool." Ralph found himself for the first time in a long time angry at his friend. Not mildly angry, but really angry. Though William had thrown snowballs at him point-blank, or taken the larger portion of chocolate bars they'd bought together, or pushed Ralph off the dock so he would suddenly find himself standing knee-deep in the lake, this was of a different order. Normally he was just being William. This was different, and all of them knew it.

William stumbled against two desks, unprepared for the act of physical violence from his good friend and frequent victim. Under normal circumstances he would have pushed back, harder. But, as was becoming obvious, they were not living in normal circumstances these days.

Trying to regain his composure, William gave Shelley and Ralph his best argument, which seemed incredibly simple and true to him. "What?! I never hit her or anything. I just wanted to see if she could draw anything else. That's all. I don't know why she's crying. Geez." The tone of William's voice changed as he spoke; it became unsure and defensive, like he was trying to defend himself but was losing confidence in his own argument as he spoke. This was unfamiliar territory for him.

"No, you wouldn't, would you? 'Cause you're too stupid." Shelley started to gently steer Danielle towards the door. "It's okay," she said to the little girl with her arms wrapped around her. "We'll take you home. Ralph, can you get her coat and backpack?"

Nodding, Ralph went to the coat hooks at the back of the room and found Danielle's familiar worn, white-turning-into-grey coat with the two rips. He noticed there was another tear, this time underneath the right armpit. He grabbed it and her bag quickly, giving his friend — if they still were friends — a piercing glare. He followed his sister out the door.

Alone in the classroom stood a bewildered and now clearly awkward William.

"Geez. You guys gonna make a big deal out of this?" he yelled after them.

There was no response. His friend and his friend's sister didn't respond.

Alone, William felt odd. It seemed the point he had tried to make had been completely overlooked. He looked at the board, at what he'd made Danielle draw, the squiggles and random lines, a very poor attempt at art. How could those lines be a dog?

"Like I said, it doesn't look like a dog. See, I was right. I don't get it...." Oddly enough, he no longer felt so exultant. For a very brief second, an unsettling thought rolled across the young boy's mind. Was it possible he, William Williams, was the bad guy here?

"William? Do you have permission to be in here?" asked Ms. Martel, standing at the door.

Great. He was now in real trouble for being in the wrong classroom and at recess.

QUICKLY GRABBING THEIR backpacks and bundling up, Ralph and Shelley took Danielle out of the school and past the schoolyard. Several kids, including Julia and Vanessa, gave the trio peculiar looks, especially when the bell went off, sounding the end of recess. All but three re-entered the school. Both Thomas children knew they might get in trouble for cutting the last part of school, but any discipline that might come their way mattered to neither one. When they told their mother their reason for leaving school, both felt sure she would absolve them of the sin of truancy. Sometimes there were more important things than knowing the difference between coniferous and deciduous trees.

"What a stupid, stupid idiot!" grumbled Shelley. Danielle looked up at the taller girl, tears forming in her eyes. At first, Shelley assumed Danielle's crying was the result of William's meanness, but then she put all the pieces together and understood. "No, no. Not you, Danielle. William. I mean William. Not you. You're okay. Honest."

Ralph saw Danielle snuggle closer to his sister, who kept a protective arm around her.

"Don't you worry about that nasty William. He's just a big, stupid kid. He needs to be kicked in the head. And he's ugly too." From beneath her arm she was sure she felt what appeared to be a giggle. That was a good sign. Glancing at her brother, she added disparagingly, "And he's your friend!"

"I'm so sorry, Danielle." It was the first time Ralph had spoken since they'd left the school. All this time he'd been listening to Shelley calm and soothe the little girl who clung to his sister. It seemed she had a knack for that kind of thing. She was a natural. He felt sad for a number of reasons, primarily because it was his friend who had humiliated her. He was used to William's rough ways. Maybe everybody was right. Maybe William was indeed a bully. He remembered reading somewhere that, legally, boxers were only allowed to fight other boxers. Otherwise, if they got into fights on the playground or in the cafeteria with everyday people, they'd get into a lot of trouble. The same should hold true for people like William, he suddenly thought. Bullies should only pick on other bullies. But that defeated the purpose of being a bully, he supposed. There would have to be a severe readjustment of their relationship when all this particular dust settled.

Danielle didn't react to Ralph's apology. Shelley had run out of kindnesses to share with the little girl. As they walked, there was only the silence of the snow-covered community to keep them company. The three of them turned on to Twin Pine Lane, an oddly named street since both the pines that had generated the name had died a decade ago and were no longer in evidence. This was where most of the dozen or so trailers on the reserve were located.

Danielle, still snugly attached to Shelley, suddenly stopped moving. She stopped so suddenly that Shelley almost knocked her over.

"What's wrong, sweetheart?"

It took Ralph a moment to realize that this was Shelley's voice and not the voice of their mother.

Crawling out from underneath the layers of coats — hers and Shelley's — Danielle emerged into the winter afternoon air. The glare of the sun off the snow made her blink a few times, and then she wiped away the remaining wetness around her eyes. Though she'd stopped crying some time ago, her eyes were still red. She sniffled and looked around, recognizing the area. Then she spoke.

"Thank you."

Ralph remembered that in their few actual moments together, that was all Danielle ever seemed to say. That seemed to be seventy-five percent of her vocabulary. Just, "Thank you." Unsure how to respond, he simply smiled at her and looked at his sister uncomfortably.

Also smiling, Shelley looked down Twin Pine Lane to the row of trailers near the end. "Danielle doesn't have to thank us, does she, Ralph?"

Again, Ralph could hear his mother's voice.

"No, not at all. Sorry we couldn't do more."

"See? And don't you worry about William. When I get a hold of him, he'll be more afraid of you than you should ever be of him." Shelley nodded her head once solidly to punctuate her assurance. "You live down here, don't you? We're almost there. Come on, let's get you home first and then we can ..."

Danielle shook her head, clearly afraid, and stepped back from the Thomas kids. Her demeanour changed completely. There was a panicked look on her face. Whatever had caused it had been triggered by Shelley's offer.

Shelley took another stab at getting the young girl home. Stepping forward, she said, "It's okay, Danielle. We just want to make sure ..."

No such luck. Danielle took another step back, now clearly looking over her shoulder. "No. Thank you, but no.

You really shouldn't. Momma doesn't like people visiting. She'll get mad. I'm okay, really." She faked a poor smile to add emphasis.

"Under the circumstances, I don't think she would ..." Shelley could see that she was about to be unsuccessful in her attempts to deliver the little girl home personally.

Danielle took another step further down Twin Pine Lane, backing away more.

Ralph felt sure she would bolt any second. He reached out and grabbed Shelley's arm, knowing she would keep trying, regardless of how Danielle felt.

"Danielle, before you go ..." he said.

Her eyes darted to him, but she still looked on the edge of running down the lane.

"We forgot to give you your present."

"What present?"

Ralph nudged Shelley, who quickly dug around in her backpack. Everything of importance to Shelley existed in that backpack. She was seldom without it, especially at school. After some rummaging around, she pulled out a small package wrapped in newspaper. Handing it to Danielle, she peeled back a layer, revealing the head of the plaster horse. "You won the Everything Wall contest."

"Again!" added Ralph with a smile.

"So this is your prize."

Danielle couldn't take her eyes off the present. She reached out and gently pulled back more of the newspaper, exposing the entire miniature horse.

"It's yours. Go ahead. Take it." With that, Shelley put the plaster cast of a horse into the little girl's hands.

Around them, the trees creaked in the winter wind, but Danielle had senses for only what she held in her hands.

"For me?"

"For you. We know it's not much, but …"

"It's beautiful."

Frequently something being "not much" was a relative term. To Danielle, this prize, this present was indeed something "much." For Danielle, this knick-knack was worth more than the six dollars and ninety-nine cents Liz had paid for it. Terrified of breaking the delicate legs on the cast, Danielle very carefully wrapped her fingers around the trunk of the animal and tucked it inside her worn jacket, close to her chest. "I want to keep him warm," she said. "You're so nice to me." With a look of contentment Shelley and Ralph had not seen before on her face, she turned to walk down Twin Pine Lane.

"Thank you." Between the dozen or so metres separating them and the sound of the wind, they barely heard her parting words. Brother and sister watched her walk down the lane, a sad and forlorn figure momentarily happy.

"Well, that was strange," said Ralph. "What now?"

Her eyes still on the retreating Danielle, Shelley took a deep breath of winter air. "Well, we could go beat up that friend of yours. He deserves it."

Though he doubted they would actually do it, Ralph found that this time he couldn't argue with his sister.

THAT AFTERNOON AFTER school, William didn't make his way over to Ralph's house. Instead, he went home to where his large family lived. He put up with his brothers' and sister's taunts, and the perplexed looks his parents gave him when they understood that he wasn't over at the Thomas home. For the rest of the evening, he sulked in his room. Looking out the window at various cars driving by, William felt kind of bad, though he would never admit it. After all, why should he feel bad? He hadn't done anything wrong. For some reason he couldn't explain, something about Danielle bothered him. It made him angry and uncomfortable. With such a big and boisterous family, he was used to feeling angry and uncomfortable, but this was in a way he wasn't used to. So he'd done what he always did when he was angry and uncomfortable: he'd lashed out. It was something he'd picked up from his older brothers. It's a commonly held belief that bullying is passed down the generations, but very seldom is it encoded in the DNA. A definite case of nurture over nature. But William knew none of these things. When something bothers you, you bother it back. It's nature.

For obvious reasons, because of his very nature, William had no friends other than Ralph. While he was frequently rough and physical with his friend, he seldom abused their relationship. He was sure Ralph appreciated the boyish companionship. They made good buddies. Hanging with William was better for Ralph than hanging around with his sister. Still, William had to put up with that sister's obvious dislike of him, though he didn't quite understand it. William didn't think he was as bad as Shelley implied. He thought of himself as quite charming and interesting. Maybe he did horse around a little too much and was rude occasionally, but who wasn't? *Girls!* he frequently thought.

In the messy room he shared with Jimmy, the brother closest in age to him, who was playing hockey in town, William leafed through a handful of comic books that belonged to his brother. Jimmy never let his younger brother read or touch any of his things, but since Jimmy was seldom home, it afforded the younger Williams boy some limited reading opportunities. Luckily for William, this sibling absenteeism helped him avoid many brotherly beatings.

Alone and quiet in his room, William wondered what Ralph was doing; was he playing some game with Shelley or eating a late-afternoon snack their mother had whipped up for them? While the Thomas family was fed and fed well, in the Williams house, with such a big family, there was seldom anything left in the refrigerator to snack on. William had already checked the fridge. Essentially, there were only condiments and pickles at the moment. Not even the good kind of pickles — bread and butter — but dill. Dill was not a flavour William enjoyed.

William was bored. None of his brothers actually played with him, unless the older ones wanted to torment their younger and smaller sibling. His sister had a life of her own with other girls, just like Shelley did. Floyd and Justine Williams, parents to the rowdiest group of relations in the village, weren't usually home. There was work and family responsibilities outside these four walls. Though it was a busy and bustling house, today it was just William, alone in his shared room. That was one of the major reasons why he spent so much time over at the Thomas house.

There was, of course, homework to do, and even though he hated both the thought and practice of math, doing it would have to be better than being bored and lonely. Almost reluctantly, William picked up his school book and casually noticed all the drawing he had done on the cover. The bottom half looked like petroglyphs and pictographs. His history teacher had done a couple classes on them, and they had briefly fascinated the young boy. He had reproduced facsimiles of Indigenous images from all across the country on his math book. Above them was the logo for the rock band Guns N' Roses. And beside it was a sketch of a horse. It startled William for a moment. He had forgotten that he'd drawn it, almost immediately after Danielle had first drawn hers. While better than most ten-year-olds could attempt, it still paled in comparison to hers. And he had tried very hard.

For a moment, he thought of the little girl that he had persecuted in the classroom. Luckily, he hadn't got in trouble with Ms. Martel for what had happened; she had missed all of what had transpired in her classroom that recess. He had been able to talk himself out of a detention as the bell rang in the midst of his scolding. But there was a little part of him, he was quite sure, that for some bizarre reason almost wished he had been punished. Everything was not what it once was. It bothered him. William didn't know where things were going and how much they were going to change. It wasn't fair.

There was something new, something different about the generally miserable way he felt. He couldn't define it, wasn't used to it, but it sure wasn't good. Guilt was a new emotion to William. The boy didn't like it. He wasn't sure what to do about it. He turned his attention to a math problem, hoping this strange emotion might be crushed under his geometry assignment. But it was not.

ACROSS THE VILLAGE, down Twin Pine Lane, sat Danielle on her mattress, which lay on the floor at the back of her mother's trailer. At the foot of the bed, almost lost in the worn and dirty sheets, stood a horse. Not her close and special friend that she'd drawn on the Everything Wall in the Thomases' kitchen, but the plaster one Ralph and Shelley had given her. Danielle had put it there when she got home. She'd been staring at it ever since. It was so pretty. She heard something break outside her door, down the hall near the living room, but she ignored the sound. There was always something breaking. Instead, she focused on the horse. It was very different from her friend, but in this particular case, different wasn't necessarily a bad thing. She was sure there was no conflict between the two.

All around the little girl on the bare wall were faint but familiar echoes of images that had been scrubbed off the white, dingy paint. Bits of a tail here, and some hind leg over by the door. Near the window she could make out, if she looked hard enough, faded lines that could be a mane. Bits and pieces of her precious Horse that couldn't be scrubbed clean. Danielle's mother had tried many times, punishing her daughter many more times for doing something so "fucking childish" as to draw on the walls of her room. For reasons unknown, her mother took her artistic abilities as a wilful and disobedient act aimed directly at challenging her parental authority.

So Danielle didn't call her special friend to come and visit anymore. Besides, the Horse didn't like it here in this small, oppressive, smelly room. He didn't like Danielle's mother and especially didn't like the man who also lived in that trailer, who occasionally put "the skinny child" to bed. The Horse disliked this trailer so much, got so angry with how the girl was forced to live, that Danielle no longer felt she should draw him here. Though she didn't know how or why, she was afraid the Horse might do something very bad. She knew the Horse was meant for better places than her tiny bedroom. It liked the house that Ralph and Shelley lived in. Very much, in fact. It came so quickly and easily when she called it into the Thomases' kitchen.

Danielle could now hear voices outside her room. Loud voices. Arguing. It was times like this she really wanted the Horse, needed him, for something she couldn't conceptualize. Without the Horse on her walls, she looked at the small, cheap — though she thought it was the most fabulous thing in the world — reproduction of a horse. It would have to do. She picked it up and stroked its cold, hard flank. She wished it was warm and soft.

For a brief moment, she had a flashback to the school and the incident that had happened earlier in the day. William had been mean to her. He had wanted her to draw a dog. Didn't he know she couldn't? Only the Horse. Dogs barked loudly and bit people. She'd tried to tell him that, but that boy didn't want to listen. He was so big and mean. It had almost hurt when she'd put the chalk on the blackboard and tried to make her hand draw something else. He didn't understand. Part of what scared her is that when something like this happened, the Horse seemed to become angrier, darker, like it was transforming into something that was fed by all the bad things around her. Luckily Shelley and Ralph had come to her rescue and even walked her home. She liked them so much, and so did the Horse. But they were so far away, and she was here.

Still gripping the horse, she looked around her dark room, lit by a small lamp sitting in the corner on the floor, and saw the faint, washed-out remains of the Horse. Even in this semi–darkness, they seemed to glow for the girl, the light from a warm and inviting home.

In another part of the trailer, she heard her name being screamed. Danielle hoped against experience it was for something good. Maybe dinner. Putting the horse down in the corner and covering it up with a towel she'd found, the little girl exited her room.

Underneath the towel in the empty room, the horse fell over.

And later that night, Danielle Gaadaw disappeared.

## CHAPTER TEN

THE NEXT DAY AT SCHOOL, RALPH AND SHELLEY KEPT TO themselves. Seldom did they spend their spare school time together, but recent events with their young friend had given them common ground. And William ... he was to be ignored. Always desperate to be the centre of attention, this did not sit well with him. For most of the recesses, he sat on one of the swings, ignoring the cold that seeped in through his jeans, patiently waiting for the free time outside the school to end. Occasionally he'd spot Shelley or Ralph across the field and would watch them, refusing to miss them.

Once, in the hallway, he'd seen Ralph walking towards him but had managed to dodge into the boys' bathroom. In class, because they often got into mischief when they were seated together, it was a long-held policy in the various classrooms to not allow them to sit near each other. That meant few unavoidable interactions today. And at the end of the day, once the bell had rung and they were dismissed, William was first into his boots and coat and out the door.

This was the routine for the next few days. Though they pretended not to notice him, both brother and sister knew perfectly well William was there. It was a small reserve and an even smaller school. Ralph missed his friend's companionship, and in a weird, unexpected way, Shelley felt the absence of It, though she would not admit it. How William had treated Danielle was so shameful, there was little chance it would be forgotten or forgiven. It was a potentially friendship-ending event. They'd seen a side of Ralph's friend they wished they hadn't.

Even William's first stirrings of guilt had made him wonder if possibly he'd gone too far in what had happened in that classroom. Lying in bed at night, eating his lunch alone, walking the snowy streets of Otter Lake, he would find his mind going back to the incident in the classroom. The more he thought about it, the more puzzled he became. Was it really that important to make Danielle draw a dog? Why? Then he remembered, he'd pushed her to the chalkboard. He always pushed Ralph, and on occasion Ralph would push back. That was their relationship. The other day, he'd pushed Shelley. That was wrong. He knew he shouldn't push girls. And yet he'd pushed Danielle.

If he'd seen that little girl somewhere at school, William might possibly have done something to try and make it up to her. But what, he wasn't sure. Definitely not apologize. That wasn't William. Something. The young boy wanted things to be back the way they were. Even if it meant he couldn't draw the best horse. He'd be more than willing to accept that. But he hadn't seen Danielle.

None of them had.

Nor would they the next day. Or the day after that. Danielle Gaadaw was not coming to school. Behind the school, Shelley found Ralph sitting on a stump that had once been a tall oak tree before it had been struck by lightning, about a year before Ralph had been born.

"Have you seen her?" Shelley was almost out of breath. The hill down to the oaks was a steep one. There had once been a fun and fabulous ice slide down it that the kids had spent their lunch hour and recesses sliding down. But in their infinite wisdom, the teachers had dropped a load of sand on it, making it virtually impossible to pick up any decent speed or a sufficient lack of friction; any attempt at sliding down the hill now resulted in ripped and torn clothing and the occasional detention if caught. Student safety and legal precautions were the reasons cited, not that it mattered to the kids. It was just another infringement on juvenile fun. Yet another memory of childhood enjoyment banned by the same adults who a few decades earlier had themselves flown down that same hill with loud and joyous abandon. The hypocrisy of adulthood was not lost on the youth. Even so, it was inevitable that these kids, down the road, would turn into adults themselves and eventually end up pouring their own buckets of sand onto the next generation's fun. One of the few real constants in the world.

This led to a unique cause-and-effect battle between the students and the school staff. On Fridays after class, some enterprising kids would mysteriously surface just before dark with pails of water and pour them down the sanded slide. The outcome was a weekend of excellent downhill skimming. But, come Monday morning, more sand would be poured down the icy hill for yet another week. It was an eternal cycle, repeated throughout each season and over the years. But this was an issue for another time.

"No, I haven't. You?"

Shelley shook her head. "Of course not. I wouldn't be asking you if I had." Shelley paused as she looked up the hill. "Should we do something?" Another earth-shattering event, Shelley asking her younger brother for advice.

"Like what?" For a moment, brother and sister said nothing, because neither knew what to suggest. What do you do in a situation like this? A shy little girl hasn't been seen in school in a couple of days. She could be sick. Wouldn't the teachers know? The principal? Would the principal have called a truancy officer? Did truancy officers still exist? These mysterious creatures had long been lorded over students as a way to frighten them into regular school attendance, but Shelley and Ralph weren't actually sure if they really existed. Were they like the Tooth Fairy or the Easter Bunny?

Shivering slightly, Shelley held the collar of her light brown coat closed. "I don't know." Once more they were silent, feeling the cold breeze coming off the lake that gave the community its name. Spring was still two months away, and already they were hearing adults complain about how tired they were of winter. "How about William? Talked to him lately?"

"Nope. I'm still mad at him."

To Shelley, that was the only good news of the day. "I always told you he was a bully."

"Yeah." The wind seemed to be picking up, focusing the

cold and helping it to find every seam and opening in their clothing, resulting in the unusual and silent wish that recess would soon end. "We could go look for her. I mean, we know where she lives. Or even just call her. Nothing wrong with that."

Shelley smiled. "Good idea. As soon as school is over. Do you know her phone number?"

Ralph shook his head. "Gotta be in the phone book." They had a plan. It was a beginning.

But it wasn't.

Finding the Gaadaw phone number was the first thing they focused on once they got home that afternoon. But there was no Hazel Gaadaw under the heading of Otter Lake. "Maybe they don't have a phone," offered Ralph.

"Who doesn't have a phone?" answered Shelley, looking as incredulous as a possible for a twelve-year-old. "Everybody has a phone."

"Hey, don't get mad at me. I don't know anything. Maybe it's listed under someone else. What do you think we should do now?"

Shelley thought for a moment. "We could go over there. They're just twenty minutes away. It's almost dinnertime, so they're sure to be home."

Though devoted to solving the mystery of the missing Danielle, Ralph put up a half-hearted attempt to postpone their doing so immediately. "Go outside!? It's cold, and we just got in. Do we have to? I mean, like you said, it's almost dinner."

"You're such a wimp. Come on, we'll be back before dinner. Or do you have a better idea?" Unfortunately,

Ralph had no such better idea, resulting in both brother and sister once again dressing for battle against the Canadian winter elements. The Thomas door opened, letting Shelley and Ralph out on their mission. And as Shelley had predicted, twenty-two minutes later they were walking down Twin Pine Lane, barely a minute away from the Gaadaws' trailer.

"What do we do, just knock on the door?

Shelley shrugged. "I believe that's how things are usually done. People do it all the time."

"Very funny, but, Shelley, we don't know these people."

"We know Danielle."

Ralph didn't seem convinced. "I've heard stories about that place. About Hazel and that guy. What if something happens?"

"Nothing's going to happen. And don't listen to stupid stories. I bet William started them all. Look, there it is, just ahead."

Indeed, the Gaadaws' trail was just two dozen frozen feet ahead, a beat-up white trailer of the long and narrow variety. It appeared to have survived many bad winters and scorching summers over the years. There was a set of well-worn steps leading up to the door and, along it, a wobbly handrail of dubious strength. The sun was beginning to set in the cold late-afternoon sky, making it gloomy. A dull yellow light could be seen coming from the front window. Taking a deep breath, Shelley marched forward. Climbing the steps, she knocked gently on the door; she could hear something rattling on the other side. Maybe something like a dream catcher was nailed to it. There was no answer. She knocked again, a little louder. Suddenly the door opened, and there stood Hazel Gaadaw framed in the doorway.

Danielle's mother was younger than they had expected, but she definitely lacked any youthful vigour that a woman of her age might normally have. She looked tired and worn, as if she had long ago passed her personal best-before date. Hazel smelled of beer, both from her breath and what had evidently spilled on her sweatpants and T-shirt over a longer period of time than the afternoon. The substantial smell of stale cigarette smoke wafted past her and out the door. Her head, for some unknown reason, was cocked to the side as she looked down at the two kids through bloodshot eyes. To top things off, she wore a look of puzzlement and annoyance, filtered through an unknown but visible haze. Both Thomas children took an instinctive step back on the small porch.

"Who are you?" Behind her, Shelley could see a portion of the trailer's interior: a couch propped up on two phone books, beer bottles that seemed to be half-filled with cigarette butts on shabby end tables, a stained and worn carpet, and a broken window covered with a black plastic garbage bag and duct tape to stop any drafts. Shelley immediately wondered if looking for Danielle had been such a good idea. She grabbed her brother's hand, pulling him close.

It wasn't the poverty of the place that scared her — she had plenty of relatives who barely got by financially. But this place in particular, the atmosphere, the sense it gave off, and the woman standing in front of them, seemed to lack everything that made a place a home. She couldn't imagine Danielle living here. Or the Horse coming from such an environment.

"Um …" Shelley was taken by surprise and didn't quite know how to respond. She looked to Ralph, who seemed to be debating the possibility of running away as fast as he could. "I … um … my brother …"

"What?!" Hazel barked.

"Danielle!" Shelley suddenly yelled out the little girl's name, trying desperately to let this woman know why they were there as quickly as possible. Collecting herself, she tried a second time, this time a little less loudly. "Danielle. We've come to see her. Is she here?" She managed a weak smile.

For a moment, Hazel Gaadaw looked confused, like she was trying to place the name. "Danielle? Why do you want to talk to Danielle?" She had a peculiar way of talking, sort of like after every third or fourth word she had to reboot her memory or her vocal cords to finish the sentence. The cold wind whistled past Shelley and Ralph into the house, but Hazel seemed entirely oblivious. Ralph blushed when he realized he could see her nipples hardening in the cold under her thin shirt. Evidently this woman wasn't wearing a bra.

Shelley tried again. "Danielle wasn't at school today. Or yesterday or the day before, either. We were kind of worried."

Seeing his sister in distress, Ralph tried to help. "We brought her homework." This was a lie, but a kind one. It was in the lie category their mother would normally forgive after proper explanation. More importantly, it gave them a legitimate reason to be there. Having a reason to be anywhere was always a good idea, but never more so than at this very moment. Seizing on the purpose of the lie, Shelley nodded enthusiastically, mentally crossing her fingers behind her back.

Hazel didn't respond at first. She continued to stand in the doorway, swaying slightly. Little wisps of her hair bobbed in the winter wind. Finally, she reacted. "No. Danielle isn't here." Her voice was flat.

"Um, may I ask where she is?"

Once more there was a pause as the older woman seemed to be formulating a response. "I don't know where she is. Haven't seen her in a while." Hazel then looked over her shoulder to make sure her daughter wasn't mysteriously standing behind her. "She'll come home when she's hungry. She usually does." Somewhere in the deep interior of the trailer, another voice, angry and loud, bellowed out. Definitely masculine. Definitely angry.

"Damn it, Hazel! Who the fuck is it?!"

Both kids flinched at the tone and volume, moving closer together. Hazel turned, looking over her shoulder as she leaned against the doorway. "Nobody. Just some kids looking for Danielle."

"Tell them to go away and close the fucking door. I'm fucking freezing! For Christ's sake, woman!"

Smiling sleepily to herself, Hazel turned around. "You heard the man. Gotta go. I'll tell the kid you were here."

Shelley only managed to get out, "Okay, our names are —" before Hazel Gaadaw abruptly closed the door. From the other side, she heard the latch go on.

"— Shelley and Ralph."

Immediately, Ralph grabbed Shelley's arm, pulling her down the steps, almost falling in the process. "Come on. Let's get out of here. Hurry."

Shelley needed little invitation, and soon both kids were walking briskly up the laneway, past where the two famed pines had once stood. "They were drinking! Could you tell?"

"Oh my god! I can't believe she lives there. That place is so horrible."

A thousand thoughts were going through Shelley's head, all about poor Danielle. Though she was perhaps too young for this kind of knowledge, Shelley now understood why Danielle had gravitated so quickly towards the Thomas household. The little bit of kindness they'd shown her at their home had been like a crust of bread to a starving little girl. It was so obvious. Even though Shelley had been very kind to the little girl, she now wished she'd been even nicer.

Ralph's thoughts were considerably more pragmatic. First and foremost, they involved getting away from the trailer at the end of the lane as quickly as possible. Though he, too, was appalled by the desperate situation of Danielle's home life, his personal safety and security and that of his sister were of a more immediate concern. There was also innate chivalry involved, a seldom-used sense of protecting his older sister.

All the way home, wrapped up in thoughts of their own, they said little. Their mission to find Danielle and talk to her had failed, and the young girl was still MIA, as William would have said. On their way home, they walked by his house. In a small community like Otter Lake, there were only so many streets, and they were mostly interconnected. Practically every house along their way was peopled by family or friends. Neither of the two acknowledged the Williams house as they passed or looked towards the large window that was still decorated with Christmas lights. They walked on in the growing cold and dark.

William, on the other side of the picture window facing the street, saw them approach out the corner of his eye as he sat in his living room watching television. He hoped that Ralph especially was coming to see him and all would be forgiven. He missed Ralph and, oddly enough, his friend's sister, though in a different way he couldn't explain. Unfortunately, the Thomas duo walked past his house and continued down the street. Putting two and two together (though math was not his best subject) William calculated where they were coming from. There were only two things further down that street: the trailer park and the hockey arena. Seeing that it was a lazy Wednesday afternoon, bingo wouldn't be starting at the arena for at least another two hours. And neither Ralph nor Shelley played bingo. That left Twin Pine Lane, and Danielle.

He too had noticed the little girl had not been around school. It made him feel vaguely uncomfortable, though again he didn't know why. Conscience was a new, odd, and unpredictable friend. Had he run into the little girl, William had no idea what he would have said to her. So far it hadn't been an issue.

William watched Shelley and Ralph disappear around the corner. He went back to half-watching television. One of his brothers kept changing the channel every two seconds, trying to annoy him. William barely noticed. In his own little world, the boy was mad at Danielle for being such a good artist and making him pick on her because of it. He was mad at Ralph for being mad at him. He was mad at Shelley for being Ralph's sister and for being her annoying self. Most of all, though, he was mad at himself.

AS FOR THE Everything Wall, it had largely been ignored. A few kids had come over during the week, intent on participating in the recently entrenched activity; however, while the door was open and the chalk sitting there waiting to be used, there was clearly a different atmosphere in the Thomas house. Everything was the same, yet it wasn't. The furniture was all in the same place. The same people lived in the house. But Liz seemed less enthusiastic about encouraging kids, thinking more about who wasn't there than who was. Ralph hadn't drawn on the Everything Wall at all, and neither had Shelley. The same went for William, for obvious reasons.

Though most of the other kids had come to find out about Danielle and her unique talent, they had not had any real stake in her involvement in the overall Thomas family affair. The shift in what was normal — no thoughts of Danielle and her Horse and lots of William's near-constant physical presence in the house, versus the current reality of the opposite — was confusing. Over the days that followed the third week in the life of the Everything Wall, fewer kids came to visit, which was just as well. The Thomas family focus was elsewhere.

Shelley, Ralph, and William each separately noticed that Danielle still wasn't to be found. But what could a couple of kids living on an obscure reserve do about that?

As it turned out, not a hell of a lot.

FOUR DAYS HAD passed without anybody seeing Danielle Gaadaw. Four days were not enough for the school to get overly worried. She could just have an illness of sorts, a cold or the flu. Nothing, they felt, to wake up the system and start the never-ending task of paperwork. This would require at least another two or three days of absence.

Shelley and Ralph felt differently. Every day they looked for the little figure of Danielle as soon as they entered the school. In every classroom. Through every recess. They had even, a few times, cautiously walked by Twin Pine Lane, not knowing exactly what they might see or what they would do if they saw something. They wanted to find the little girl, and achieving this goal had somehow become a part of their lives.

At the end of each school day, Liz Thomas had taken to asking her children about her favourite little artist, and she was rapidly getting concerned herself. She knew of Hazel Gaadaw, having gone to school with her long before children were a fact to either of them, before the death of Hazel's husband, and before her descent into what she was now. That made her even more worried.

By Saturday morning, the disappearance of Danielle became too much to bear.

"Please, Mom."

Two sets of eyes pleaded with Liz, and Liz, being who she was, couldn't say no.

"Very well." Though she protested, Liz too was curious as to where Danielle was and the story behind her so-called disappearance. So being forced to call the Gaadaw house by her children was merely accelerating what she would have done eventually. It was seldom both son and daughter agreed on anything. Perhaps she should have made the call before now.

And she, too, was feeling the absence of William in her house.

These were indeed odd times.

The Gaadaw phone number came from somebody at the band office. It rang three times before a male voice answered, taking Liz by surprise. "What?" Loud and gruff, it made Liz momentarily forget who she was calling.

"Uh ... uh ... is Hazel there?"

In the background she could hear the man coughing, loud and unpleasant. "Of course she's here." Silence.

"May I speak to her?"

Liz heard the man clear his throat one more time before yelling, "Hazel! Some woman wants to talk to you." A second passed before the man's voice returned. "Who is this?"

"It's Liz Thomas. I'm a very old ..."

"Somebody named Liz Thomas."

Through the crackle of the line, Liz could hear the hints of a conversation stuttering. Ralph and Shelley watched their mother expectantly. What was difficult for them to achieve, their mother frequently could. Suddenly the voice was back. "What do ya want?"

This was not the conversation the woman had expected. "Uh ... I just wanted to ask about Danielle. Maybe she could come over and have lunch with my kids. I understand she ..." Once again, the voice was gone and there were more indecipherable mutterings.

"Hazel's busy." The line went dead.

Liz looked at her phone, puzzled and concerned about the context of the conversation. "Well, what did she say?" asked Shelley.

"Nothing. Didn't speak to her. Some guy answered. Said Hazel didn't want to come to the phone. And hung up when I asked about Danielle."

"Mom," Ralph spoke. "You look worried."

Putting on her best smile, Liz hugged her two children briefly. No need to share her concerns with her kids. She considered them too young to warn about the evils of the world, or even just Otter Lake. They would learn those truths eventually. Today, she decided to let them think the world was still a fairly nice place, though cracks were already beginning to form in that philosophy. But deep in her mind, it bothered the woman. The rumours about Hazel and her friends. The missing Danielle. The undercurrents of the voice of the man on the phone. Her kids had opened the door to this problem, but it looked like they were all about to walk through it together.

THAT AFTERNOON, A spike in the Danielle mystery graph appeared; it came from an unexpected source.

Splayed out on an overstuffed armchair, Ralph was leafing listlessly through one of the books that he and his sister had forgotten to return to the library. The book explored cave paintings in Lascaux, France. Because the paintings were supposedly twenty thousand years old, the author marvelled at the technique, the imagination, and the artistry that were abundantly evident — and all from what were once called "primitive cavemen."

Page after page showed large animals of many varieties; some Ralph recognized, many he didn't. When he glanced up from the book to where the Horse on the Everything Wall still guarded the kitchen and beyond, the boy was surprised at the number of similarities between the horses in Lascaux and Danielle's Horse in Otter Lake, particularly the shading used by the artists to create texture. Danielle's innate ability to master such a complex practice continued to astound him. Instinctively, Ralph understood there was more than just talent involved in Danielle's creation. There was something deeper. But, like everybody else, he had no idea exactly what that extra something was. It was difficult to believe that the thin young girl with pretty much nothing to say other than her polite thank-you had such depths to her.

Shelley, meanwhile, was making a feeble attempt at some homework. She had planned to go over to Vanessa's in the afternoon, but she'd lost the impulse around the time her mother left. Instead, she turned her attention to the annoying social studies project she'd been putting off. It was due on Thursday, so she set her mind to the task and sank her teeth into it. She could think of a hundred things right off the top of her head that said "Saturday afternoon" way more than studying the migratory patterns of the Amish.

Piled-up books and a couple of maps spread out on the coffee table before her, Shelley was sitting near the front window of their house. Trying to put her mind in the heads of a contemporary Amish family, she had idly glanced out their living room window at the world she was increasingly having difficulty understanding or appreciating. Why would somebody voluntarily want to use outhouses instead of bathrooms in the house and horses for transportation instead of cars and trucks? She had no appreciation of the outhouses, but did have some for the animal that appeared to be running free in the Thomas family kitchen.

While she was thinking about the Amish horse and buggy and the Horse in the kitchen, wondering if there was anything more than an ephemeral connection, she was almost positive that she spotted a familiar figure in a familiar parka.

"Ralph, is that William … I mean It … out there?"

"What? Where?" Ralph jumped up off the chair and hustled over to the window near his sister.

"Over there. Across the road, near the big pine tree. I think I saw him." Both siblings looked hard out the window, squinting against the bright white expanse between the house and where the forest began. They saw a small flock of chickadees looking for food and a woodpecker making its way up the pine tree. But that was all.

"I don't …" Ralph didn't have a chance to finish his sentence. He saw the distinctive brush cut sticking out from behind the big pine tree, looking at their house.

It hovered there for a second, then disappeared out of sight. Perhaps he saw the brother and sister staring back at him.

"That was It, wasn't it?"

"Yeah, but why is he hiding?"

"I don't know. He's your friend."

"That doesn't mean I know how he thinks."

They watched the pine tree for a few seconds longer, and then William's head darted out again, this time on the other side of the tree. Because of the angle of their window and the storm windows attached on the outside, the glare off the multiple panes of glass made it impossible for William to know he had been spotted. Still, two seconds later, he pulled his head back to safety behind the big tree. Brother and sister looked at each other and shrugged. Then they nodded.

A few moments later they had put on their winter boots and jackets and were out the door, walking down their driveway in the direction of the big tree just ahead. Ralph was in the lead. "Hey, William! Might as well come out. We saw you!"

"Yeah, quit hiding. I don't want to have to climb through that snow bank to get you, and scuff my boots."

They stopped at the side of the road, three or four metres away from William's not-so-well-chosen hiding place. The sun had begun to descend in the northern afternoon sky, resulting in a blinding glare. Even in the full sun of a cloudless sky, it was cold. Shelley fidgeted and shuffled, trying to keep warm. She slapped her brother's arm, nagging him to call out to his reluctant buddy.

"William!" yelled Ralph again.

There was a pause, and then William appeared, sheepishly stepping out from behind the tree.

"Hi."

Shelley and Ralph looked at William, and he looked back at them, no one really knowing how to proceed. "So, any particular reason you're just standing out here in the woods, staring at our house?" Shelley couldn't decide if she was angry or not.

"Nothing. Just hanging around."

"Behind a big tree across the street from our house?"

"It's not your tree."

William's logic was absurdly simple, but true. No matter how true it was, though, his answer was not really a response to their question.

Frustration, anger, and a host of other emotions forced Shelley to take the initiative. "This is so silly. Do you know all the problems you've created?"

William didn't respond. He shrugged his shoulders.

"I'm talking to you, William Williams!"

The breeze rustled the branches above, and Ralph imagined that the sound was the tree holding its breath, anticipating an answer.

William crossed the street, his head down, not wanting to face the angry girl almost directly in front of him but knowing it was inevitable. "Yeah."

"Danielle's missing! She hasn't been at school for a week. We don't know where she is. Nobody's seen her. Even her mother doesn't know where she's gone, so she was no help. I don't think she even cares where her daughter is. All because of your stupid actions! Are you happy, William?! Huh, are you?"

By this point, Shelley's nostrils were flaring and her chest was heaving. She took a step forward during her rant, her brand-new boot almost toe-to-toe with the boots of the object of her anger. William continued to look down, not knowing how to respond. Ralph was characteristically silent, deciding it was better to let his sister get her anger out of her system and direct it at William rather than at him.

"No. I'm not happy. Okay? I'm sorry." The words sounded so quiet and sad the way William said them. He was obviously unused to uttering apologies.

"And what are you going to do about it? When you spill milk, most people know enough to clean it up."

Now Shelley went silent. She had said what she'd wanted to say and now she was done. From a few driveways away, they all heard a car door slam, the sound carrying well in the crisp atmosphere. Somewhere further away, a snowmobile was racing down the frozen lake.

William struggled to speak. "Yeah."

Once more, Shelley rose to battle. "Yeah? Yeah? That's all you have to say? Give me a break. You're just a —"

"I think I know where she is."

"— stupid little …" Shelley stopped once what William had said registered.

Ralph took a step forward, attention focused.

"You know where she is?" he asked. "Is that what you said?"

William nodded, finally looking up from the snow.

"How do you know where she is? Tell us."

William took a deep gulp before answering. "Earlier I was going out with my brother Jay ice fishing. I was kind of bored, not used to spending all this time at home, so I sort of invited myself along. He's usually kind of mean to me, but this time he said ..."

"Danielle, William. Where is Danielle?"

William realized he was getting off topic and quickly got to the point. "We were walking down by Henry's Landing, and I saw a trail of boot prints cutting across, almost hidden by the blowing snow, heading towards the camp fort. They were kind of small and had no tread, like they were old and had been worn for a long time. I remembered that she had boots like that. I told my brother I would meet him out on the lake later."

"You followed the prints?" asked Ralph.

William nodded. "And, like I said, they led to the camp fort. I looked in through the window and I saw something move under that brown blanket that's there. I saw a flash of white, like her jacket."

This time, Shelley asked the question. "Did you go in?"

Looking back down at the ground, William shook his head.

"Why not? If that was her?"

"Shelley," interrupted Ralph. "Let him finish."

"I am finished. I came here right afterwards. I didn't know what I'd say if I went in. I thought she might be scared of me. So I thought I should come get you guys. But I didn't know how to tell you. Now I've told you." He looked up furtively, then back down.

Abruptly, Shelley turned around and started walking rapidly south, away from the two boys.

"Hey, where you going?" shouted Ralph.

"Boys can be so stupid. Where do you think? The camp fort. Are you coming?" To show her determination, Shelley wrapped her favourite blue scarf tighter around her neck. Ralph looked at William and immediately started running after his sister. Once he'd caught up to her, he whispered something in her ear. She nodded and stopped. Yelling over her shoulder, she locked eyes with William. "And you — you're part of this. You started it. You'd better come, too."

Relieved to be a part of the gang again, William smiled and ran after them, catching up almost immediately. In fact, so excited was he, William took the lead. "I know a shortcut. Follow me." He broke into a run, forcing Ralph and Shelley to follow him at a greater speed. Halfway down the street, he turned abruptly to the right, where he disappeared into the woods, leaving behind a narrow trail of broken snow.

Shelley stopped at the edge. "My new boots!"

Ralph ran by her and was past the line of bushes quickly. "Hurry up," he yelled back.

Reluctantly acknowledging the importance of the situation, Shelley gritted her teeth and left the calm and ploughed world of civilization and entered the snow-filled and chaotic woods, following her brother and the boy who had started all this, the boy she called It.

To anyone observing the reunited triumvirate, it appeared that the underbrush of Otter Lake had swallowed them up. But they were not about to get lost. This was the path William had already broken to get to the Thomas house to tell Ralph and Shelley the news about Danielle being at the camp fort. Being third on the trail, with William leading Ralph just up ahead, Shelley had an easier time because the snow was fairly broken and trailed. That was something, at least. But it was a good kilometre and a half to the location, and Shelley hoped her precious boots wouldn't be scuffed, marked, or otherwise marred. She knew it was a stupid thing to think about right now, but the boots were new.

Ralph was trying desperately to keep up with William, but Shelley was having no part of that competition. She knew where the camp fort was, roughly, and if she got lost, there was the well-established trail to follow. If Danielle had been there all this time, a few more minutes of responsible and measured walking wouldn't change anything. So Shelley plodded on, slow and deliberate. Twenty minutes later, she came upon William and Ralph, each leaning against their own cedar tree, breathing heavily. Running in loose snow can be very taxing work. She smiled as she passed them. "Waiting for a bus?" she asked innocently. *Boys*, she thought to herself, yet again.

For the rest of the journey, William and Ralph followed her. William began to talk incessantly, seeming to pick stories and memories randomly, catching up on days of missed conversation.

"Remember when we used to come up here all the time, Ralph? One night your father took us, and we stayed overnight, and we heard all those spooky noises. The next morning we made scrambled eggs for breakfast and fried some pickerel we'd just caught. That was so cool. Best breakfast I'd ever had. We should do that again, huh?"

For the remainder of the journey through the woods, Shelley and Ralph said nothing, allowing William to work at re-establishing a friendship he had damaged so badly. William's lone voice startled the silence of the wilderness that surrounded the town.

The camp fort was located some distance down by the eastern shore of Otter Lake, where families would camp or fish. There was a good place in this particular location to put the boat into the water from a trailer, and it was generally believed to be one of the prettiest sights on the reserve. Thirty years earlier, a group of enterprising teenagers (Tye Thomas being one of them) had built a fort. It was a loose conglomeration of scavenged boards, planks, siding, and other assorted panels. They'd even managed to put a small window into one wall. The structure, no taller than six feet, had been weathered by thunderstorms, snowstorms, winds, baking sun, and two generations of bush parties. Every spring, it was repaired faithfully. It was, however, rarely used during winter — a perfect place for Danielle to hide.

Another twenty minutes later, the trio wandered out of the woods and stood in front of the camp fort, breathing hard. Though it was cold, with a stiff and miserably biting breeze that was now blowing in directly off the lake behind the camp fort, they were sweating from their exertion. The cobbled-together fort looked dark and empty.

"You're sure she's here?" asked Shelley.

William nodded. "Yeah, pretty much. Inside, though. See!" Directly in front of the warped door were small, clear footprints. Fairly recent. Evidence of older ones was still barely visible in the blowing snow.

"Danielle!"

Shelley shouted out the little girl's name as she approached the makeshift structure. Just last fall somebody had put up an ad hoc fence around it made of cut poplar. She slipped between the railings and stood in front of the weathered door, which seemed to be a normal door like one found in any house, except the top third had been sawed off.

"Danielle?" she called again.

There was no answer. The boys slowly followed Shelley and were soon by her side, debating their next course of action.

"Should we go in?" asked Ralph.

"That's why we're here." Without hesitation, Shelley opened the door and entered. The two boys watched her enter, unsure if they should follow. It was Ralph who decided they should, brushing the shoulder of his friend as he leaned over and entered. William, now once again part of the gang, followed, narrowly missing hitting his head on the upper frame.

Inside it was dark. The only sources of light were the small window to their right, completely frosted over, and the half-open door behind them. The floor was basically sawdust, with cigarette butts, beer caps, and what appeared to be the odd used and frozen condom scattered around. The place smelled of pee. Generations of it that had seeped into the sawdust and the ground beneath it.

In the corner they saw an old saggy and stained mattress, and gathered into a pile on it what appeared to be some ratty looking blankets, no doubt as old as the building itself. But it was what was above the mattress, spread across the ceiling boards, that suddenly stole their focus. It was the Horse. Looking bigger and stronger than they'd seen it in the Thomases' kitchen. Slightly different again, though they couldn't quite understand how. Ralph searched his mind for the words to describe it. Ominous, he decided, might be the best way to put it. The Horse spanned the entire length of the ceiling. It looked down on them through one eye. Danielle had brought pencil crayons she had found or stolen to the camp fort. She certainly hadn't brought them from her home. She'd drawn the Horse on the ceiling of the frame roof. Had she done this to keep her company or to protect herself? But all that was important to Ralph was the fact it was even more awe-inspiring in scope than its previous incarnations on the Everything Wall. On the shoulder, just below the Horse's mane, was a handprint in red. About the size of a little girl's hand. It was the first time they'd seen that on the Horse.

Her eyes still on the image, Shelley called out one more, "Danielle!" This time a little quieter. There was a stirring on the mattress that startled them.

"That's her."

At the sound of William's enthusiastic voice, the figure under the blankets wedged itself closer to the wall. Ralph could hear her whimper.

Shelley gave William a sharp glance, making him mouth the word "Sorry" and step behind Ralph, as if to hide.

Shelley moved closer to the girl hiding under the meagre pile of old blankets. "It's okay, Danielle. It's me, Shelley."

Danielle didn't move.

"I won't let William hurt you. Honest. Are you okay? We haven't seen you in a long time. We were worried. Weren't we, Ralph?"

Ralph nodded, until he realized the little girl was still hidden beneath the blankets and couldn't see his nod. "Yeah. Real worried."

"Have you been here all this time? You must be freezing. Come on, can I see your pretty face? Please." Kneeling on the old mattress, Shelley gently tugged on a blanket. At first it didn't move, then gradually it fell away, revealing the person they'd been worried about. If possible, Danielle looked smaller, tinier. It appeared that the little girl could, if pushed, almost fit through the cracks in the wall, if not for the wild and busy nature of her unwashed and uncombed hair.

"There you are. We are so glad to see you." Shelley's smile was huge and genuine, making the place seem a little less gloomy.

Danielle, radiating a combination of embarrassment and shyness, still hid behind the blankets. She was blinking her eyes at the brightness of the winter sun pouring in. Then she saw William and pulled the blanket back over her head.

Shelley crawled across the small space of mattress to the bundle of blankets.

"Don't worry, sweetheart. William won't hurt you. Will you, William?"

She gave him a warning look that froze Ralph's blood.

For a moment, William struggled with what he was feeling and how to say it. "No. I won't. Honest." He struggled further, looking for better words, finally ending with an uncomfortable, "I'm sorry. I won't do it again. Really."

"See. He's sorry. Now, sweetheart, what are you doing way out here?"

Though her full attention was on the little girl, she couldn't help glancing up at the Horse above her. Neither could the two boys. It watched over them like an avenging angel, ready to swoop down upon them if necessary. It reminded them of a big stained glass window in a church, something that was supposed to instill either confidence or fear, depending on who was looking at it.

A small, quiet voice came from under the blankets. "You came to look for me?" Danielle's face emerged from behind a checkered blanket.

"Of course we did."

William and Ralph were content to let Shelley do most of the talking. "We looked everywhere for you. Didn't we, Ralph?"

Resisting the urge to nod, he answered, "Oh yeah. We even went to your house."

"Did you see my mother?"

"Yeah."

With what Ralph would later remember as huge, hopeful, puppy dog eyes, Danielle asked him, "Was she worried about me?"

It was time for another lie their mother would no doubt absolve them of. "Yeah. Real worried. Wasn't she, Shelley?"

Danielle might have appeared to be meek and uncertain about many things, but she knew her family. And to a certain extent, she was beginning to understand the kindness of her new friends. Before Shelley could answer, Danielle nestled into the corner of the fort, pulling the blanket more tightly around her. "No, she wasn't."

None of the three quite knew how to respond to that.

"It's because I'm a bad girl."

Shelley reached out and took her hand. It was bare and cold. "Why do you say that?"

"That's what Mommy says. That's why Santa didn't bring me any presents this year."

All of them, including William, couldn't believe the statement just uttered by Danielle. It was like sacrilege, if that was the correct word. Though they were at the age where knowledge of Santa Claus and belief in him were precarious at best, they knew no parent should tell a child something like that. Santa was supposed to be like Jesus, he had to like everybody, even though he knew who was naughty or nice. Everybody in the camp fort knew that Danielle definitely did not fit in the naughty category. William, whose brothers and sister had said similar things at various times to him, knew very well his parents would never utter those words. And, regardless of his family's financial situation or his level of "being good," William had never been deserted by Santa. For an unexpected moment, he felt sad for the little girl.

Shelley was first to break the silence. "That's horrible. You are not a bad girl. No."

"No. Not at all," Ralph agreed.

Even William found himself nodding in agreement, mentally promising himself that somehow, someway, he would get this girl a present. Even if it meant giving her one of his.

Danielle gave a faint but seemingly accommodating smile. "Do you like my Horse? He's gotten bigger, huh?"

"Oh, he's beautiful." Secretly, the bigger girl was beginning to find the Horse's growing evolution a little overwhelming and intimidating. Shelley sat down beside Danielle, hoping to put a couple extra feet of distance between it and her. Instinctively, Danielle huddled against her. Shelley could feel her trembling.

Ralph felt himself nudged by his friend. He looked at William as the husky boy gestured up to the Horse. "Am I crazy, or is the Horse glowing?" Ralph looked up, and to his surprise, it was true. The Horse drawn across the parallel slats seemed to be glowing and shimmering, even glistening. It was beautiful and eerie.

"How did she do this?" asked William. Shelley shared their astonishment. It was truly awesome.

Ralph answered, "I don't think she did. Remember that bus trip our school took last year to that hockey game in Baymeadow, when the heater in the bus was broken."

"Yeah," responded William. "Man, that was a long, cold ride."

"That's what happens when your heater breaks. Anyway, I noticed inside the bus there were little tiny snowflakes falling. Remember, I pointed that out to you."

William was still looking towards the roof, but listening. "Yeah."

"And then Mr. Barton, who was sitting just ahead of us,

turned around. Do you remember what he told us?"

"Uh-uh. I don't think he likes me."

"There's a surprise." That was proof Shelley was still listening.

"He told us the condensation from our breath rose up and got colder. Eventually it turned into snow near the top of the bus and fell back down." All three looked up again at the glimmering Horse.

The bigger boy shivered. It might have been imagination, but it seemed a good five degrees cooler inside the fort. "And you think something like that is happening here?"

"I think so. I don't know the science of it, but Danielle's breath rising up the past few days must have somehow turned into ice crystals instead of snow." Once more, they all looked around. It was like the Horse was made of diamonds or stars.

"Yeah. Yeah. That's what I thought."

Amazed by the Horse, Ralph reached up to touch its forelock, mesmerized by what the girl had created, this time in near-darkness, and how nature had improved it. It looked so real, he almost felt like he could pet it, angry and defiant as it looked. His hand connected with the pencil crayon–covered cedar plank and, for a brief second, that crack between the worlds that Danielle had somehow forged opened for him, and he could swear that he felt the Horse's hair. He didn't know how or why, but he also thought it was warm.

"Don't touch him!"

The scream came from Danielle, cutting through the cold and dark, startling everyone. Bolting from the corner, she pushed Ralph away, knocking him with remarkable strength directly into William; they both went down.

"You can't do that. He's mine."

Breathing heavily and looking weak, she stood over the two boys. "Please. I don't have anything else." Then, leaning back, she began to cry. It was the second time she had shed tears in front of them.

"I'm sorry." Struggling to his knees, Ralph didn't know what else to say.

Shelley took Danielle's hand and led her back to sit beside her on the stained mattress. "Don't worry. Ralph won't touch your Horse." In a world that was obviously askew, it was hard for Ralph to know what to do. He stayed on the cold, sawdust-covered ground next to William, who was equally perplexed. Out of nowhere, the tiny little girl had briefly frightened the bully.

Danielle had definitely not acted this way the last time Ralph had touched the Horse. But then, as he remembered it, the little girl had been finished with her creation and had left their home. Evidently, she wasn't completely done doing whatever it was she had to do with it. Or her attachment to the Horse, or it to her, was lasting longer. Maybe getting stronger. All these questions were way out of Ralph's level of understanding. He wondered if his mother would understand. If she could explain it to him. So he just sat there, amidst the sawdust and cigarette butts, hoping his sister could help the little girl.

Danielle's sobbing increased, and Shelley began to look like she was on the edge of panic herself. All she could think of doing was getting closer to the little girl, wrapping her more tightly in the worn blanket in an attempt to keep her warm. She repeated, "It's okay. It's okay," rocking her back and forth.

The four of them were aware that things were indeed not okay. After a few minutes, Danielle's sobbing seemed to subside. Her tear-streaked face appeared from Shelley's shoulder. She wiped her nose with her sleeve, sniffling loudly.

"I'm sorry. That was rude. I'm sorry." She tried to smile and managed a small one. "I'm just so hungry."

That's when it occurred to the trio. She'd been hiding in here for the past few days, was it already five in total? Was it possible? She'd not had anything to eat in that entire time?

"Danielle, when's the last time you ate?"

She shrugged. "I don't know. I don't remember."

Cursing herself, Shelley wished desperately she'd brought something for the little girl to eat. But she hadn't. It hadn't occurred to her, and it sure wouldn't have occurred to William. Maybe her brother. "Ralph, do you have anything to eat?"

"No. I don't." *Why would I?* he thought. Instinctively, he rummaged around in his pockets and found one piece of gum. Quickly, he pulled it out. "I got this! A piece of gum. Want that?!"

Shyly but hungrily Danielle nodded, and Ralph crawled across the floor and gave it to her. Eagerly, she took it, unwrapped it, and swallowed it without chewing. It wasn't much, but it was something.

William cleared his throat. "Um. I've got two ham and cheese sandwiches. And an orange."

Shelley and Ralph both looked at him in surprise. "I was going out ice fishing with my brother, remember?"

Out of his big snow jacket pocket, he pulled a paper bag stuffed with food.

"It's yours. If you want." He held it out for Danielle, not wanting to come closer and perhaps scare her.

"Go ahead. It's okay." He even managed a hesitant smile for her, wanting Danielle to accept his gift more than he could explain.

Ralph took it from him and handed it to Shelley, who reached into the crumpled brown bag and brought out the sandwiches and orange. Unwrapping the plastic wrap, Shelley offered her half of one of the sandwiches. Like a cat pouncing on a mouse, Danielle grabbed it and, as small as her mouth was, managed to fit the half completely into her mouth.

"Danielle! Take it easy. You'll choke." Shelley held the rest of the sandwiches out of her reach. "You can have the rest as long as you promise to eat it slowly. It isn't going anywhere. Promise?"

Danielle nodded eagerly, swallowing the last of what was in her mouth. Shelley, with a stern look, handed her the remaining portion of the sandwich. Danielle attacked it, too, though she ate it more slowly and more deliberately, a bite at a time. Taking out the orange, Shelley started to peel it for her.

Danielle looked at William, who was still sitting on the frozen ground, watching her. "Thank you."

William managed another smile and nodded.

Shelley finished peeling the orange and offered it to

Danielle. Taking it, she then said, "Thank you" again and began to tear the sections apart. She offered all three an opportunity to share a wedge, but all declined for obvious reasons.

"Feel better?"

Danielle burped, causing everybody to laugh. She was halfway through the orange when Ralph asked a question that had been bouncing around in his head ever since Danielle had first appeared at their house.

"Danielle. If you don't mind me asking, why do you draw this Horse? Over and over again? Obviously it's special to you. I'm just curious. Why?"

Looking and feeling relieved, she raised her free hand up to point to the image hovering over her. "My Horse. I like to draw my Horse."

"I know, but why? Why do you make him so big, so colourful, and so ..."

"... incredible," finished William. This was a question he had wanted to ask, too, but had never had the opportunity. They all knew there had to be a story behind such a creation, behind Danielle's obsession.

With the last of the orange gone, Danielle savoured the remaining flavour in her mouth before answering. "He's my friend, like you. But the Horse wasn't always there. Sometimes I had to go find him. Now he always comes when I call. He's always here when I need him. I think he likes me, too."

Ralph took note of the faraway look on Danielle's face. He asked another question. "Where does your Horse come from?"

"Campbellford, I guess." That was a small town just a few hours' drive to the southeast of Otter Lake. They had all been there once or twice for the big agricultural fair held every fall.

Danielle looked up at the ceiling of the camp fort. "He reminds me of my father."

Ralph and Shelley nodded, wanting to hear more. They remembered their parents talking about Danielle's father and how he had died. It was a tragedy that no child should have to remember. It was clearly a tragedy her mother couldn't get over.

William knew the town of Campbellford very well since two of his brothers played hockey there quite frequently and he would tag along, but at the moment his interest lay above the four. He was positive the large image dangling over their heads was staring at him. Positively glaring, and it seemed specifically at him. He was feeling increasingly uncomfortable.

Stroking Danielle's hair, Shelley tried to coax more of the story out of her. "It's okay. You can tell us." She smiled encouragingly.

The dam had been breached. Though she was known as a small and quiet little girl, Danielle Gaadaw's story sprang forth like it had been waiting for a spring thaw to break up the ice jam.

Nestling up against Shelley again, drawing the older girl's warmth like a thermal vampire, the past poured out of Danielle. "Back when my dad was alive, he took me to that town ... Campbellford." Not wanting to interrupt her, the siblings and friend acknowledged her by nodding encouragingly. "Well, they have pony rides there, and my father knew I liked ponies. I remember this big lineup of kids ... and there was only one pony for them all. We had to stand in line for a long time before I had a chance to ride. All the time I kept watching that poor pony. They put one kid after another on his back, and he would go around and around in a circle, around and around, wearing out a path in the grass. Sometimes his eyes weren't even open. That's all he ever did. Just went around in the circle all day, every day. And I felt sad for him, very sad. He looked so old and unhappy, and his back was bent real low from all the kids sitting on it, kicking him in the sides with their heels. When it was my turn to ride, I started crying. I felt so sorry for that poor pony, I didn't want to ride him."

All Ralph could say in response was, "Yeah, I've seen ponies like that," which was more than the others did. "What's that got to do with your Horse?"

"A couple months later my dad died. And things got different at home. Mom changed. Everything did. But I never stopped thinking of that pony, thinking how sad its life must be. I wondered if he dreamed of better things when his eyes were closed. Then he began to change when I thought of him; he grew bigger and got stronger the more I thought of him. He grew to be really beautiful and strong. I could see him so clearly, it's like he was waiting for me. Then I began to draw him. At first, he didn't look very good. Kind of like a stick figure, but it was still him. And I began to wonder if all things could change, be different, if they had better places to live, people who loved them a whole bunch."

This time, William broke the silence. "Wow, your art teacher must love you."

Danielle shook her head violently. "No. No. It doesn't work like that. Not on a small piece of paper. Then it becomes the pony again. Has to be someplace special or big. Your house is special. Mine isn't. I tried there a few times and got punished real bad. So I don't do it there anymore. The problem is He wants to come more and more, and I've got few places to let him come anymore."

"Maybe if we talked to your mother? I'm sure maybe we —" Shelley was still at the age where she thought all things were possible.

For the second time since they'd arrived at the camp fort, Danielle seemed agitated. "No, you can't. No. She wouldn't like that. Her and her boyfriend don't like people coming over." For a second, she paused. "I miss my father. I miss my mother."

"But your mother is still alive."

Danielle remained silent. She no longer looked at the Horse, nor did she look at them. It was like she had retreated deep into herself. "She's not my real mother. She changed after my father died. She used to be so nice, then she got sad. Then she started drinking. Last year her new boyfriend showed up. Now I'm afraid. I don't like it there. I don't like him. He scares me."

They could barely hear her voice.

A cold and dry silence hung over the occupants of the camp fort. Ralph could see the steam coming from the mouths of the others, but he couldn't hear them breathe.

In the short time they'd been there, the sky had clouded over outside, and it was growing dark. Perhaps Danielle's story had depressed the world.

"Danielle, I'm so sorry." Shelley was on the verge of tears. "I wish there was something we could do."

"Could I come and live with you?" Danielle looked up at them, jumping to her knees, hope filling her eyes for the first time. "Please. I'll be good." The intensity of her stare briefly startled the older girl.

Shelley and Ralph looked at each other. They didn't know how to respond. This was not a matter they had any power of decision over, but both knew their mother would bring this hurt little girl into their house and quite probably shower her with all the love and gifts possible. Sadness and want would become a thing of the past for Danielle for sure. Ralph wanted to help, he was sure of that. After learning her story, he knew he needed to help her, somehow. At his age, he had figured out that the world primarily consisted of good people and bad people; there were no shades of grey in between. Up until this silent moment, it hadn't occurred to him, to any of them, that someday they might have to make a choice between the two. And, he had to admit, he kind of liked the idea of being somebody's big brother.

"I don't know. I don't think things work that easy." Growing uncomfortable, Shelley shifted her seat on the mattress, hoping the move would help. It didn't.

Reaching out, Danielle grabbed Ralph's shoulder. "I'll let you touch him. My Horse!" she said eagerly to Ralph.

Once more, Ralph was at a loss for words, glancing nervously at the Horse. Then he looked to Shelley and then William for any kind of support.

It was Shelley who uttered for the first time the panacea used by all mothers to placate anxious and excited children. It was a foreshadowing of her life to come as a wife, a parent, and a minor executive in charge of child welfare on the Otter Lake reserve. "We'll see." For only a brief moment, the wattage of Danielle's enthusiastic smile dimmed. But "we'll see" was something. And something is always better than nothing. Her new best friend would see, whatever that meant. She would have to be content with that for the moment.

"As for right now, young lady, I think you should be going home." Shelley tried to put some confidence in her voice.

This brought another puzzling response from the runaway. "Why?"

It was an uncomfortably good question. The definition of "home" varied widely among the four of them huddled together in that fort. Based on everything she knew about Danielle's family, her current situation, and what that home held for her, Shelley struggled to find an adequate and honest response. "Uh, well, it's probably a lot warmer than in here, for sure. And this isn't the place for a young girl to stay." From what Danielle had told them, her house wasn't much better than this place, but they knew they couldn't leave her here. The trailer she called home was truly the lesser of two substantial evils. But it was the only crutch they had to rely on. The options available to these well-meaning children — and they were still children — to save the day were severely limited.

"Come on, we'll walk you home."

Succumbing to Shelley's urging, Danielle rose shakily to her feet. Her head hung with resignation. One by one the four of them left the small building, heading back into the woods to follow their trail to what could thinly be called civilization. Ralph led the way in the deepening darkness this time, followed by Danielle, who kept looking over at Shelley, who would occasionally put her hand on the little girl's shoulder. Then came William, protectively watching their backs.

It had been a very strange afternoon for all of them.

As they walked through the poplar and cedar trees, William debated asking a question of the young girl. Purposefully, he had kept quiet during much of this encounter, not wanting to aggravate the situation any more than he had already. But there was a question that the emerging artist in him needed to ask. It had been bugging him since they had entered the camp fort and seen the new version of the Horse. Now was as good a time as any.

"Um, Danielle. I noticed, on your Horse this time, the red hand, I guess it was your hand, on it. You've never done that before. I was just curious …"

Breathing hard from the exertion of walking in the snow, Danielle struggled to find the breath to answer. "That's me. Being part of the Horse. Joining it. I saw some pictures of old-time Indian horses in that book Shelley's mom gave me. There were handprints from warriors on their war ponies. I guess it means I am always going to be a part of the Horse now, and he's always going to be a part of me."

William thought this explanation was kind of odd. "Always is a long time," he said.

The little girl shook her head, almost stumbling off the trail at one point into the deep snow. "Not for me. Someday, when I'm older, I'm gonna have a real horse, too. Maybe a bunch of them. I'm gonna ride them and pet them and feed them. Yep. I know it. And ... and ... and ...," she added almost too quickly to get all her thoughts and hopes spoken coherently. "I'm gonna have a place for tired ponies to rest and stop walking in circles."

It was a relief to all of them to hear Danielle sounding happy again. Though nobody could see, Ralph's fingers were crossed in a silent prayer that if the art, horse, and little girl gods were kind, Danielle's happiness would last and her situation would get better.

As the sun made its final descent on that part of the world in order to rise somewhere else, they arrived at Twin Pine Lane. "Just a little further now." Shelley took Danielle's hand and stepped towards the beat-up trailer where Danielle lived. Danielle didn't move, and her hand slipped out of Shelley's grip.

"No."

This was the second time they'd heard Danielle use that word, and just like the first time, it sounded awkward. Like it was a word that she didn't use all that frequently. It was a word she was probably not allowed to use. She shook her head. "I'd better go home by myself. It might be better. I don't want to get anybody in trouble. I'll see you all at school." With that declaration, she walked down the lane alone, the almost-set sun casting a long, cold shadow on the icy snow of the road. Shelley desperately wanted to make sure she got home safely, but it was obvious to all of them that Danielle wanted to go there alone. Her wishes had to be respected.

They stood there at the side of the road watching her walk away, the cold beginning to seep through their clothes as the warmth they had generated walking through the woods dissipated.

Danielle was passing the first tree when she turned around and yelled to them. "Ralph! I'm sorry. I should have let you touch my Horse. I should learn to share more." Then she resumed her trek to what was dubiously called her home, leaving behind three increasingly depressed kids. For they all knew, the person growing more and more distant from them had nothing else she could possibly share with them. She was still so giving, even with nothing to give.

"She's so pathetic," said William. This time, it wasn't in a snarky or brutal fashion. It was just his way of expressing the fact there was someone in the world who had things worse off than he did. Something he hadn't thought was possible. And that's what was so pathetic. He actually felt sorry for her.

"Yeah," responded Ralph.

Shelley didn't say anything.

Together, they turned and started to walk back to the more populated section of the reserve. They were silent, lost in their own thoughts. All were different, but all revolved around the ten-year-old they had just walked away from. After ten minutes, they came to a cut-off in the road that led to William's house. Deeply embroiled in his own thoughts, William turned towards home without a word of goodbye.

"Hey, William!" called Ralph. "If you want, you can come home with us."

Uncharacteristically, Shelley nodded in agreement.

William stood at the fork in the road, momentarily processing the offer. He shook his head. "No. I don't feel like playing. Or anything. Maybe tomorrow. Bye." With a sad smile, oddly reminiscent of Danielle's, he turned back to his street and left his friends.

*If you want, you can come home with us.* It struck Ralph how much Danielle would have loved to have heard those words. And how much he would have loved to have said them to her. The last thing Ralph and William wanted was another sister, but Danielle would have been different.

The siblings watched William turn in to his driveway, then disappear inside the Williams house. Without much reason to stand there at the side of the road, they resumed their journey home.

High up on a tree, a crow watched them pass. It knew nothing of horses or little girls or much of anything regarding the complex human world, which, judging by today, was a good thing for those in the crow world.

## CHAPTER ELEVEN

HIS TWO-WEEK RESPITE FROM TRAVELLING THE ROADS OF northern North America was rapidly coming to an end. In two days, Tye's employer, Sawyer Transport, wanted him to haul three thousand units of maple syrup to the Prairies. Chuck, his boss, loved the idea of a Native man hauling such a uniquely Canadian item across the country. Tye, on the other hand, didn't care much. Maple syrup, toilet paper, brass fittings, women's underwear. It was all the same. All came with a location, a deadline, and the necessary papers. Once there, though unconfirmed, there was a good chance he was coming back with a truck full of discount socks and maybe some underwear.

He loved his family deeply, but Tye found his time on the road peaceful, almost Zen-like. He could think his Tye thoughts, listen to his Tye songs, and enjoy the growing homesickness that gradually overtook him, knowing full well it would soon be eased, like an itch or a sneeze, though he would never use those metaphors in front of his family.

"Maple syrup? Socks and underwear? Your ancestors would be so proud." In retaliation, a pair of Tye's own socks quickly bounced off Liz's head, landing on the floor near the closet.

She was helping her husband to pack for this trip, as she did every trip. It had practically become a ritual. He wasn't scheduled to pick up his truck till day after tomorrow, but experience had long taught the couple it was better to be prepared in advance. Many a time deliveries had to be rushed and there was only time for the rapid grabbing of random clothes. On one such occasion, somewhere on the other side of Thunder Bay, Tye had discovered an odd assortment of Liz's underwear in his bag. It made for an uncomfortable drive the next day till a Giant Tiger outlet was quickly located.

At this moment, Tye was picking out his travel jeans, as he called them, loose, comfortable, and warm for long stays in the truck's cab. Meanwhile, Liz was picking out his shirts that fit the same description. On the bed in front of them was a familiar large duffle bag.

T-shirts were next on his list. A frequent problem he had as he packed them was that he'd notice several were missing. In many ways, Tye was a sentimentalist. Each T-shirt in his possession came from a place and time in his past, and he remembered the origins of each fondly. Would he wear a random T-shirt with no backstory? Never. The problem was that, like many stories, frequently they got old, uninteresting, and needed to be replaced with something new. Liz took that awesome responsibility upon herself, frequently weeding out those shirts and stories that sported holes and loose threads. On occasion without telling her husband.

"Have you seen my yellow powwow T-shirt?"

On their first trip together as a couple, Tye had taken Liz to the yearly powwow at Curve Lake, near Peterborough. They had camped there for two nights, and generally a good time was had by all. He distinctly remembered singing songs till three in the morning with a couple in the next tent. Some Creedence Clearwater Revival, some Johnny Cash, some Beatles, and he couldn't remember what else. The police had shown up. Ever the acoustic experts, the local rez cops told them that sound tends to travel unusually well over water and that this campfire karaoke was keeping quite a few people up in the local community. They had to shut it down. Not the best or the most original story in the world, but definitely one worthy of a T-shirt.

"Threw it out."

"What! I love that T-shirt. Do you remember I took you —"

"It was full of holes. There was a large grease stain on the side from when you were working on your car that, try as I might, I could not get out. And it was faded. Very faded. You have better T-shirts. You don't need that one."

"But I liked that shirt."

"I am sure you did, but the T-shirt industry needs more sales to survive."

Knowing there was little point in arguing, Tye sighed his disappointment.

"I heard that."

"I know. You were meant to."

Downstairs they heard the door open and the distinct sound of two young adults entering the house, though in a somewhat subdued manner. Tye checked his watch. "The next generation is home. Together. They're spending a lot of time together these days."

Liz had finished with the T-shirts, including managing to eliminate one advertising a popular Canadian beer brand that she personally found problematic but that Tye loved due to the fact he had been invited to the product launch after hauling a trailer full of it into town. Technically the term was "swag", or as he called it, "Stuff We Aboriginals Get."

"Yeah, I think it's because of the Everything Wall. And that Danielle Gaadaw."

Pausing for a second, underwear in his hand, Tye looked to his wife. "I've been meaning to ask about that. What are you going to do about that thing ... sorry ... the Everything Wall of yours?"

Liz stopped what she was doing. "I don't know. It's not doing what I thought it was going to. I mean, it did originally, but now ... I just don't know. It may be causing more problems than anything."

"I know everybody likes that Horse thing, but seriously, it gives me the creeps. Sometimes I feel like we have a fifth person living in this house. And I'm not including William. Speaking of him, where's he been lately? Not that I'm complaining."

Liz moved on to the underwear, making sure hers was as far away from the duffle bag as possible, liberally lining the well-travelled bag with Tye's. "Kids' politics, I think. Nothing serious."

"Liz, is it just me or has the feel of this house completely changed in the last little while? I'm almost afraid to go away this time."

"I know what you mean." Packing momentarily forgotten, Liz sat on the edge of their bed. "I have to admit, sometimes when I look at the Horse, I feel a combination of things. I don't know, fifty percent total amazement that a ten-year-old could create that."

"Agreed. And the other fifty percent?"

Liz thought for a moment. "Twenty percent envy. Twenty percent incomprehension. And ten percent uneasiness, I guess."

"I feel all of those, but in different percentages." Tye sat on the bed beside her, idly bouncing a sock ball in his right hand. "Here's an uncomfortable question, my sweet. Have you ever tried to think about where that Horse came from?"

Brow furrowed, Liz cocked her head to the right, not unlike a cocker spaniel puppy she'd once had. "I don't understand. It came from Danielle's imagination."

He shook his head. "No. I mean yes. But where inside that little girl did such a huge thing come from? I think maybe it's some sort of cry for help. Or worse. It's not just a horse. It's more than a horse. Am I making any sense?"

"I don't know. This is not my area of expertise."

"Mine either. Maybe you can contact one of your weird friends and ask them."

This time a sock bounced off Tye's head.

Most of the small talk gone, Liz hovered on the edge of confessing something to her husband. It had been bothering her all day, and she wanted to get it out of the way. Taking a deep breath, she said, "Tye, I went over to see Hazel."

This generated a perplexed look from the man. "You did? Hazel? Danielle's mother? When? And why would you do that?" Tye knew his wife seldom had concrete, three-dimensional, concise explanations for many of the things she did, but this definitely required some clarification. Patiently, he waited for an answer.

Formulating her thoughts, Liz pulled a loose thread out of one of Tye's socks.

"I was worried about that little girl. I didn't want to tell the kids, but I needed to do something."

"Okay. What happened?"

"I knocked on the door. That Arthur guy answered." Liz went silent.

Putting down his favourite jeans, Tye turned to his wife and leaned on the bedpost. He wanted to hear where this story was going. "And?"

More silence followed his question. Then Liz found the words to continue. "They invited me in. I think they felt they should, rather than they wanted to. Once I was inside, I sure didn't want to be there. The place was a disaster zone. Horrible."

"Did you see Hazel?"

That question caused a short bark of laughter from Liz. "You could say that. But it wasn't the Hazel I remember. She's changed a lot. I doubt she could really see me. They offered me a beer, but I said I couldn't stay. I asked about Danielle. Evidently our kids had been there yesterday, asking the same question."

"They were? They didn't say anything."

"Doesn't matter. Hazel said Danielle was sleeping and she didn't want to wake her up."

"Do you think that was true?"

There was a creak of wood somewhere in the house, filling in the silence of understanding.

"No."

Tye went back to packing. Liz went to the closet, rifling through a series of neatly hung winter sweaters. Nothing more needed to be said.

"Mom, Dad?" Ralph and Shelley entered their bedroom, sans winter wear. For the first time in a long time, Liz noticed how quickly her children were growing up. In five months, her little girl would be a teenager. Liz's mother had always warned her about the terrible twos, but it was those mid-teenage years that struck Liz with their own form of subtle concern. Her son was shooting up, already as tall as his older sister.

Tye looked up, ready to get back to the important task of choosing socks for the road. "Hey, you two, what's up?"

"We want to talk to you about something."

That subtle fear Liz had thought about earlier suddenly had a growth spurt. "About what?"

Looking at each other for support, both kids entered the room. "It's about Danielle."

Tye mumbled to himself, "Again?"

Though the children had initiated the conversation, there seemed to be a clear reluctance to further it.

"Yes?" said Liz.

As usual, it was Shelley who stepped up to bat, wetting her lips before speaking. "Mom, Dad, about Danielle …?" That was as far as she got. Once more there was an uncomfortable pause.

Slightly irritated, Tye broke the silence. "What about Danielle?"

This time, Ralph spoke. "We think you two should adopt her."

"Or foster her. Or whatever you think is best, but she needs a place to stay." The words started to come out fast and furious. "She's been living at the camp fort, down by the shore. You should have seen her. Oh my god!"

It was Ralph's turn. "She hadn't eaten in days. I don't think her mother looks after her. William said she looked pathetic. She needs our help."

"She could have my room. I could move back in with Ralph." Ralph gave his sister a quick, puzzled glance — that had not been previously discussed — but that was something to be dealt with later. "I'm worried for her."

"Me too," added Ralph. "We'll look after her. Feed her. Everything."

This drew a small elbow from Shelley. "She's not a dog, Ralph." She turned her attention back to her parents. "Well?"

Now it was the parents' turn to hesitantly respond. A slightly amused but still concerned Tye looked to his wife, who was looking down at the wood floor. Two seconds passed before Liz spoke. "I'm afraid things don't work that way." She looked as sad as her children, having secretly considered the same thing. Though her heart ached for Danielle, especially after what she'd just been told, the law and the world just didn't allow for her family to scoop up the little girl and adopt her. To the best of her knowledge, there was precious little she could do.

"But, Mom, she's so miserable there. They don't want her and ..."

"... we do." Shelley finished her brother's sentence.

Liz Thomas wished desperately the world was as simple as her daughter and son seemed to believe it was right at this moment, but she knew differently. She opened her mouth to speak, but it was Tye who came to her rescue.

"It doesn't work that way, sweetheart. Hazel is her mother. That's the way things are. It's not always right, and frequently it sucks." Tye stopped, aware he'd almost sworn in front of his kids. There was also the fact he was unsure what else to add. While his children's argument was not exactly a detailed one, it had a clear moral purpose, a forceful superiority that he couldn't deny.

"Your father's right. If I could, I would. We would."

The attitude from the Thomas kids began to change from their original hope to sadness, and then to frustration. Holding on to the purity of a child's sense of right and wrong, Shelley and Ralph couldn't understand why what they were suggesting wasn't possible. Their plan would be good for everybody. It was a win-win situation. The best kind. But their mother, who was usually their biggest supporter in most things, was oddly becoming their biggest obstacle.

"There must be something we can do! Mom, Dad, it's not right." Shelley had the floor, but her brother was fully behind her.

Liz was silent for a moment, obviously weighing what her children had told her. She totally agreed with her daughter and was proud of her sense of judgment, but society had a way of interfering with a person's moral compass. "Maybe ..."

Both siblings jumped at the breach in the dam. "Maybe" meant something. Seldom had more hopes been pinned on a two-syllable word.

Liz's visit with Hazel had raised some very serious concerns but had provided no answer. There were always possibilities, as Liz had frequently tried to impart to her children. Life was not a series of dead-end lanes.

Though definitely sharing his wife's concerns about Danielle — what normal parent wouldn't be troubled about the precarious welfare of a child? — Tye had learned to be suspicious of his wife's brainstorms.

"I suppose I could have a word with Marilyn. It doesn't hurt to chat, I suppose. Tye?"

That earned a firm nod from her husband. "Good idea."

Marilyn was the local Children's Aid worker, the woman in charge of making sure as many of the homes in Otter Lake were as happy and fit as was humanly possible. It was a hell of a job for just one woman, because a good part of her job involved making enemies. But Liz trusted her and felt sharing some of the information provided by her children might have an overall positive outcome.

Tye was more than a little relieved that they would be

handing this particular ball off. This whole subject, from the Horse to legally extracting a little girl from a potentially abusive home, was in a decidedly grey area. And for all his strengths, Tye was not a fan of grey areas. The blacker and whiter the world, the better he understood it.

Saying her children were pleased would be an understatement.

"Really!" Shelley knew Marilyn. Shelley's good friend Vanessa was her daughter. Though both girls thought the woman's clothes were a little out of fashion and she needed a better haircut, this was definitely a step in a more proactive direction. "Are you gonna phone? Like now?"

More an observer of the story than a participant, Tye contributed his own curiosity to the conversation. "Yeah, you gonna?"

Standing up from the corner of the bed, Liz appeared obviously more fortified. There was a direction to move, and she was the one everybody expected to do the moving. "This is important. This needs a personal touch. I'm gonna go see her."

Both kids, considering themselves way too old to jump up and down in happiness, merely smiled and cheered. But deep inside, they were indeed doing handstands and somersaults.

"Uh, Liz, it is a Saturday, you know. I think she's off the clock."

Walking out the door, Liz dismissed her husband's concern. "Child welfare workers are never off the clock." Tye heard his wife's voice say, as she walked down the hallway, "I assume you can finish packing by yourself."

The kids raced after their hero, leaving Tye behind, an unpaired sock in each hand.

"No problem."

Downstairs, Liz got on her coat and shoes. It was the second time that day that Liz had suited up for battle. Hopefully this time there would be a victory involved.

Her children started to don their winter attire, but Liz stopped them.

"No. I should do this alone. You two stay here."

Almost in unison, both kids said, "But we can help!"

"Ah, that's so sweet that you think you have a say in this. We'll talk when I get back. Stay here. Look, there's some soup on the stove, and feel free to make yourself some toast or a sandwich if you get hungry."

"Uh-huh." The two high-fived each other. For all their mother's embarrassing faults, the Thomas siblings knew she would ride to the rescue. That's what mothers were supposed to do — except for those like Hazel Gaadaw.

Buttoning up her coat, Liz kissed her children goodbye and promptly left the house. With a determined stride, she walked out to the road, down four houses, and then up Marilyn's driveway. It was one of the benefits of living in a small reserve. Glued to the window, they watched every step their mother took until she disappeared from their sight.

"I've gotta phone William, let him know."

Oddly enough, Shelley didn't say anything snarky.

When Ralph called him, William seemed quite delighted. He hadn't been able to think about much else since he'd returned home. Sitting in his room, he'd occasionally looked out the window towards the trailer park. Once his mother had looked in to see if he was feeling better. A sedate and solemn William was an unusual event, enough to warrant investigation. After some parental interrogation, William was allowed to be introspective.

On the desk in front of him was a blank piece of paper. Beside it, a pencil. A seemingly innocuous pair of inanimate objects. For a second, the boy's fingers pushed the pencil back and forth on the desk, wondering why he was doing this. Then, in a burst of conviction, William sat in the chair. Pencil in hand, paper in front of him, he tried to remember what Danielle had said about the Horse and how it came to her. What had she said? She ... called ... it. William wondered, just how was he supposed to call an imaginary horse? His mind wrestled with the concept. Maybe he was thinking about the question wrong. "Too literally" was how one of his teachers would put it. A person usually called something when they wanted it. So, maybe, if he wanted something, something good and amazing, and just somehow put it out to the universe, something might happen. It sounded silly when he thought of it that way, but he'd seen it work. Really work. Danielle's Horse was the proof.

Instinctively he knew he couldn't, shouldn't, call on the Horse. He was hers, and William had no right to try. But there must be something. For the next hour, he tried. Dogs. Cats. Motorcycles. Cars. Boats. A multitude of different things, using up a fair stack of white paper. All were well drawn and showed imagination — William had always been a good artist — but nothing really leaped off the page and into the world around him as he'd seen happen with Danielle and the Everything Wall. Whatever he was looking for wasn't there.

Though only ten, William had been slowly developing an interest in drawing. He was experiencing just an inkling, a tiny seed of awareness: there was to be more art somehow down his youthful road. He knew there were real artists out there, even a lot of successful Native ones. His siblings would, of course, ridicule him for such a thing, but that would be a battle for later years. At the moment, he was desperately trying to find *his* Horse. Maybe his Horse was deaf.

If it was okay with Danielle, maybe he could ask her about how she was able to draw like that. Maybe she could teach him, but only if she wanted to.

WHEN LIZ GOT home, Shelley and Ralph were on her like she was carrying an armful of freshly baked pies. Even a curious Tye came down the stairs. "Well?" they all asked in one manner or another.

"She's gonna look into it."

All three of them looked at each other, but it was Tye who spoke. "She's gonna look into it? What does that mean?"

Liz took her coat and boots off, showing an unusual amount of weariness. "It means she's gonna look into it. That's all she can do. Hazel and Danielle have been on her radar for some time. So, she's gonna look into it. She'll keep us posted."

Tye hung his wife's coat up. "I thought all this stuff was private, confidential."

"Yeah, you'd think so, huh? I need a tea."

Without saying much more, Liz went about making herself some tea. She didn't ask her husband or her children if they wanted any. This one time, this moment and this tea was to be hers entirely.

WILLIAM RAN UP to the siblings as they walked to school. "Hey. Anything happen with Marilyn and your mother? About Danielle?"

Ralph shook his head. "Not really, but she was there for about two hours. You know adults, there's a … what was the word Mom used, Shelley?"

"Protocol."

For a second, William's consciousness focused on that word. It didn't sound like a good word. "What the heck does that mean?" There were some words the boy instinctively had a dislike for. The way the syllables of those words were strung together were unpleasant to his ears. He reacted to the sound of words as much as what they meant, and this generated his overly negative response. *Protocol* was such an uncomfortable word for William, as were such equally distasteful things as yogurt, caterpillars, and people who smile with their lips parted, showing their teeth.

Shelley listened to William's questions, equally disliking the word *protocol* — along with shrimp, snakes, and people who are too touchy. "She says there's a process for dealing with things like this. There are things to do. Doors and hoops, stuff like that. She told us it takes time."

William, another Otter Lake individual cut from the

same black and white cloth as Tye, mumbled aloud, "So nothing then? That sucks."

Ralph shook his head. "Not right now. Luckily, Marilyn had heard stories about Hazel Gaadaw and that guy who lives there, and what kind of shape the trailer is in. She said she's gonna look into it today."

"Look into it?"

"That's what she said."

"Well, I guess that's better than not looking into it." William made the choice to be pleased at the outcome. "All right."

They continued their walk to school, their camaraderie re-established, with the added bonus of their joint interests making Shelley a little less critical of William. Casually, William picked up a chunk of hard snow and threw it against an aged oak tree, where he watched it dissolve. Ralph followed his lead but missed, his snowball falling into a bush at the side of the road.

"So, what did you do last night?" Shelley seemed oddly uninterested in tossing portions of snow at flora.

William searched for another chunk of suitable snow. "I tried to draw."

"You always draw." Ralph tossed him a good-sized, apple-shaped piece of ice.

"I tried to do that Danielle thing," William said.

This caught both Ralph's and Shelley's attention.

Shelley spoke first. "Did you draw the Horse?"

That got a very emphatic response. "No way. That thing scares me. No, I just tried to, I forget how she put it, but I wanted something really good. Really impressive."

Ralph spoke. "And?"

Without looking at either of them, William shook his head. "Nope. What about you guys? I mean, have you ever tried?"

Looking down at the snow, Ralph shook his head. "I was never good at art to begin with. I don't need to prove that."

Shelley's eyes were on the school in the distance. "Almost. A couple days ago, I was looking at the Horse. And I wanted something of my own. But I couldn't." They were all quiet as they walked the rest of the way.

As they crossed into school territory, skirting past the parking lot where Ralph and Danielle had had their first run-in a scant three weeks or so ago, Shelley caught William's eye. "William, I'm a little confused. Last week ... you hated Danielle."

Immediately, the boy looked down to the dirty snow under their feet. "No. I don't hate her. Not anymore. I just ... I don't know. Just never mind." An uncomfortable silence descended on them as they crossed the playground. It was there that Shelley saw a lone little figure walking up the road coming from the trailer park, slowly making her way to the school.

"I think ..." Shelley then started shouting, "Danielle! Hey! Danielle!" Both boys pivoted in the direction of Shelley's gaze. They saw the little figure start running towards them. William actually smiled as Ralph spoke.

"Looks like she's going to school today."

"Yeah. Look at her run," commented Shelley. Out of breath, Danielle practically ran into Shelley's arms with a thud, knocking her back a foot. It was an interaction worthy of William's physicality, but for a far different reason.

"Hi," was all she said. They assumed that's what she said, as it was difficult to hear her with her face buried in the bigger girl's coat. Shelley hugged her back. Still feeling a bit sheepish over his earlier treatment of the little girl, William stepped back for fear of spooking her again. Reluctantly emerging from Shelley's arms, Danielle then hugged Ralph and even managed a small smile for William, who felt a genuine glow inside, though he was unsure why. And he didn't care. As the school bell rang, signalling another day of education, all four finished their walk to the school entrance.

During the rest of the day, Danielle spent both recesses and the lunch hour with the three of them. At one point, Julia and Vanessa came up to Shelley to invite her to participate in some recess activity. The Thomas girl begged off, astounding everybody, saying she was busy. Even William struggled to be friendly in his own way; discovering that Danielle had a lone bag of chips for lunch, once again he magnanimously gave her one of his sandwiches. It was ham and cheese on brown with lots of mustard. He also gave her half his orange. Danielle really liked it, and William was pleased. By the end of the day, Danielle ended up hugging him goodbye after they all walked her to Twin Pine Lane, where, as usual, she demanded they leave her. Waving enthusiastically, Danielle disappeared down her street, leaving the three friends to think about their day.

"Well, that was a good day," summed up Shelley. The boys heartily agreed.

Though it was a cold day, they all felt comfortably warm as they made their way to the Thomas home. Equilibrium had been restored in their lives, in their homes, and on the Otter Lake reserve.

Walking up the driveway, they saw Liz in the big bay window, looking out at them. They all immediately had the same idea and went racing in, hoping there was good news on the other side of that glass window.

The first words out of Liz Thomas's mouth were, "There's nothing Marilyn can do."

Simultaneously, all three of the kids' hearts sank. "She went over and interviewed Hazel and Arthur — that's her boyfriend's name — but —"

"Couldn't she see —" argued Shelley.

"Listen to me. Yes, she saw everything. But the Children's Aid Society can't just yank every kid who lives in poverty away from their families. It wouldn't be right to the parents. The way the CAS official policy puts it, you can't fault a family for not giving a child what they don't have. It's not deliberate neglect."

Shelley wasn't buying this. "It's not just because they're poor. They told Danielle that she was a bad girl and that's why Santa didn't bring her any presents. I don't care how poor you are, that's not right. And they drink —"

"No, it isn't right, and I told Marilyn that. She promised me she'd help them with stuff."

"What stuff?" Now it was Ralph's turn to question authority.

"Marilyn said she'd help them with social assistance and counselling."

"That's it?"

"I'm afraid so. CAS policy is to try and keep families together as much as possible."

Admittedly, this was a far cry from the CAS of Liz's parents' and grandparents' time, but supposedly society marches forward. The arc of justice and all that. But one thing was for sure: at some point in their development, children begin to become disillusioned with the adults around them. Monsters under the bed and Santa coming down a non-existent chimney get replaced by different kinds of monsters and shopping mall Santa Clauses. Children's loss of belief usually begins around the ages of ten or twelve, but not with a loss of faith in government agencies.

"I'm sorry." And Liz truly was.

The problem with children is they often can't see beyond their own disappointment. The problem with parents is they often take on their children's disappointments and magnify them under their adult lens. This was a situation where truly nobody was happy. Even William, deep in his own funk, went home early.

LATER, AS HE was preparing to go to bed for the night, Tye, who was the most distantly touched by what was going on under his roof, felt the pangs of impotency. Originally he had had no interest in having another child in his house, they both had long ago accepted that, but under the circumstances, if everything he had been told was true — and he believed his family wholeheartedly — he'd be the new villain in this scenario if he chose not to take Danielle in. More importantly, he would feel that about himself.

"And that's where Marilyn is gonna leave things? I don't think I like that."

Brushing her hair, Liz concurred. "I absolutely do not like it, either. I don't like it so much, it almost burns."

"You know, I've met that Arthur guy once or twice."

"You have? Where? I can't imagine you wandering around in the same social circles."

"At the bar in Bayfield."

"I stand corrected. And …"

Tye pulled back the sheets on the bed and crawled in. "I haven't seen him there in a while. He was barred."

"Barred from the bar. Even better." Liz put her brush down and looked into the mirror. She saw herself. She also saw the woman she used to be, as well as the woman she one day wanted to be. But, most of all, she saw what she wasn't: a woman with the power to fix this situation.

"The kids are really disappointed in us. I'm disappointed in us." Her eyes could not leave her mirrored reflection. Maybe on that side of the mirror, she could have been more effective.

Had this all started with the Horse? Or had it all started with the Everything Wall? It had been such a good idea. And look what it had caused. Part of her, on this side of the mirror, wished she'd not created the Everything Wall. Nothing would have changed. Would that have been better? It is often said that ignorance is bliss. Would she, Liz Thomas, have been happier not knowing about Danielle and the awful living conditions she herself had seen? After everything — the drawing, the children's friendship — nothing on either side of the mirror would have changed. Was it wrong for her kids to get Danielle's hopes up? To get their own hopes up? Only to have them come crashing down, a terrible lesson in the reality that not everyone grew up in happy homes. Maybe maintaining the status quo was the right path in life, a statement Liz never thought would enter her mind.

But, on the other hand, maybe she was grossly misjudging Marilyn. After all, she was a professional. This was what Marilyn did for a living — and had been doing for a good seventeen years. This had to be the necessary step, the right one, a good one, the first in forward movement. She had the wisdom and knowledge of decades of CAS experience to back her up — again, another sentence Liz had never thought would enter her consciousness. Marilyn did say she was going to do what she could, that she was going to help.

Help is always good.

It has to be.

"What are you thinking?" asked her husband, noting the silence.

"Nothing I'm sure you haven't thought." Later, after a bad night's sleep, in the early hours of the morning, while the house slept, however restlessly, Liz descended the stairs to the kitchen. To the Everything Wall. As silently as possible, she poured herself a bucket of warm, soapy water. The Horse watched her as she stood before it: It seemed to know, and to acknowledge, that it was to be the object of artistic euthanasia. Swipe by soapy swipe, the Horse left the Thomas home.

"I'm so sorry," Liz said. As she spoke the apology, she

wasn't sure if she was addressing the Horse as she made it disappear or if she was addressing herself. About an hour before dawn, the kitchen was pristine and ready to face the new day. Both the Horse and the Everything Wall had been retired.

THE NEXT MORNING on their way to school and then standing around in the schoolyard, Ralph and Shelley and William did not see Danielle. At recess they could not find her, and at lunch hour, the same. It seemed that once again, she had disappeared.

"I haven't seen her anywhere," William said as he and Ralph met up with Shelley at lunch hour.

"Me neither. I'm worried," said Shelley.

"So am I," admitted Ralph.

"Being worried ain't gonna do anything. Let's go find her." This time, it was William's suggestion. And it was a good one.

Eagerly, Ralph expressed a thought. "Should we check out the camp fort?"

Shelley shook her head. "Yeah, we can try there. But maybe you guys are over-thinking this."

"We are?" William didn't understand the concept of over-thinking this or anything.

"Maybe she's at home. Kids have been known to stay at home. Maybe she's just sick or something. If she's not there, we can go and check out the camp fort. Eliminate the obvious first." Ralph did not like the idea of going back to the trailer at the end of Twin Pine Lane where Danielle's mother and Arthur were.

"Let's go," said William, more to himself than anybody else. For a second, Ralph balked at the idea. His sister was older and William was tougher. Both were better suited to tangling with these particular drunken and fearsome dragons. The other two were half a dozen strides gone before Ralph found himself following them. As frightened as he was, the thought of being useless, of not mattering, of not being one of the good guys and letting bad things tell him what he could and couldn't do, galvanized him. He followed his sister and friend into the discomfort of the unknown and unpredictable.

Leaving the schoolyard behind, they ran down towards Twin Pine Lane. Except for when they took the sobbing Danielle home a few weeks earlier, Shelley and Ralph had rarely ever skipped school before. William had, of course, but only when it was absolutely necessary. They were all becoming uneasily aware that the world had different priorities than the ones they had for themselves. Learning about the root causes of the First World War just did not hold a candle to whatever might be happening to their friend Danielle. As they got closer to their goal, the trio slowed down. Concerned about encountering Hazel and Arthur, not knowing what condition or mood they might be in, the three children circled around the trailer to its back, not exactly sure how to proceed. As driven as they were, this was seriously new territory for them.

Not a one of them wanted to knock on the pale green door. Once again, they were so close but so far. Somewhere on the inside of that weathered aluminum panelling was their friend, who just might be in trouble. William tapped Ralph on the shoulder and pointed. At the back of the trailer, framed by her bedroom window, was Danielle, looking out at a world that did not seem to want her. There was a faraway look in her eyes, and even though she seemed to be gazing towards the forest, they were all sure she didn't see it. Danielle also didn't seem to see them.

One by one, they all crept out of the woods, coincidently in sequence of height. One by one, they stood under her window, looking around nervously, then up to her. Ralph whispered loudly upwards, "Danielle."

She didn't move. The snow-filled world they were currently standing in still did not command her attention.

He tried again. "Danielle!"

In response to Ralph's louder yell, the little girl was jolted out of her daydreaming. Looking down, she saw the trio beneath her, amidst an old stone-ringed firepit and two cast-off rubber tires.

At first it seemed like Danielle was having trouble correlating the world inside her bedroom and her friends outside of it. These were disparate images that did not appear together in her limited experience. It took another second for her to fully understand that her new friends were in her backyard, looking up at her. Reluctantly, she opened the window, still not convinced she was seeing what she was actually seeing.

"Why weren't you at school today?" asked Shelley, trying to keep her voice down.

"I wasn't allowed," Danielle whispered back, adding a nervous glance over her shoulder.

"Why weren't you allowed? You didn't do anything."

She gave a sad shrug. "Some woman came for a visit yesterday. Now I'm in trouble. Now we're moving."

*Uh-oh*, thought Ralph. "Moving where?"

"Toronto, I think. My mom's boyfriend may have a job there."

It was William's turn to ask a question. "When?"

"Today."

Shelley's breath evaporated. "Today?! So soon?!"

"Yeah. 'Before some other bitch sticks their fucking nose in our business.' That's what my mother said. Seems like a lot of other people have been asking about me, and my mom doesn't like it."

All three had heard swearing like that before; in fact, in William's house he'd heard a lot worse before breakfast. Still, it was completely incongruous to hear it coming out of Danielle's tiny mouth. Shelley and Ralph had become painfully aware once again that, by knocking on the door and asking for her, they might have contributed to Danielle's unfortunate situation.

There was an odd silence as her words registered. Then Danielle spoke again. "I was just looking at these trees again. I'm going to miss them. My father put a swing up on that one, so long ago. The branch rotted off and the whole thing fell last spring."

William was the only one who looked over his shoulder at the tree. If she stayed, he would put up another one for her, he was sure of that.

Ralph took a step closer to the trailer. He was now standing directly under Danielle's window. "Danielle, we tried to help. Honest we did."

The little girl smiled sadly at Ralph. "I know. Thank you. I think you were the only one who could really see my Horse, he wanted to meet you, but ..." Suddenly her head swivelled around, and the loud, angry voice of Hazel Gaadaw could be heard.

Instinctively, the Thomas and Williams group ran to hide. William hid around the corner at the end of the trailer, while Ralph jumped behind a snow bank. Shelley found the comfort of a large tree to conceal herself, the one Danielle's father had put the swing on so long ago. Though hidden safely, they all peeked, seeing Danielle suddenly disappear and Hazel's head jut out of her daughter's window, curious to find what her daughter was either looking at or talking to. Her hair in a rough, greying bun, Hazel noticed nothing of particular interest to her in the backyard. Angrily, she closed the window with a loud thud. Still hiding, the three friends waited a few minutes, hoping Danielle would appear again, but she didn't.

On their way back to school, a dark cloud hung over them, darker than the cloudy winter sky. William broke the silence. "What should we do?"

"I don't know," said Shelley.

"I think we've done everything we could. And it wasn't good enough."

Of the three, Ralph looked the most dejected.

"This isn't right." Perhaps it was William who summed up their last few days the best. Neither of the other two could argue. Silence was their only comment. They slowly made their way back to school, despondent and defeated.

Later that afternoon, after school had let out, all three

were standing by the swing set wondering if there was anything more they could do when they saw Arthur's beat-up pickup truck driving down the reserve's main road. The back was loaded with boxes, bits of furniture, and black plastic garbage bags obviously stuffed with clothes and pillows. Danielle was sitting squashed in the back of the cab. She looked out at them with a resigned expression. The vehicle was moving, the windows were dirty, and there was a fair distance between her and them, but it appeared to all three that she had a black eye. Three sets of eyes locked on her as the pickup approached. The little girl put her hand up to the side window for a brief moment. When she took it down, it left an imprint on the frosty window. All three later agreed that it looked like the same image of her hand on the side of the camp fort Horse. The pickup passed them and turned a corner. Danielle slid out of view.

Continuing its journey out of the village and the children's lives, the truck disappeared over the big hill at the edge of the reserve. Seconds and minutes passed, yet they stood there, continuing to watch the crest of the hill. They didn't really expect her to reappear, but they didn't know what else to do. They were frozen to the spot. Even when the four o'clock school bell rang, they didn't move. They were each lost in their own thoughts.

Ralph was torn up over their inability to do anything. It was a sense of frustration or of impotence — their failure to accomplish something no matter how hard they tried. There are fewer things sadder than a child realizing how unjust the world can be. He took a deep breath, his body telling him he hadn't drawn one for too long. The boy hated the feeling of not being able to do anything. Of not being able to make a difference. Somehow, someway, he or his sister or William should have been able to do something. Someday, he thought, he would become somebody who might be able to do things. To help people like Danielle.

All the ten-year-old boy could do was stand in front of his school in the dark Canadian winter cold. Staring at an empty road. Twelve years later, Ralph Thomas would receive his shield and weapon.

Beside him, Shelley's heart was breaking. Every fibre in her body wanted to run after the truck and beat the two adults senseless, then take the little girl home and make the world a better place for her. The image of Danielle, her eye black and swollen, watching her as she was driven slowly by would haunt her for a very long time. She too could do nothing about it. There had to be better answers in the world. She didn't hear herself cry. Why does the world have to be that cruel?

Across the road was the daycare. Every day on her way to school, Shelley passed the fence and building that housed the next generation of Otter Lake people. Three dozen children, most of them related to her, played and learned in the building. Was there another Danielle in there? Somebody who needed a hug? A little girl or boy who needed a better champion than a twelve-year-old girl could be? It pained the young girl to think that. Eighteen years later, Shelley Thomas would find herself sitting in an office with a sign on its door that would read *Executive Director, Otter Lake Day Care*.

It was William who had the most visceral reaction. He stood on the packed snow, watching the weathered pickup drive by, his fists tightly clenched. In that little girl, he saw the worst in himself. When and if a book was written about that girl's sad and sorry life, he knew that he would have contributed a few unpleasant pages. And he was ashamed. So ashamed and angry he clenched his fists tighter. So tight his nails cut into the flesh of his palms, making them begin to bleed. But he was oblivious to it.

Since the event in the classroom, William had hoped to redeem his actions, not just to the little girl but to himself. It's been said we make our own hell, and for many like the Williams boy, knowing what you are capable of is frequently the most damning.

Other thoughts crowded his head. Maybe all his brothers and his sister and his parents didn't hate him after all. Two years ago, he'd been down by the shore of Otter Lake jumping from frozen snow and ice mound to frozen snow and ice mound, even though his father had told him repeatedly to stay away from the shoreline due to the unstable nature of the melting spring ice. And, as is occasionally true, sometimes fathers do know more than their children. As predicted, William went through the weakened ice and landed chest deep in the still remarkably frigid water. He felt a cold that felt burning hot. In a state of both physical and emotional shock, he literally froze.

He dimly recalled hearing the front door of his house burst open with a bang and his father run down the hill to the lake. Jumping into the water, breaking through the ice himself, the man pulled William out of the water and dragged him up to the house, where he was warmed. At the time, the only thing the young boy had remembered was the spanking and scolding he got that night for doing something so incredibly stupid. Now, however, he realized that was the only time he'd ever seen his father, a large Native man with an immense belly and short legs, run. His body wasn't built for speed, yet the man had seen his son fall through the weak spring ice and he had run down to the lake, jumped in himself, and saved his son. Now William realized his father would never have let him drown in that lake if there was anything he could do about it. And he remembered behind held close, the man's big arms around him as his father took him up the hill into the warmth of the house.

And there was that time last year, at a nearby hockey arena, two white kids had roughed him up in the boys' washroom. Crying at home, he'd told his brothers about it, and they'd teased him for being a girl, so weak and defenceless. But two days later, at that same arena, he'd noticed those same white kids stayed far away from him, looking at him with a certain kind of fear. It didn't take long for William to realize his brothers must have had a rather aggressive word with those two boys. Two minor tormentors in his life had definitely done something to protect him against other possible dangers. He wasn't as alone as he thought. Nor was he as alone as Danielle was in that pickup.

At this point, having watched Danielle disappear into the distance, William was transformed into one of the rarest creations. In the blink of an eye, William Williams became

a bully who would bully bullies. While hardly the super-
hero type, William knew that he might not be able to
change the world, but there were little things he could do
to make it somewhat better. For him, that included keeping
an eye on those who were in a position of power and used
it to torment those who were weaker or different. It wasn't
a calling or a question of morality, it just became part of
his personality. It was something he did because it needed
to be done.

William didn't have Ralph's uniform or Shelley's job,
he merely had his conviction. And that was good enough
for him.

Lost in her own world, Shelley looked down to her new
boots, a little more scuffed now. They were the same colour
as Danielle's jacket. That's when she first noticed the little
droplets of blood dripping onto the pale snow directly
below William's ten-year-old trembling hands. Pulled out
of her own reverie, she took out a napkin she had in her
pocket and grabbed William's right hand. She had to use
all her strength to pry his fingers open and wrap his palm in
the napkin. Luckily she always carried tissues with her and
found another for his left hand. He was barely conscious
of what she was doing, only at the last minute looking at the
blood on his hands. He looked confused, unable to process
what he was seeing. Then, noticing her hands holding his,
he gazed into her face. They saw each other's pain.

Ralph saw this happening and noticed a certain amount
of caring as his sister did her best to halt the bleeding.
Shelley closed William's hands around the napkins. Then,
in the silence of the dark and cold afternoon, they went

back to the Thomas house, where the rest of the day would wind down with all three lost in their own thoughts. Largely silent. No play. Just a lot of wondering what they could have done differently.

Outside, it began to snow, and soon the tire tracks left by Arthur's pickup would be lost to the elements. Like so many other things.

LYING ON AN aged motel mattress in a nameless truck stop just across the Manitoba border, Tye was watching television. For reasons unknown, he kept looking at the large blank wall adjacent to his bed, half expecting to see something either on it or peering out at him. On television was some inane American sitcom that once, he might have found funny. Now he was watching it without watching it. His thoughts were completely detached from what was spitting out of the television. He missed his family. Tye always did when he travelled, but he had left just yesterday and the deep longing usually didn't kick in for four or five days. To save money, he and Liz had worked out a plan of talking every two days to catch up. They weren't due to chat until the following night.

Tye dialled the Otter Lake phone number. It rang three times before Liz answered. "Hey, it's me. I was just missing you and thought I would call early. Is everything okay?" He could hear Liz taking a deep breath. That was not good.

"Something's wrong with the kids." Instantly Tye swung his feet off the mattress and onto the floor, hand tightening on the receiver.

"Are they okay? What happened?"

"They're fine, Tye. They're just sad."

"Sad? About what?"

Liz took another deep breath. Tye could imagine her sitting on the stool beside the phone. "Danielle is gone."

"What do you mean she's gone? Like lost?" Tye was getting a sick feeling in his stomach. He did not like the direction this conversation was going.

"No. Hazel and her boyfriend and Danielle just disappeared. The kids said they saw them driving out of the village in that old pickup of what's-his-name …"

"Arthur …," Tye answered absent-mindedly.

"They just drove away. Disappeared. Marilyn is guilt-ridden. She's beside herself. She contacted a bunch of CAS officials about this, and they're going to look into it."

There was that phrase again. It promised so much but usually delivered so little.

Liz continued, the worry evident in her voice, "But since technically her mother and Arthur haven't done anything wrong to this point, she's unsure how seriously they will assess the situation."

Tye could hear the slight quiver in her voice that made itself known when she was stressed.

"And what about the kids?"

"It's hard to get anything out of them. I think they feel guilty."

Puzzled, Tye tugged at the collar of his T-shirt, which announced a 1995 Tragically Hip tour. "Okay, I'm getting a little lost here. What do they feel guilty about? They didn't do anything."

"Sure they did," answered Liz. "They made friends with Danielle. And now this little girl they wanted to help is gone." She paused for a second. "I feel guilty. We should have done more."

Tye wanted to say, "What more could they have done?" but he knew that would not be the right answer at this moment. "Do you want me to come home?"

"Can you?"

Now it was Tye's turn to take a deep breath. "Ray will kill me. He'll have to get a replacement driver out here, and I'll have to pay a penalty, but ..."

He could practically hear her smile on the other end of the phone. "Thank you, Tye."

The Native man, alone in a nondescript hotel room in a town he would never remember, smiled to himself. He had made his wife happy and grateful. He was not sure what he would be in a position to do for his kids, but he would try. According to rumour, that's what a good parent does.

"I have no idea how to get home from here without the truck, but I'm on my way. I'll keep you posted."

"Love you, Tye."

"Love you, too."

Hanging up, Tye immediately began to repack his toiletries and tomorrow's T-shirt, socks, and underwear that he'd laid out just half an hour ago. Once he had everything together, he would call the front desk about finding the best way to get out of here and back home. He also wanted to pick up the nifty T-shirt he'd seen in the lobby, something about a bass — the fish — playing a bass — the musical instrument. And there was the issue of presents for his kids. He hadn't brought back any from the last trip, maybe something from here might cheer them up. Tye remembered seeing some stuffed animals in a big bin when he'd checked in. A giraffe, he remembered, a dog, a cat, a horse ...

Tye stopped packing. No horse.

FROM THAT POINT in their lives, Danielle Gaadaw and the Horse passed into legend. Never forgotten, but hidden in the shadows. The Everything Wall, after three glorious weeks of existence, also disappeared into history. At one point, Tye tried moving the refrigerator over the bare spot on the wall in what he thought was an innocuous attempt to put behind them the events of that winter, but by the time he came home a few weeks later the appliance had been moved back to its natural home. Very little was said about the little girl they had come to know briefly. It was better to remember her kneeling in front of the Wall, excited and happy, instead of wondering what might have become of her wherever Arthur's pickup truck had stopped.

Another family moved into the Gaadaw trailer shortly after, as housing on the reserve was a precious commodity. The Horse lived on in the camp fort for another season, but the structure stopped being a focal point for adolescent mischief. Little partying could be done while the Horse stared down on them, seemingly passing judgment. Later that fall, a fire consumed the building, and the Horse with it. It was now as if there was no trace left of Danielle.

Ralph, Shelley, and William grew up, as children tend to do. Their lives became more complicated, and thoughts of old friends, both human and equine, began taking a back seat to more current and pressing adventures. Tye and Liz grew old together, with Liz still occasionally throwing her family a curveball. One year, she bought a yurt.

Some twelve years after the incident with Danielle, Tye's journey on Mother Earth came to an end. It was a slow death, made not too painful by modern science, but still one of anguish for the family. William and Shelley had just become engaged, and the wedding had to be postponed.

## CHAPTER TWELVE

THE PARAMEDICS HOISTED HARRY ONTO THE PORTABLE gurney, marvelling at how light the man actually was. The layered and worn clothing gave the impression of far more substance than Harry carried on his bones. Ralph was standing beside him as they strapped him to the ambulance. People around the donut franchise looked on with curiosity.

Struggling weakly against the restraints, Harry looked at the two medical professionals as they went about their work. He could tell the woman paramedic tightening the strap around his body, someone the other one called Molly, was only weeks away from resigning her position. He was sure by the way she glowed that she was on the edge of a breakdown. Too many calls, too much stress, too much pressure was making her self-confidence ooze out — that was the best way Harry could describe it. She was leaving bits of herself on the floor of the Tim Hortons as she packed up the medical equipment. The other paramedic appeared okay. His eyes were where they were supposed to be, and he didn't seem to be radiating anything negative. He was indeed a man who wanted to make the world a better place, and that was always a good thing.

Harry's blood pressure was high, and his heartbeat was irregular. The paramedics kept asking him very annoying questions, none of which he wished to answer. He just needed to stop talking and thinking and he'd be okay. Yes, he knew he had made the decision to call over the police boy to talk, not thinking it would take such a toll on him. Now he just wanted to be left alone.

"Just leave me be. Take me to my grate." Both paramedics looked at each other. They were trained to handle street people, who frequently had a different value system. Their voices were gentle but firm.

"Ah, no, sir. Can't do that at the moment. Do you know where you are?"

Deciding not to answer, Harry let his head fall back onto the stretcher. This wasn't his first encounter with Toronto's medical shock troops. Every once in a while, his latent diabetes would end up giving him some unwanted attention, but today he just wasn't in the mood.

"Look, just give me a donut and let me go!"

Ralph stepped up to the prone, anxious man. "Harry, just go with them. They'll make you better."

"Better than what?"

Maybe if he finished what he'd started, he might feel better, like closing the door on an unpleasant smell or getting off a bumpy plane — though Harry had never been on a plane, he felt the metaphor was just — would ease the nausea.

"Police boy, you want to know about the Horse?"

Ralph nodded.

"Don't look. You may not find what you think you will. They change. People change. Horses change." The paramedics tried to calm Harry down, but he barely saw them. "Go home."

Ralph stepped up to the stretcher, despite the protestations of the medical personnel. "I can't. I have to find out what happened. See if I can help ... even all these years later."

"Why?"

"Because. That's why I became a cop."

For financial reasons, Ralph had spent the morning, one of several, pacing back and forth in front of a construction site. That didn't fit in with his reasoning at the moment, and when the time came, he would have to reassess that stone in the foundation of his life. But right now, in front of Harry, he was so close to solving a mystery that had haunted him his entire life.

"I wanted to be one of the good guys. I didn't like being ... impotent."

Harry's head was now throbbing. Distant memories and images of a long-ago life began to pop up. Once again, he heard the police boy's voice.

"Tell me, Harry, where can I find Danielle?"

Focusing on the Native man's face through the haze of his past life, with errant memories of long-forgotten people and a barely remembered language bombarding his consciousness, Harry uttered his last words.

"Where would you be if you were a horse?"

The paramedics pushed the policeman aside as the man on the stretcher suffered a seizure.

Once again, Ralph could only watch from the sidelines.

## CHAPTER THIRTEEN

HIGH PARK IS THE LARGEST PARK IN CANADA'S LARGEST city. Stretching several square kilometres from the Bloor subway line all the way down to Lake Ontario and across three subway stops, it provides samples of many of Canada's landscapes, from rolling fields covered in snow to bushy areas to forested enclaves.

Somewhere near the centre of the park sat a Native man, his back to the sun and his face to the openness of the grounds. Though it was still deep in winter's embrace, the city was experiencing a brief warm spell, enough to feel the distant kiss of an approaching spring. Ralph did not know why he was sitting here. This was the second day he'd come to the park. Did he trust that crazy homeless man? If so, why? Perhaps that man wasn't any crazier than anyone else he'd met in his travels. Wisdom and knowledge come with many faces. He'd read that somewhere. And, as he'd learned on the job, it didn't hurt to investigate all possibilities.

The hot chocolate in his cardboard cup could no longer be legally called "hot." How long he'd been sitting here, watching the population at winter play, he couldn't say. A fair percentage of any person's job in the police force involved doing nothing; it truly was a hurry-up-and-wait career. Spending hours watching the world pass by was pretty much second nature to Ralph. But he'd lost track of the multitude of joggers, strollers, and dogs. After two days, Ralph felt as much a part of the landscape as the park bench he sat on. He'd turned down an offer to return to the condo construction, saying he was reassessing his priorities. Instead, he sat here getting colder and colder, wondering if he should have his sanity reassessed.

Shelley and William had been amazed. Currently in the third trimester of child number four, they were unable to jump into their minivan and race into the city, as eager as they were to view the Horse. The picture Ralph had taken with his cellphone and sent didn't do it justice, he had told them. Instead, they wished him success in his plan. All three had reminisced for a good hour when they'd finally connected on the phone, reliving every remembered moment. The two of them doubted, and to a certain extent so did Ralph, that doing what he was doing would produce any reasonable result. Still, it was better than doing nothing, and that was something he would not do anymore.

If by some miracle Danielle was around, what would he say to her? Even this he did not know. The sun was setting typically early for this time of year, casting long shadows in front of him, reminding him of winters at home. Currently the young man was trying to decide if he was an idiot for sitting here so long or if he should return to the park later in the week when he had another free day and take the opportunity to confirm his idiocy. After all, this whole situation was a long shot. Definitely a shot long enough to be measured in years. He took a sip of his drink then just as quickly spit out the half-frozen beverage. Disgusted, he placed it on the bench beside him without looking. Surprised, Ralph felt his paper cup knock something over that hadn't been there when he had sat down.

Looking down to his right, he noticed a small figurine that had somehow materialized on one of the bench's wooden slats. It looked like a small plaster horse. One leg was broken off, and both ears looked damaged. It was discoloured in a particular way; it was scorched. But somehow, it seemed familiar. Picking it up delicately, he rolled it over in his hands, unwilling to believe what his memory was telling him.

Looking up from the horse to the ground in front of him, Ralph noticed something else different. He now had two shadows. He was fairly sure he had arrived with one. It hovered there on the snow before him, slowly shifting weight from one foot to the other. Occasionally he'd see the head flip and long hair, almost like a mane, swirl in the air. Behind him, he could hear light breathing.

"Hey, Danielle ..." His tone was husky and a little cautious.

Behind him, he heard a voice.

## ACKNOWLEDGEMENTS

This story has been decades in the development. It has had many different forms: first a short story, then a one-act play for young audiences, and, finally, a novel. Since the concept first appeared to me back in the early 90s, there have been a lot of influences in its evolution, both conscious and direct and some not so conscious and direct.

Let's start with Ms. D. Kappele, who provided me with the original concept oh so long ago. See what you caused! From a vague dinner party discussion, it grew, eventually ending up in a collection of my short stories, *Fearless Warriors*, published by Talon Books, originally christened "Girl Who Loved Her Horses". Thanks to Karl Siegler and Talon Books for giving both Danielle and the Horse their first opportunity to run free.

But the story, and Danielle's plight, wouldn't leave me alone. One story in a collection of other stories wasn't enough for it. It kept nagging me … if that's the correct word. Eventually I wanted to explore the universe of the story more. *Girl Who Loved Her Horses*, the play, came out a few years later. For that I have to thank Theatre Direct. Thanks to those who helped me further develop the story, I'm talking about the late Larry Lewis (a personal mentor) and Richard Goldblatt, who directed the first production. The following year, the play was also published with Talon Books as part of two one-act plays, along with *Boy in the Treehouse*.

When asked, I would frequently say this story, in both forms, was one of my favourite things I have ever written. Every once in a while, when I would for one reason or another reread either of its forms, I would frequently say to myself, somewhat surprised, "Wow, I wrote that!" Now I get to say that again.

Danielle and the Horse lay dormant for a number of decades, but they would not leave me alone. They had more to say. At one point a few years back I said to myself, "Just write it as a novel. See what happens." So I did. Alas for a while I thought I was alone in my enthusiasm for their unique tale. I had great difficulty finding a home for that book. Then one afternoon, in a rather lovely hotel bar, I had a conversation with Marc Côté, publisher of Cormorant Books. Actually I had meant to pitch him another story I thought might make a half decent novel, but as I settled into that first glass of wine, I found myself talking about this secret dream/project of mine lying unappreciated in both my computer and my mind. I still remember my delight when he looked me in the eye, a definite expression of immediate interest, saying "You mean there's an unpublished Drew Hayden Taylor novel out there?" I would have married him right there. So thank you, Marc, and Cormorant Books for giving my little girl and her mighty Horse a larger pasture to explore.

And of course, a special thanks to those who have supported and encouraged all of my literary efforts for as long as I can remember: my agent, Ms Cheeseman who has guided my career through its ups and downs. Also the lovely Janine, who has always been incredibly supportive of my flights of fancy, and my mother, whose efforts in the real world provided me the opportunity to play in my make-believe world.

I thank you all, and if I have left anybody out, my apologies. The older I get the more details seem to fall between the floorboards of my mind. I blame it on the 80s.

*Drew Hayden Taylor*
Curve Lake First Nation
June 2019

Drew Hayden Taylor has done many things, most of which he is proud of. An Ojibway from the Curve Lake First Nations in Ontario, he has worn many hats in his literary career, from performing stand-up comedy at the Kennedy Center in Washington D.C., to being Artistic Director of Canada's premiere Native theatre company, Native Earth Performing Arts. He has been an award-winning playwright (with over seventy productions of his work), a journalist/columnist (appearing regularly in several Canadian newspapers and magazines), short-story writer, novelist, television scriptwriter, and has worked on over seventeen documentaries exploring the Native experience. Most notably, he wrote and directed *Redskins, Tricksters, and Puppy Stew*, a documentary on Native humour for the National Film Board of Canada.

We acknowledge the sacred land on which Cormorant Books operates. It has been a site of human activity for 15,000 years. This land is the territory of the Huron-Wendat and Petun First Nations, the Seneca, and most recently, the Mississaugas of the Credit River. The territory was the subject of the Dish With One Spoon Wampum Belt Covenant, an agreement between the Iroquois Confederacy and Confederacy of the Ojibway and allied nations to peaceably share and steward the resources around the Great Lakes. Today, the meeting place of Toronto is still home to many Indigenous people from across Turtle Island. We are grateful to have the opportunity to work in the community, on this territory.

We are also mindful of broken covenants and the need to strive to make right with all our relations.